Dropped Third Strike

A Portland Pioneers Novel

By Micah K. Chaplin

Cover by Stacie Ricklefs Photo + Design

ISBN: 978-0692623169 (MKC)
ISBN-13: 0692623167

Dedications

For Amy, who helped me develop a deep love for baseball before leaving this world far too soon.

For the many other baseball fans in my life who have imparted upon me their baseball theories, wisdom, and opinions.

For my readers – Rachel, Jamie, Jill, Bruna, Nikki, Bridget, Laura, Angie, Candace, Alicia, Jessica, Courtney, and Will – for your invaluable support and feedback.

Special thanks also to the Texas Rangers, who seduced me into the tumultuous relationship of being a fan of the game. Despite all the heartbreak, I wouldn't trade a minute of my fandom. It has lead to some incredible friendships and given me many moments of pure joy.

A dropped third strike occurs when the catcher fails to cleanly catch a pitch, which is a third strike (either because the batter swings and misses it or because the umpire calls it). The pitcher gets credited with a strikeout, but the umpire indicates verbally that the ball was not caught, and does not call the batter out. If first base is not occupied at the time, the batter can then attempt to reach first base prior to being tagged or thrown out.

Author's note: There's a glossary of more baseball terms used in this story at the back of the book.

Chapter One

Kate hung up the phone with a sigh and swiveled her chair halfway around to face away from her desk. She sat up straighter, arching her back slightly as she tried to work out the tension that had amassed while she was getting chewed out over the phone.

She let out a long breath and looked out the floor-to-ceiling window. Her view was magnificent – flawlessly manicured grass and crisp reddish dirt. For six months out of the year, this picture also included dozens of fit, agile young men running, hitting, and throwing. Kate was proud of where she'd gotten, and while the road to being general manager of the Portland Pioneers hadn't been easy or altogether pleasant, she believed it had been worth it.

Portland, a three-year-old franchise, was one of the newest additions in Major League Baseball, and Kate was one of the few female general managers in the history of the game. When her hiring was announced, the press and message boards immediately made her gender an issue. Surely, no woman could – or should – handle a man's sport. There were comments about the trade deadline being too near her menstrual cycle and her inability to accurately assess talent instead of just a nice physique. A few insults masked as compliments were peppered in as well. Some speculated that she used her well-toned legs, low-cut blouses, and sparkling green eyes to negotiate a contract that saved the owner a million here and there. There was no proof to support that theory. Or debunk it.

Kate did her best to ignore her critics. She knew she'd earned this opportunity, as did the people who had hired her and those who had helped her along the way. College internships with the Arizona State Athletic Department and the Arizona Diamondbacks provided her with experiences and contacts. She continued on with the Diamondbacks after college, working as an assistant in the front office. She never shied away from speaking up in meetings and sharing her opinions. Brian Dockery, the assistant general manager, took note of her skills and insights and then took her along with him when he moved on to Pittsburgh, giving her a small team of scouts to manage. It was a huge step up for such a young person, especially a woman, but Kate handled it quite ably, and built a reputation as a hard-working woman with extensive baseball knowledge. A few other organizations tried to lure her away to their operations teams, and while they were tempting, she stayed where she was. The offers were not only flattering; they helped her standing in Pittsburgh, as the general manager gave her raises and promotions to retain her. She had inched her way to role of assistant general manager for the AAA affiliate when James Scott approached Brian and told him he was buying a baseball team in Portland and was in need of a general manager. Brian connected James with Kate, albeit a bit reluctantly. He told Kate he hated to lose her but felt she was ready to move into a position of more prominence.

As she surveyed the grounds in Portland, she smiled. So far, she had managed to prove most of the naysayers wrong. She had made more smart deals than bad ones. Sometimes she lamented the few times she'd made a mistake, but she told herself that every GM had a bad trade once in awhile.

She couldn't count the number of times her father, a long-time Mets fan, lamented the 1971 trade that sent Nolan Ryan, Don Rose, Frank Estrada, and Leroy Stanton to the Angels in exchange for Jim Fregosi. The move did nothing to improve the Mets' infield, and Ryan went on to become one of the game's greatest pitchers.

More recently, she remembered the shock of seeing Atlanta move Jarrod Saltalamacchia, Elvis Andrus, Neftali Feliz, Matt Harrison, and Beau Jones to Texas in exchange for Mark Teixeira and Ron Mahay. A few years later, the Rangers went to back-to-back World Series with three of the players in that trade and Atlanta had nothing to show on their side of the deal.

She took comfort in the knowledge that her mistakes hadn't been quite as bad as those, and the team had not suffered too much in the end. In fact, the Pioneers were gradually moving out of newbie status and into the realm of being legitimate contenders. Opponents no longer looked forward to the Portland series as an easy and automatic sweep. Just last season, her boys had played the role of spoiler for two teams making late-season runs at the playoffs. Indeed, the Pioneers were coming along, and it was all because Kate and her colleagues had made the most of a moderate budget and assembled a fine group of athletes.

Today, none of those athletes were running around on the field below. It was only early January after all. The field wouldn't be busy again for several more weeks. Occasionally, she'd see a handful of the players who lived locally jogging laps around the perimeter of the park or climbing the stairs, but most of the athletic activity was contained to the weight room and cages, which were three levels below her office.

Opening Day was a few months away, but to Kate, it still felt too close. The club's hitting coach had resigned just before Thanksgiving citing family obligations. Had he resigned right at the end of the previous season, Kate might have found his replacement swiftly, but the late start in her search meant a lot of potential candidates had already been scooped up by other teams. So far, a dozen candidates had been considered but none of them felt right. Kate didn't like the thought of hiring someone who was merely "OK," especially coming off a season in which their club was third in the league for home runs and second in runs scored. Offense was their centerpiece and the only thing that saved their mediocre pitching. They hadn't made many improvements in the pitching staff, so they would need to rely on the bats again in the season ahead. She needed the perfect candidate, but she was quickly running out of time.

Her job put her every move under many microscopes. Currently, however, it was her lack of movement that was drawing ire from all angles. The media was on her back, the owner was calling her daily, and the manager stopped by whenever he was in town, which was becoming more frequent as the new season loomed closer. The club president made his share of calls as well, including the one she had just hung up. None of these individuals or entities were pleased with her answer of, "I'm still searching." If she didn't make a hire in the next few weeks, the players might report to camp without someone to tweak their timing and adjust their batting stance. And she might find her employment status hanging by a thread.

She sighed and turned back to her desk as Bart, the mailroom clerk, strolled in with the day's correspondence.

"Looks like there might be a few more candidates for the hitting coach job, Ms. Marks," Bart said. "There are some big envelopes here. I put them on top for you."

Kate smiled at the young man in appreciation. Other GMs might have snapped at the college sophomore for prying, but not Kate. Bart had been a genuine find. His head was full of baseball knowledge – and not just the generic everyday kind. He knew more about VORP, OPS, and range than most men 10 years his senior. Bart had made no secret about his aspirations to work in Major League Baseball full-time one day, and while the mailroom was hardly a place to utilize Bart's knowledge, he had taken the low-paying job just to be around the sport. Recognizing his value early on, Kate happily worked around Bart's college schedule to get him the hours he needed. On top of that, she listened to his insight and let him have access to people and information no other mailroom employee in the league probably had.

"Let's hope they're good ones," Kate said. "We're running out of time, Bart."

"I know," Bart said. "And the Mariners just hired Stan Beasley this morning."

Kate groaned. Beasley had been on her fallback list. Instead, he'd taken a job with one of their division rivals in the American League West. She couldn't blame him. They'd offered the job first while she was still waiting for the perfect candidate. Beasley hadn't been perfect, or even great, but he would have been adequate. She only hoped her hesitation wouldn't come back to bite them in the standings.

"Great," Kate said. "Well, there's another name I can cross off the list."

"He probably wouldn't have been right anyway," Bart said. "He enjoys small ball a little too much for the Pioneers' style."

Kate smiled as the young man once again showed off his knowledge.

"That was my hang-up too," she said.

"Someone better will come along," Bart said. "Anyway, I need to get moving. I have stats class in an hour. See you later, Ms. Marks."

Kate waved as Bart left her office and continued on his mail route. Mentally crossing her fingers, she opened the first big envelope. She scanned the résumé – a triple-A bench coach and former AA player who specialized in outfield defense. *Next*, she thought. The second one yielded even less promise. She found no inspiration in the third, fourth or fifth either. An hour of reading and re-reading was gone, and Kate was no closer to finding her coach.

Her phone intercom buzzed, and her secretary said Mr. Scott was on the line. Kate took a deep breath before answering. She already knew how this call would go.

"Why is it that the Mariners have a hitting coach now and we don't?" the team's owner barked.

"Beasley wasn't right for the Pioneers," Kate said confidently, or at least that was the tone she tried to convey.

"The Mariners have the worst offense in the division, and I'll be damned if we swap places with them because you're waiting for the 'perfect' candidate to fall into your lap," James snapped.

"I don't think that's possible," Kate said. "Not with Tanner and Davis coming back. Those two don't need a hitting coach to replicate what they did last year."

Kate knew throwing out the names of the Pioneers' All-Star middle infielders would help mollify the owner. Justin Tanner and Ian Davis had been two of her earliest signings, and they quickly became the cornerstone of the franchise. Their bat speed and power was rivaled only by their ability to turn at least two fantastic double plays in every game. She couldn't count the number of times their defense had saved a pitcher from being overworked, to say nothing of the number of runs they'd driven in. They were the Pioneers' version of the Bash Brothers and the most fearsome three-four hitters in the league. The owner loved them.

"I suppose not, but they can't carry the offense again this year," James said, sounding a bit less edgy. "And Castaños and Walker still need a lot of work."

"I know, sir," Kate said. "I've been monitoring their work in Mexico this winter, though. Castaños has become a lot more patient at the plate, and Walker is starting to drive the ball to the opposite field more often."

"That's promising, but their progress may be for nothing if you don't get someone to keep them going," James said.

"I know, and I will find that someone," Kate said. "I plan to narrow things down later this week."

The owner guffawed on the other end of the line, and she couldn't blame him for having doubts. Kate had made the same statement a few times since beginning her search. She had yet to deliver on her word, and she hated that. Kate prided herself on following through.

"I promise," she added, using those two words for the first time.

"You better," James said. "I'm counting on you, Kate. I didn't hire you to dilly-dally around. Pitchers and catchers report in 45 days. Workouts are ramping up. I expect you to have an announcement before Fan Fest at the end of the month."

Kate glanced at her calendar. That gave her less than three weeks. Her stomach rolled a bit.

"I will," she said. Her tone conveyed more confidence than she possessed.

Kate hung up and slumped in her chair. She wasn't completely defeated yet, but she was definitely feeling the pressure. She supposed she should be thankful she only had one boss now instead of four or more as she had endured in previous jobs. Even though there were many people waiting on her decision, she only had to answer to James Scott. But that didn't do much to ease the pressure on her. Not when you considered the power her boss had – he could ruin her easily. And not even blink an eye while doing it. He wasn't the only one leaning on her either. He was the most vocal, but certainly there were others waiting to pounce on every failure.

A week later, Kate had conducted a handful of interviews. The résumés had underwhelmed her, but the impending deadline usurped her hesitation so she had brought in the most promising from the stack.

Two of the candidates were older men with respectable baseball careers. They had each played minor league ball in their prime and had since managed a few AA teams. They also shared a confidence in their ability to add to the Pioneers' offense. Kate listened patiently as each explained in detail some of the exercises he would use to improve the hitters' patience and timing. Their methods sounded good, but Kate was unmoved by their interviews. They were smart enough and certainly experienced, but her instincts told her to hold off.

The other three candidates were far younger and completely new to coaching. Their vigor and energy was their main appeal, but when asked about how they could impact the Pioneers hitters, they stuttered and spat out clichés in their answers. Their lack of conviction left Kate feeling uneasy.

After the last interviewee left, Kate put her face in her hands and let out a long breath. Over the course of her career, she had never sweated this much over a hiring, and that was saying something. When she came on board, the Portland franchise was brand new, so she had to start from scratch – hiring a manager and an entire coaching staff, not to mention assembling a 40-man roster and building a farm system. James Scott had been tied up in the financial dealings, so he let her take the reins on all the staffing decisions. It had been empowering and also a lot of work, but she couldn't remember feeling this stressed during that process. Since then, she had made countless decisions – more good than bad. Many of the faces in the organization had stayed the same. She liked consistency, and it had worked well for her. Despite all of her success, she knew her job could be in trouble if she did not hire a hitting coach before her deadline. On top of that, she had to make up for this delay. The candidate she contracted had to be worth the wait. It had to be someone with a recognizable name and reputation. Someone James Scott could get excited about. Someone the fans would embrace.

She rubbed her fingertips from her forehead down to her temples and back up over and over, racking her brain for a name. She had worked in other organizations before landing with the Pioneers, compiling an extensive contact list in her journey to the front office. She opened up the address book in her e-mail and perused the names. Surely there was a lead on a hitting coach in there somewhere. After several moments of simply reading names, she composed a brief message about what she was looking for in a hitting coach and sent it to a few of her most-trusted former colleagues. Kate hated asking for help. It made her feel vulnerable and out of control — two things she worked hard not to feel — but desperate times called for desperate measures.

As soon as the e-mail was sent, she closed down her computer and gathered her things, anxious for a bit of an early exit. It was nearly five. Even if someone read her e-mail immediately, she wasn't likely to receive a response until the next day. She might as well take advantage of a full evening. With the hitting coach search coming down to the wire, she had been putting in a lot of long days. Those were usually reserved for the trade deadline and post-season meetings, and they always left her feeling weary. Today felt like one of those days. Regardless, she intended to hit the gym on the way home to work off a bit of her frustration as well as some of the winter weight she'd put on — not that anyone could see it except her. There wasn't anyone to notice anyway.

Kate was a bit of a loner — partly by design and partly as a result of her profession. She worked a lot of long hours and traveled frequently from February through September. This didn't leave much time for a social life, let alone a love life. Her career choice gave her plenty of opportunities to meet available men — some more desirable than others — but it hadn't really lent to dating success. Of course, most of the men she met wanted to talk baseball all the time, so their dates ended up feeling like an extended workday. Her well-intentioned best friend, Jill, tried introducing her to a few men outside of her professional circle. Unfortunately, the few Kate actually liked were unprepared for the rigors of her work schedule. They were looking for marriage and family, and those things were not on Kate's immediate agenda.

That hadn't always been the case. Although the baseball business had long been her dream, Kate had once envisioned herself trading wedding rings instead of outfielders. More than once, actually. Kate had twice given her heart to the same man, and twice he'd returned it to her in pieces. After the second break, Kate decided she couldn't go through that again. Not with him or anyone else. It wasn't worth it.

Following the second round of misery, she'd picked herself up, threw herself completely into her career, and never looked back. Her efforts had paid off handsomely. She had a prestigious role in a sport she had loved for most of her life. It came with an equally impressive salary, as well as chances to travel, talk with baseball legends, and meet people from the entertainment and sports worlds. Her job was her life, and she was happy with it, even if most people didn't believe her when she said as much.

All four of her sisters were married, and between them there were nine grandchildren for her parents to dote on. Still, that hadn't taken all of the pressure off of Kate. The Marks elders were still concerned about their first-born daughter's single status. They didn't think it was healthy for her to spend so much time at work and alone, even though she insisted she preferred it that way. They wanted to see her happy and settled, and she seemed so far from that at the moment. Her love life was still among the first subjects discussed whenever Kate ventured or called home. She never seemed to have the right answer for them either.

Then there were Kate's friends, all of whom were married or coupled up. They were even worse than her parents. On top of the constant inquiries about her dating calendar, there were the not-so-sly set-ups masked as dinner parties and game nights. Kate accepted the invites and was never surprised to hear comments like, "oh, John is here and he's single too. You two should talk." At first, Kate was irritated and angry, but after she spent some time thinking about it, she learned to just let it go. She could have stopped accepting the invitations, but then when would she see her friends? And she knew they had good intentions. Plus, her social life was pretty minimal already, and she wasn't willing to ditch her friends just because they chose to keep ignoring Kate's objections to their set-ups.

While she was at peace with her relationship status, Kate occasionally missed the perks of having a significant other. At times she felt like the only single among couples. Logically, she knew that wasn't true, and fortunately she was often too busy with work to dwell on these thoughts for long. But even at work, she couldn't completely escape being inundated with images of couples. At the ballpark, her gaze was inevitably drawn to the screen during the "kiss cam" segment. A bit of jealousy surfaced whenever the focus was a young twosome obviously in the early stages of their relationship. Kate remembered those days, when it seemed like you were the only two people in the world and the electricity between you would never fizzle. She was also decidedly touched by the occasional elderly duo caught on the cam that were clearly as enamored with each other as they were comfortable. It was hard to look away, and the scenes often made her wistful. She missed the affection and companionship of a relationship, but not enough to chance having her heart broken again.

Every time she started longing for a boyfriend, she reminded herself of the pain one man had caused her. She remembered the tears, the countless boxes of tissues, the sad songs, and the ice cream. She recalled the shattered dreams, the broken promises, and the lost sense of hope and self. Upon the recall of these memories, the longing for a boyfriend quickly disappeared.

Besides, if she wanted to maintain and even improve her professional reputation, she needed to stay focused. A boyfriend would only distract her from her work. She couldn't afford a distraction – especially not one as worthless as a man. The only men she was allowed to focus on were those whose checks she signed – the players, the managers, and the coaches. Those were the relationships that would benefit her on her mission to build a championship team.

That was the long-term goal.

The short-term goal was to hire a hitting coach.

She mulled over her options and contacts in her head again as she hit the treadmill at All-In Fitness. There was a gym at the stadium available to her, but she thought sweating with them or in front of the ballplayers she employed might compromise the professional barriers she had carefully crafted. Kate had specifically sought out a 24-hour gym to accommodate her unconventional work schedule. She preferred to work out before heading to the office, but occasionally a late meeting or game would keep her in bed later in the morning. On those nights, she opted for a late-night workout. They weren't ideal, but they were necessary. Working out had become a staple in her life after her break-ups. If she wore herself out, there wouldn't be any energy left to cry herself to sleep. As the years went on, she'd found them to be a great way to fight stress and her brain a break from the business of baseball.

As her brisk walk turned into a slow jog, Kate plugged her headphones into the treadmill's console and looked up at the television in front of her machine. Her feet pounded against the belt as the one-liners and laughter of *The Office* chased work concerns from Kate's mind. She didn't watch much TV, but one of the guys she briefly dated had mentioned this show. While the relationship hadn't worked out, his sense of humor had been one of his most endearing qualities, so Kate checked it out one night. She loved it immediately, and since the episodes were only 30 minutes long, Kate found it easy to catch up and keep up.

When the credits rolled, Kate began flipping through the channels. Unable to find anything else she could get into, she finally stopped it on the MLB Network, where they were discussing some of the latest transactions. It might have been a little too work-related for what was supposed to be off-time, but Kate couldn't resist. Even before she'd entered the baseball industry as a professional, she'd had a hunger for constant information on the sport and the business behind it. As a GM now, she was always interested to see what her colleagues were doing. Most of the topics were old news to her, as she'd received calls and e-mails about various transactions and happenings all day. However, there was one announcement that nearly made her trip on the treadmill.

"After designating him for assignment early last week, the Mets have released outfielder Reid Benjamin. A one-time top prospect, Benjamin's stock has been steadily dropping since his debut. He hit .250 with 30 walks and 120 strikeouts in his second season as the starting centerfielder after signing a five-year contract worth $100 million. Despite tallying 89 RBI, 20 home runs, and 40 doubles last year, he has not been able to put together a full season without injury or incident. His troubles off the field have also undoubtedly influenced New York's decision. In the last few years, Benjamin has been arrested a handful of times on charges ranging from public intoxication to disorderly conduct. Just two weeks ago, he was kicked out of a popular nightclub after punching a bouncer. That appears to have been the final straw for the Mets. Benjamin now becomes a free agent. Between the size of his contract, his offensive troubles, and the late off-season nature of his release, finding work will be quite the scramble for him."

Kate's gait stuttered a bit as the segment started. Fortunately, she was able to stop the treadmill and find the side rails with her feet before looking like a klutz in the near-empty gym. For several long moments after the TV had gone to commercial, Kate's gaze remained on the screen, letting the name resonate through her brain – Reid Benjamin.

From a professional standpoint, Kate was not all that surprised by the news of Reid's release. His off-field headlines combined with his declining value and a saturated outfielder market would likely leave Reid without a job this season. She actually felt a bit sorry for him, and that sympathy annoyed her. Why should she feel sorry for Reid? He certainly hadn't done anything to deserve it.

Kate knew Reid well – far better than any of those scouts, managers, or GMs who had been drooling over him for years. Reid also knew her quite well – in ways she preferred not to think about. Much to her chagrin, they occasionally snuck up on her. Usually on nights when she let her mind wander a little too far into the past.

This is not going to be one of those nights.

She unplugged her headphones and went over to the free weights section of the facility. For the next hour, Kate drove Reid Benjamin from her mind with every lunge, squat, and curl. After she stretched and cooled down, she showered and headed home for a quick late dinner and bed.

Kate's reprieve from hearing Reid Benjamin's name didn't last long. Even though she was at her office by the ungodly hour of six, she already had three voicemails mentioning his name. The last one was from the team's owner. She shook her head and took a sip of her coffee as she picked up the phone to dial his number and set him straight.

"Please tell me you've already set up an interview with Benjamin," Mr. Scott blurted out, almost before Kate could even say "hello."

"I haven't," Kate managed to answer.

"And why not?" Mr. Scott demanded. "He would be perfect."

"For what?" Kate asked. "You're aware of his history, right? On and off the field, he's a huge liability. I wouldn't sign him as a player, and I definitely don't want him coaching and mentoring. Even if he wasn't such a bad influence, he has no experience."

"Clearly, you are the one who has not looked at his résumé," the owner replied. "During the off-seasons, he went to his alma mater and helped fine-tune the mechanics of many players there. Most of them have been or will be drafted."

"Then why was he so horrible at the plate?" Kate asked.

"You know what they say – those who can't do teach," Mr. Scott said. "Interview and sign him. Fan Fest is in two days. I want to make the announcement then."

"OK, I'll interview him, but I can't guarantee I'll hire him," Kate said.

In her mind, the possibility was very doubtful. Her personal bias against Reid Benjamin aside, she could not imagine him as a proper fit for the Pioneers – professionally or otherwise. Neither his batting stats nor his rap sheet inspired her. Besides, who was to say he would be interested in a coaching position? Regardless, the owner had given her an order. She had to carry it through. Honestly, it wasn't as though she had many other options. The other candidates had failed to impress her. Reid was likely to follow suit, but at the owner's command, she had to at least interview him.

Now she needed to figure out how to get in touch with Reid. His information was still in her phone contact list, but she wasn't sure the number still worked. Years had passed since she'd even attempted to use it. Trying to shake that memory, she turned on her computer and opened her e-mail. The answer was in her inbox. More than one of the replies to her plea for help had suggested Reid and included his contact information. Some of them were time stamped before the evening announcement, so either they had insider information or they'd seen the writing on the wall. Interestingly enough, his number was still the same as it had been five years earlier. She took a deep breath and picked up the phone, dialing the number slowly.

When he answered sounding sleepy, Kate inhaled quickly. Knowing how his voice had once affected her – particularly when laced with the sexy, barely awake tone it carried now – why hadn't she rehearsed something to say?

Fortunately, "Professional Kate" mode kicked in.

"Reid Benjamin?" she asked in a cool, even manner.

"Yeah," he mumbled. "Who is this?"

He didn't recognize her voice. Given their history and the time that had lapsed since their last conversation, this shouldn't have shocked her or even bothered her. But it did. She felt a distinct and familiar twinge of pain. Somehow, she found a way to push on without sounding affected.

"Kate Marks, general manager of the Portland Pioneers," she said. "I'd like to talk to you about the hitting coach position in our organization."

There was a silent pause on the other end, and she wondered what was going through his head. Then she heard a rustle of fabric, which suggested he was sitting up or getting out of bed. The mental picture rattled her as much as his voice had. She closed her eyes, but that only made the image more vivid. She snapped them open and turned to look out the window, nearly pulling the phone off the desk in the process. She scurried to catch it and reposition it smoothly. She wondered if he had heard any of the clatter in his silence.

"Sorry, you woke me up," Reid said finally. "Can you repeat that?"

Kate repeated what she had said, though she could hear a slight tremor in her voice that hadn't previously been there. She hoped he didn't notice it. The odds were in her favor though as Reid had never been particularly observant where she was concerned.

"Oh," Reid said. "I guess the good news of my release traveled fast."

She heard a catch in his voice. She couldn't tell if it was hurt or annoyance, maybe a combination of both. Kate, in turn, felt a little bad for her negative thoughts about him.

"Yeah, I heard it last night," Kate admitted. "I know it's probably too soon for me to be calling you about this opening, but I felt like I needed to jump on you before someone else did."

Kate immediately regretted her choice of words, especially when she heard him chuckle. Apparently, he heard the unintended innuendo as well.

"Well, you might be a bit late for that," he said in a low voice, still clearly amused. "Except in terms of employment; I'm still open on that front. I could fly out next week."

"Actually, I'd like to talk to you sooner than that," Kate said. "I could make arrangements for you to be here this afternoon. We would cover the costs, of course."

"This afternoon?" Reid asked. "Wow…you must really be desperate. Well, OK, but I can handle the costs. As you know, I made a pretty good living while I was employed. I'll call the airline and get back to you with my ETA. What was your name again?"

Kate rolled her eyes and gave him her name again along with her number.

As he hung up the phone, Reid smiled to himself. He hadn't heard that voice in a long time, but he'd recognized it instantly. He'd never heard the woman speak in such a business-like tone – but he still knew who was on the other end of the line before she identified herself. Despite the years that had passed and the substances he'd ingested in the interim, Reid had never managed to erase Kate Marks from his memory, even though he preferred to have her believe that was the case. He would have preferred that to be the case too, but it hadn't happened. Clearly. His reaction to hearing her voice on the phone was unsettling, to say the least. And now he would have to face her in a matter of hours. He really wasn't in any shape for a reunion or a job interview, but he had already agreed, and now he had to go. Plus, he needed a job, and for the first time in his career, there weren't multiple teams fighting over him.

Scouts had drooled over Reid, the third overall pick in the 2005 draft. Managers begged their GMs to trade large chips for him. Many GMs had tried to do just that, but the Mets had clung to their prize prospect. They'd invested millions in him immediately and saw the fruits of their investment returning as Reid's raw talent and well-developed skills materialized on the field. Reid started in Low A, but found himself in AA by the end of his first professional season. The following season, he spent just two weeks in AA before being promoted to AAA. He remained there for a few seasons, waiting for a call-up. Unfortunately, Reid's rise was stunted by a crowd of very talented outfielders already on the big league roster, and none of them were performing in a way which put their jobs at risk. Several teams continued trying to pry Reid from the Mets organization, but New York wasn't keen on giving up on their investment, even if they had no immediate need for his services.

Reid's big break came when the Mets' All-Star right fielder dislocated his shoulder and strained several muscles on a highlight reel diving catch. Facing at least a few weeks of recovery time and a tough August schedule, the Mets brought Reid up to the majors. For the first few games, he remained on the bench, but finally the outcry from the public – and undoubtedly the GM – won out, and Reid made his much-anticipated major league debut against the division-leading Philadelphia Phillies. Reid lived up to his hype in that first game. He went 2-for-4 with a double, one RBI, and one fantastic outfield assist to nail the Phillies third baseman trying to get home during a tense eighth inning. Reid managed to maintain that performance for the rest of the season, impressing the front office enough that they traded one of their veteran outfielders for a couple pitchers and let Reid have a shot at the starting nod. He earned the centerfield duties during spring training and was standing in Citi Field on Opening Day the next spring.

Reid's sparkling September had set the expectations very high with very little room for the typical rookie growing pains, so when they inevitably hit, fans grew agitated. At first, the Mets faithful were quiet about it, merely mumbling when Reid struck out. As the weather grew hotter, so did the fans' temperament. Reid was no longer just striking out; he was flailing at horrible pitches outside the zone. Occasionally, he would have a good game with a bomb of a home run or timely double, but this success only further angered the masses, as they got their hopes up about his struggles ending, only to watch him strike out four times in the next game. The Mets missed the playoffs that year, and while a team certainly isn't made of one player, much of the blame fell on Reid's shoulders. Fans and local media argued the traded player would have made all the difference and Reid was a waste of money. He bounced back a little in his second full season, but Reid was still the most popular target of message board ire. His extracurricular activities rivaled his on-field failures, making him the punch line of nearly every bad Mets joke told. His rise had been short-lived, but his fall seemed as though it would never end.

He glanced at the woman in his bed and sighed. After he'd learned of his release, Reid had sought solace in the only two things he could count on – alcohol and women. He turned to the two more often than most people liked, but they were always available and willing to take his mind off his worries. He was several drinks in when Megen showed up at his place. She had knowingly planned for his level of inebriation and wore minimal clothing that was easy to remove. He divested her of it pretty quickly, and then she turned her attentions on him while he continued to down vodka like it was water. Before long, his mind was numb and his body was alive. And that was just what he needed. He was grateful for his two vices. They'd both gotten him in some trouble, but he could quit either one when they were done serving their purpose.

With a dull ache in his head, Reid wandered into the living room of his condo and called his usual airline. He was able to book a ticket on a noon flight. That gave him two hours to get Meg out of his place, nurse his hangover, and get to the airport. He took a deep breath and padded back to the bedroom to take care of the first of those tasks. It wasn't actually that difficult of a feat. Meg knew how their arrangement worked, although she did talk him into a quickie before he hit the shower. When he emerged clean and shaven, she was gone, but she'd left him a plate of eggs and toast along with aspirin and big bottle of water. He ate in his towel and made a mental checklist of what he needed to pack. He didn't really know how long he'd be gone, but he figured he should prepare for a few days. Easy. As he rode in a cab to the airport in a suit with just a carry-on in tow, he realized of all the things he'd learned in his time as a ballplayer, packing for a road trip was certainly a contender as the most valuable.

Settled in his seat on the plane, it occurred to Reid that he'd never interviewed for a job before. He knew he should be nervous, but he'd detected a bit of desperation in Kate's voice that morning so that took some edge off. Plus, he knew how to charm her. There was little need for him to be nervous. He held all the power in this situation, and as soon as the aspirin kicked in, he would be able to walk into Kate Marks' office full of confidence.

Kate's stomach was a bundle of nerves as the clock approached two-thirty and her appointment with Reid grew closer. She'd been on the phone when he called back with his flight information, but he left a message. With the time difference between New York and Oregon, he would arrive around two and head straight to her office. A few hours didn't seem like enough time to prepare for this meeting. Then again, she wasn't sure any amount of time would be sufficient in preparing to see Reid again.

She had listened to his message multiple times, and Kate tried telling herself it was only to double-check (OK, quadruple-check) the details. But she couldn't even fool herself. It was about hearing his voice – especially the part where he said her name. It still sounded so familiar on his lips even though he'd made it clear he didn't remember her at all. She was still bothered by that fact … and annoyed that it bothered her. How could he have forgotten her? Despite her best efforts, she'd failed at erasing her memories of him. There were just too many, and most of them still qualified as significant moments in her life. Those were the kind of memories that never went away. Apparently they were not as significant to him. She shook her head before her thoughts could go down that road. She was sure it would catch up with her later, but for now, she needed to focus.

Reid didn't have an actual résumé, so Kate had spent the morning researching his playing career and calling the coaches at the college where he'd reportedly tutored players on their hitting. The staff members at North Carolina practically fell all over themselves to praise Reid. As soon as she finished telling them who she was and why she was calling, the positive words about Reid came pouring through the phone. She had a hard time getting the men off the phone. The head coach was the most fervent in his support for Reid.

"Look, ma'am, I know Benjamin's got a reputation, and his own offensive numbers don't show it, but he knows how to hit," the coach said. "He's helped a lot of my boys, not just on the field, but in the classroom. I'm not sayin' he tutored them himself, but he got 'em to care about their grades and work a little harder. He's a good guy, and he can relate to players who have ego as well as those who don't quite believe in themselves. I hope you'll give 'im a chance."

This did not help support Kate's belief – or hope – that Reid was underqualified for the job.

Kate thanked the coach for his time and hung up with a sigh. Looking for another out, she called a few contacts she had in the Mets organization. They offered their support of Reid as well. Many of them were dismayed by their GM's decision to let him go. They still believed Reid would turn a corner and become the All-Star so many had projected. They echoed the UNC coach's sentiments that Reid knew more about hitting than his stats conveyed.

By the time Kate's assistant buzzed her to announce Reid's arrival, Kate already had a strong sense about the outcome of this interview. This was probably a blessing, since his presence was likely to wreak havoc on her ability to think clearly. She told Sara to send Reid in and took a deep breath before the door opened. Silently, she began to prepare herself for the sight of him. She felt calm and collected as she stood and crossed toward the door. But then he walked in and any illusion she had of feeling of calm and collected walked out.

Reid wore a simple but well-tailored charcoal grey suit

with a black shirt. He had skipped the tie and left the top few buttons of his shirt undone. It might have been a bit casual for a typical job interview, but on him, it worked. Then again, Reid looked good in everything. He also looked good in nothing, but Kate quickly squelched that recollection. Her gaze drifted up from his attire to his face, where his lips were curved into a slight smile and his hazel eyes were full of amusement and recognition.

He closed the door behind him, and Kate only hoped her intelligence wasn't on the other side of it.

"Kate," he said, holding out his right hand.

"Reid," she responded, shaking his hand and praying he couldn't feel the slight tremors running through her.

"It's been awhile," he said.

"Yes, it has," Kate said. "I wasn't sure you remembered me."

"Of course I do," Reid said. "I'd ask how you've been, but I don't think I have to."

He gestured to their surroundings and Kate nodded, grateful for the excuse to avert her eyes from him and look around her office instead. Yet even the carefully-chosen artwork and fine furnishings tastefully done in the team's colors – brick red and grey – could not distract her from the fact that Reid was standing so near. His scent had invaded her personal space, and Reid had always had a presence about him that was hard to ignore.

"You could say I'm doing well, I guess," Kate said, hoping her breath sounded steadier than she felt.

"I'm not surprised you landed here, in the front office," Reid said. "You always did know your baseball."

Kate smiled politely at the compliment and took a seat behind her desk, glad to give her shaky knees a break and put something of a barrier between herself and Reid. He sat down opposite her, folding his six-foot-four frame into the plush grey suede chair. He had filled out more since high school, unsurprisingly, but otherwise, Reid still looked like the same boy Kate had noticed on their high school diamond. And he appeared every bit as calm as she wished she felt.

"Thanks for coming out on such short notice," Kate said.

"Not a problem. I'm technically unemployed, so I

suddenly have a lot of free time on my hands."

He said it lightly, but Kate didn't miss the underlying hint of rejection and disappointment. The sympathy she'd tried to eliminate earlier in the day snuck up on her again. She did her best to keep it out of her face though. In her mind, he still didn't deserve it.

"I'm sure you won't stay jobless for long, which is why I insisted on bringing you here today," Kate said. "As you know, I'm interested in seeing how you might fit in as hitting coach for our organization. Have you given much thought to the idea of coaching?"

"Sure, but I thought those days were a few years down the road," he said. "I'll be honest and tell you I'd rather be playing. But since that doesn't seem to be an option right now, I guess I'll be happy if I can just stay involved with the game. Baseball is all I know."

"You have a degree in business though," Kate said. "At least you have that to fall back on."

Kate had been impressed that Reid held a degree. He'd had a chance to enter the draft midway through college, but he'd waited. By the time he graduated, he'd also raised his draft stock. Not many pro athletes put their education first, and it made her respect him more, despite her reservations.

"True, but I don't want to fall back," Reid said. "I want to move forward."

Blunt. To the point. Typical Reid.

"Do you think being a hitting coach would qualify as moving forward?" she asked.

Reid paused for a moment, clearly considering her question. Kate waited as he appeared to weigh the option in his mind. This gave her more time to study him, which wasn't necessarily a good thing, although it wasn't wholly unpleasant. His dishwater blonde hair looked the same as it had in high school – buzzed on the sides and slightly longer on top. The ends were blonder than the roots, and Kate couldn't decide whether it was obtained from a salon or the sun. His seemingly permanent tan complemented his eyes, which were a color that could only be described a hazel, though Kate thought that label failed to do them justice. Indeed, they did look hazel from a distance, but anyone fortunate enough to get close enough to him would see they were actually golden brown rings with the faintest flecks of green. She remembered the first time she had looked into those eyes up close. She was pretty sure she'd melted on the spot. And he had seemed completely unaware. That was a long time ago, but the youthful sparkle still seemed to be there as she looked at him now, and that surprised her. Knowing what he'd been through over the years – to say nothing of the professional setback that brought him to her office today – she would have expected that sparkle to be missing. She wondered how he kept it around.

"I don't know," he said, abruptly ending her study of him. "It's not necessarily a step back. The position would be an honorable one, but playing again is going to be my ultimate goal."

"If you don't mind me asking, do you have reason to believe another team might pick you up right now?"

He shrugged. "I haven't heard anything from my agent, if that's what you're after. In fact, when I told him about your call, he told me I should give it serious consideration. He thinks this would be a great move for me."

"I believe it would be too," Kate said. "But I also need to know why you would be a great move for this team and, specifically, our offense."

"I'm glad you asked that," Reid said. "I pulled last season's batting stats and studied them on the flight. We both know stats don't tell the whole story, but they can at least give an outline. I'm also familiar with your former hitting coach and his style. That fills in a few more gaps for me. He seemed to focus on a lot of power and big home runs. Your players embraced that, but they also struck out a lot. I would like to see if we can get them to take more walks and be more selective about the pitches they go after. Obviously, I say this without watching any film of the team, and it's been two years since I've seen the Pioneers in interleague play, but I think it's a good start."

Kate nodded. Reid's insights weren't earth-shattering, but he had hit some very key points, which showed he had done his homework. Also, it wasn't so much what he said, but how he said it. He had a confidence in his words and yet didn't claim to know all the answers without further investigation. Kate knew from experience that Reid would take his research on the offense seriously. He hadn't necessarily been at the top of his class in academics, but when it came to baseball, he was a top scholar.

The interview lasted a full hour, and Kate learned more about Reid's work with the college players as well as the different methods he tried in attempt to repair his own batting woes. She could tell the latter was a tough subject for him and clearly something he thought about often. Maybe too often. Perhaps that was his problem, but Kate knew no one could tell a baseball player he was thinking too much; he had to figure it out and loosen up on his own.

Throughout the interview, Kate felt her calm returning, and she was all business. Discussing baseball had corralled her nerves and kept her thoughts from drifting to her history with Reid. Then again, baseball had always been a safe subject for them. As long as they both stuck to that, they'd be fine. Kate shook his hand to close the interview, and as they walked to the door, she told him she expected to make a decision quickly.

"Great," Reid said. "And since I'm in town for the night, maybe we could get dinner."

"Excuse me?" Kate said, caught off-guard by his suggestion.

"I know there's a possibility that you'll be my boss soon, but what would be the harm in two old friends having dinner?" he asked.

Talk about a loaded question.

The interview was one thing – but dinner for two was a completely different story. They were so much more than simply "old friends" and he knew it. She wasn't sure she could keep her serene façade in check in a social setting, and she definitely didn't want to unlock an emotional flood – a very real risk where he was concerned.

"No harm," Kate said, even though it felt like a lie. "But I have a lot to do. I need to go over my notes from our interview, make a few calls, and finalize some details for Fan Fest. I'm not sure I'll get off work in time for dinner."

Work was her standby out, always there to help her in

uncomfortable situations. And this most certainly qualified as uncomfortable.

"I understand," he said with a shrug. "With the time change and the travel, I'm pretty beat. I plan to catch a nap, so I probably won't eat until around eight. If you change your mind, give me a call."

"Sure thing," Kate said, opening the door to let him out.

"It was good seeing you, Katie," Reid said, offering his killer smile.

Kate did her best not to show how the familiar nickname shook her as she merely nodded in response. He waved to her assistant and continued on down the hall. Just before stepping into the elevator, he turned and smiled back at her. Kate struggled to make a quick retreat into her office without blushing or scurrying away like a scared mouse. Behind her closed door, she fanned her face, but the heat wasn't due to his smile or even the warmth of his hand enveloping hers in greeting and departure.

He'd called her "Katie."

There it was.

Katie.

No one called her that.

Except Reid.

What's more, the familiar nickname rolled off his tongue with such ease, you'd never know he hadn't used it in years. She sat down at her desk and stared down at his stat sheets and the notes she'd taken during phone conversations with his references, the closest thing to a résumé she had. With great effort, she tried to re-focus on why Reid had just been in her office. The Pioneers needed a hitting coach, and despite her personal issues with him, Reid would be a very good fit. With a sigh, she began drafting a formal offer to e-mail to Reid and his agent. The one-year contract was decent but the salary was nowhere near what Reid was used to making. It also included a clause about his alcohol use. The contract could be voided if he was intoxicated in public or behaved in a way that would embarrass the organization. The team's legal counsel flinched a little when she added it but assured her it wasn't illegal. As badly as they needed a hitting coach, she also wanted to protect the team's investment. She hoped Reid wouldn't balk at the stipulation.

James Scott was thrilled when he called to check in on Kate and learned of her progress. He had expected her to drag her feet on even contacting Reid, so he was surprised she was acting so fast. He had done a bit of his own research on Reid, and he believed the signing would be huge for the organization. Not only would Reid satisfy the hitting coach role, but he would also bring some publicity to the team, something James was always trying to generate. He didn't even try to mask his excitement about the new hitting coach, and he kept Kate on the phone for even longer than usual. It was one of the more pleasant conversations they'd had recently though, so she didn't mind one bit. She soaked in his praise, letting it make up for all the pressure he'd been putting on her in recent months.

By the time Kate finally hung up with the owner, Reid's agent had responded. He was happy with the contract and had already conveyed his opinion to Reid. Now, Kate just had to wait for a call from the man, himself. This certainly wasn't the first time she'd been in this position.

Not by a long shot.

Chapter Two

Reid Benjamin had caught Katie Marks' eye with the ease of tracking down a routine fly ball. It just took a bit longer – and a bold move on her part – for him to notice her. A senior in high school with scholarships on the line, he was too busy working on his bat speed and keeping his grades above water to pay much attention to the quiet brunette who sat in the front row next to the dugout at every home game.

Even if he had noticed her sooner, Reid probably would have written her off as another jersey chaser. Sure, he'd enjoyed the attentions from a number of those girls, but he never let any of them get too close. He found them to be a distraction. Reid, and others, noticed that his batting average took a bit of a dip whenever he was involved with a female. Even in high school, he couldn't afford that. His athletic talents would earn him the opportunity to be the first member of his family to go to college. Several college coaches had watched him and visited him over the last few years. A few pro scouts had come and gone as well. They all agreed he had talent, but the consensus was that a season or two of college ball would best benefit him, an opinion that pleased his parents.

Sam and Kathy Benjamin were certainly proud of their son's athletic accomplishments, but they longed to see Reid earn a college degree. He knew it, and he felt an obligation to give them that since he'd been the reason neither of them had a degree. His parents' educational journeys had been cut short when Kathy became pregnant during their junior year of high school. Thanks to night classes and help from their parents, they both finished high school, but medical bills from Reid's premature arrival had eaten up every extra penny they had, eliminating their already dwindling post-secondary options. Both had worked hard to provide Reid a comfortable childhood, and a college degree would be the culmination of their dreams for him.

But school didn't come easily to Reid. He had to work twice as hard as many of his classmates to pull a low B average. Early in the fall semester of his senior year, Reid found himself struggling in pre-calculus. The first few assignments took him all night, and he completely bombed the first quiz. He knew he needed help. Badly. He stared at his quiz with a frown for most of the class period, barely noticing when the bell rang.

Katie was in the same class, and since she was always watching Reid, she'd noticed his reaction to the quiz scores. Clearly, he hadn't done well. The confidence she saw him exude on the field was not present in pre-calculus. She could only assume his prowess didn't extend to math, which was one of her strongest subjects. When the bell rang, she hesitated only a few moments before doing something she'd never done before – she spoke to him.

"That quiz was pretty killer, huh?" she said, coming up beside Reid as the classroom emptied into the hallway.

"An average-killer for sure," Reid grumbled, not even turning to see the source of the voice. "But someone must have done well, because I sure didn't see any curve in my score. Even a curve wouldn't have gotten me into passing range though."

Katie blushed and bit her lip a little. Reid shifted his glance to look at her in attempt to read her silence.

"Let me guess - you got an 'A,'" he said.

Katie nodded shyly.

"Math is pretty easy for me, I guess," she said with a shrug. "I could help you if you want."

She was working hard to keep up a nonchalant exterior as her insides quivered with anxiety. Katie had never approached any guy in school, and now she was offering to tutor Reid Benjamin. She had been watching him on the baseball field and in the school hallways for almost three years. He was one of the hottest guys in school, and he wasn't lacking in female admirers, most of whom were far less subtle than Katie Marks.

"Really?" Reid asked. "I don't know. I wouldn't want to take up your time."

"It's no big deal," Katie said. "Meet me at the coffee shop after baseball practice tonight. We'll get started on tomorrow's assignment."

Not leaving him the option of telling her "no," Katie walked away and disappeared into the crowd of students. Even as she left him behind, she could feel her heart pounding. It took the entire next class period for her to calm down, and as soon she did, she began questioning her offer. It was entirely possible that she had just made a fool of herself. Reid Benjamin was probably sharing the exchange with his buddies at this very moment and having a laugh at her expense.

By the end of the school day, she'd convinced herself he wouldn't show up for help. She was certain he'd laugh it off and steer clear of her for the rest of their high school careers. But just in case, she went to the coffee shop anyway. If nothing else, it was an excuse to get her favorite latte and a quiet place to get her other homework done.

Even though she repeatedly told herself not to expect him, she looked up from her books whenever the bells on the door chimed. From her spot at a corner table, she had a clear view of the entrance. Her heart sank a little every time the new customer was not Reid Benjamin. Her history homework was largely neglected. It was hard concentrating on the women's suffrage movement when she thought the school's baseball star might be joining her at any moment.

By seven o'clock, she'd decided he definitely wasn't coming. Ignoring her unwarranted disappointment, she was finally able to zone in on her reading. *It's better this way anyway*, she thought. At least she would get some homework done in peace and quiet, two things that were hard to come by at her house with four younger sisters who were constantly chattering or bickering.

She was five pages in when she heard someone nearby clear his throat. She looked up and there he was – all 6'4", 205 lbs. of him. (Well, that's how the baseball program listed him, but Katie always suspected it was a tad generous.) For a few moments, Katie couldn't speak. She could only look at him. His dusty blonde hair was still damp with sweat at the temples and his brownish eyes looked down at her with a bit of uncertainty, as though he wasn't sure he should be there.

"Hi Reid," Katie finally spit out. "I wasn't sure you were going to make it."

His shoulders appeared to slump in relief as he pulled out the chair next to hers and sat down.

"Yeah, I was in the cages, and I lost track of time," Reid said. "Sorry about that."

"It's fine," Katie said. "It gave me a chance to get some of my history reading done."

She closed the book and pulled out her pre-calc book and notebook. Reid quickly followed suit, retrieving a bottle of water as well. Katie watched as he took a drink and then opened his materials.

"Alright, let's get started," Katie said, mentally shaking herself out of her reverie. She had offered to help him, not stare at him. She needed to deliver on her offer.

"First, I need to ask you something," Reid said. "And I feel stupid asking…but what's your name?"

She wasn't at all surprised he didn't know her name. Katie and Reid didn't share any mutual friends, and although she hadn't missed a single game in his high school baseball career, she knew she wasn't on his radar.

"Katie," she said. "It's Katie Marks."

"I'm sorry I even had to ask," he said. "You must think I'm a jerk."

"Nah," she said, shrugging. "Why would you know it? Pre-calc is the only class we have together, and Mrs. K doesn't take roll."

"I still feel like kind of a tool," Reid said. "On my way here, I hoped I would be able to recognize you since I didn't know your name to ask for you."

"Well, you did," Katie said, smiling a little. "And now you know my name. Let's see if we can introduce you to pre-calc too."

Over the next few weeks, Katie and Reid spent three evenings out of every seven at that same table in the coffee shop. Occasionally, after they finished pre-calc, they would both linger to work on other assignments. Katie found herself looking forward to doing her homework, although she tended to still have plenty to do when she got home from the coffee shop. She had difficulty focusing with Reid around, but she wasn't about to call an end to their study sessions. She enjoyed her time with him, knowing it probably wouldn't last long. At least that's what the realistic voice in her head told her. It was usually the loudest one. But that wasn't always the case when it came to Reid.

Katie felt butterflies every time he spotted her in the coffee shop and smiled as he headed her way. When their arms would accidentally brush, she felt a tingle run all the way up to her brain. She'd never experienced anything like it before. At 17, she'd had crushes before and even a few adolescent "relationships" at summer camp, but none of them had shaken her like this. Until

Reid, she figured those sensations were made up for romance novels and movies. Now that she knew they were real, she hadn't yet decided if she was better for the knowledge or not.

Too often, she had to remind herself that she was just his tutor, and if it weren't for pre-calc, he still wouldn't know her name. He said "hi" to her in the hallways and gave her a thumbs-up gesture in pre-calc when he scored well on his assignments. But that was it. Even when they studied together, they didn't talk about anything but school. Yet she somehow still managed to cling to this tiny hope that he might start to feel the way she did. At times, she felt foolish for having that hope, but as long as she periodically gave herself a reality check, she was certain she could avoid getting hurt.

After their next big test, Reid ran up to her in the hallway and gave her a hug. His warmth enveloped her and although it was only brief, it was enough to weaken her knees. Reality check shredded.

"I got an 'A'! You are amazing."

When he let her go, Katie smiled and adjusted her t-shirt, still reeling from the surprise of his action. She looked around to see if anyone had seen them embrace, but no one was paying attention.

"That's great," she said. "But don't give me all the credit. You worked hard."

"I know, but there's no way I would have figured things out without your help," Reid said. "We should get pizza or something to celebrate. How about Friday after I get done with practice?"

"Sure," Katie said easily.

Meanwhile, her mind was racing.

Did Reid Benjamin just ask me on a date?!

"Great," Reid said. "Let's meet up at Valerio's at seven. See you then."

He rushed off without another word, but that was okay with Katie. She wasn't sure she could keep a smile off her face much longer and she didn't want to look foolish in front of him. She wore a permanent grin for the rest of the day and on through Friday as she rushed home from school to get ready for her date with Reid.

Dressed in a brand new shirt, her favorite jeans, and a pair of trendy boots, Katie arrived at Valerio's a few minutes before seven. She looked around, but Reid wasn't there yet. She went ahead and found a table, ordering water and looking over the menu as she waited. More than a few times, she checked her reflection in the silver napkin holder on the table. So far, her meticulous curls and makeup were holding up just fine. If only she could say the same about her nerves. As the huge clock opposite her ticked to seven and then to five after seven, she began to wonder if he'd forgotten – or worse, that he'd changed his mind.

Finally, nearly 15 minutes later, as Katie was convincing herself to leave, Reid rushed in. Any anger or disappointment she had felt melted away when he spotted her and grinned.

"Sorry I'm late," he said. "Coach kept us a little longer than usual."

Katie merely nodded. She wanted to be mad at him, but he made that impossible. Especially with that smile.

"Thanks for getting a table," Reid said. "We'll need a few more chairs though."

She frowned in confusion. "Why?"

"Doug, Jake, and Lee are coming too," he replied.

"Oh, they are?" Katie asked. "I didn't know. I thought…"

"It's no big deal. I got it," Reid said, pulling over another table and more chairs. "They should be here any minute."

As if on cue, three of Reid's teammates entered and headed straight for their table. Wound up from a vigorous fall baseball practice, the boys were noisy. Introductions were mixed in with general conversation about baseball and pizza toppings, and Katie wasn't even sure her name or presence registered with them. Once they ordered, baseball and other school gossip dominated the table. Katie tried to keep up, but the boys barely let her get a word in.

After most of the two pizzas were gone, Katie pulled some money out of her purse and set it on the table.

"Well, this was fun, but I have to get going," she said, standing up.

Reid looked surprised, and for a moment Katie wondered if he'd forgotten she was there.

"Do you want to take any of the leftovers?" he asked.

Katie shook her head. "No, you guys split it up. I'll see you in school on Monday."

"OK, bye Katie," he said.

She barely heard him as she pulled on her jacket and exited the pizzeria as quickly and nonchalantly as she could. She hoped no one saw the embarrassment on her face as she walked around the

31

block to her car. She started it and pulled away from the curb, but she didn't go straight home. Instead, she drove around aimlessly, analyzing the situation. After more than an hour and lots of emo songs on the radio, it all came down to one thing – she felt ridiculous.

How could I have even let myself believe it was a date?

Why would Reid Benjamin ever be interested in dating me?

Then, she began analyzing herself. She hated the way she acted around him. She had catered to his schedule, never called him out on being late, and turned into a quiet mouse whenever she was around him. That wasn't her. Being with Reid had been an emotional boost, but he had effectively killed her confidence and turned her into someone she didn't know.

Well, those days are over.

By the time Monday rolled around, Katie had re-discovered her confidence and self-esteem. A weekend of hiding in her room watching her favorite movies helped her get back in touch with the real Katie Elizabeth Marks. The one who didn't go gaga over some guy just because he looked good in a baseball uniform and had a smile brighter than the Arizona sun.

The hard part was pretending not to notice Reid when she passed him in the hallway. He gave her his usual wave and smile, but she averted her gaze and ignored the way her stomach flip-flopped. It took considerable effort to put Reid out of her mind. He made it particularly difficult by taking the seat behind her in pre-calc. That alone was enough to unnerve her, but then he went a step further. She heard him lean forward and then his voice was right in her ear, sending a shiver through her. She hoped it wasn't visible.

"You left in such a hurry Friday," he said. "Are you mad at me?"

"Of course not," Katie said. "Why would I be mad?"

"I don't know," Reid said. "You just didn't seem … well, as talkative as usual."

"There wasn't room for everyone to talk," Katie said. "And it was clearly a boys' night out, so I just let you all have your fun."

Reid sighed. "I'm sorry it turned into that. I really did want to celebrate that 'A' you helped me get. I guess I shouldn't have invited the guys. Either way, you shouldn't have tried to pay for your pizza. Dinner was my treat. I picked this up after you left."

He held the folded bills over her shoulder, but Katie brushed them away.

"I can pay my own way," Katie said. "You didn't owe me anything."

Reid withdrew the money and leaned back. He was quiet for a few moments and Katie wondered what he was thinking. She heard him lean forward again and she could tell he was just about to say something when class started. Katie was somewhat relieved, and as soon as class was over she left quickly, wanting to avoid any further conversation with him. She successfully evaded Reid for the rest of the day and felt a rush of relief when she arrived home later that day. Admittedly, she also felt a twinge of sadness as she sat down at the desk in her bedroom to do her homework that evening. She was usually at the coffee shop by now, waiting for Reid.

She wasn't the only one troubled by the change in her routine. Around eight that night, her mother called for her and said she had a visitor. Katie made her way downstairs and was surprised to see Reid standing in the entryway of her house.

"What are you doing here?" she asked.

And how did you find out where I live?

"I could ask you the same thing," he said. "I've been waiting for you at the coffee shop since six."

"Oh, I guess I thought we were done now that you got an 'A' on that test," Katie said. It wasn't the complete truth, but she figured it was a passable lie.

"It was just one test. I still need your help."

"Fine. We can start again on Wednesday."

"Why not tonight? I'm here now, and tomorrow's assignment is hard."

Katie sighed. "Fine. I'll go get my books from my room and meet you in the den."

She'd used the word "fine" twice in a short span of time. If Reid had been older and a little bit wiser when it came to women, he might have gotten a clue that she was not being completely honest. But the boy's mind was filled only with thoughts of pre-calc and baseball, so he missed the signs that anything was amiss.

She pointed him toward the den, and she heard her mother offering him popcorn and soda as she went back up the stairs. She had finished her pre-calc homework already, but she picked it up along with her history book. Before she left her room, Katie couldn't resist giving herself a once-over in the mirror. After school, she'd traded her jeans and blouse for yoga pants and a t-shirt, and she'd pulled her long hair back into a low ponytail. Katie decided it was acceptable for studying with Reid – especially since he'd made it clear he wasn't going to notice anything but her math skills.

When she returned, Reid had one hand in the popcorn bowl while the other held a pencil over his notebook. His attention was on his open pre-calc book, so he barely noticed Katie's return. She sat down next to him on the floor, using the coffee table as their desk.

"So what are you stuck on?" Katie asked, opening her notebook to her homework.

"The third problem," Reid said.

"Ah," Kate said, finding the problem in question. "That one was a little tricky."

She explained her process of finding the answer, and Reid listened carefully, working through the problem. They repeated this cycle a few more times, and between help sessions, she was able to finish reading her history assignment. She expected Reid to leave once his pre-calc homework was done, but he surprised her by hanging around to do other homework, just as he had when they worked together at the coffee shop. It was after 10 when he stood up and stretched.

"I still have reading to do, but it's getting kind of late so I should go," he said.

Katie nodded and stood. She yawned, surprising herself. She hadn't even felt tired until that moment.

"And that's definitely my cue to go," Reid said. "Sorry for staying so late and keeping you up."

She shrugged. "I don't go to bed very early anyway. I'm kind of a night owl."

"Me too," he said with a smirk.

She often stayed up late reading and watching bad TV. Somehow she doubted his nighttime activities were as tame. She'd seen the girls who hung all over Reid and his friends. She'd also heard about some of the parties the athletes and popular girls attended. She was certain Reid could have his pick of female companionship even though he always appeared to be single. She had to will herself not to let her mind wander too far as she watched him pack up his things.

She walked him to the door, and he insisted on thanking her parents before he left. Moments later, he was gone, and she went back to her room to do a little more reading before finally calling it a night.

They continued meeting at her house to study from there on out. Katie's parents liked Reid, and they always had snacks ready when he arrived. They were also good at keeping Katie's sisters out of the way while the two studied.

Katie wasn't all that surprised when her mother asked if there was more to their relationship than math. Katie quickly and thoroughly denied any romantic interest, which seemed to disappoint her mother, but only briefly. Her father never asked, although Katie suspected he hoped there was something going on. A former athlete, he was undoubtedly disappointed when none of his daughters had elected to participate in sports. At that point, there was still hope for the younger girls, albeit a slim hope. Katie often watched games with him, which was how she first got into baseball. They'd bonded over baseball for years – her father was a lifelong Mets fan, and Katie was true to her hometown Diamondbacks. Still, Katie supposed he was excited at any opportunity to discuss sports with another male, and Reid was all-too-happy to oblige a brief exchange on the latest sports headlines before their study sessions began.

Katie noticed she was making a conscious effort to be dressed casually whenever Reid came over. In her mind, it was a way of preventing her imagination from getting carried away again. She saw the kind of girls who fawned over him at school. If they couldn't get his attention, there was no way she could. Besides, she didn't want to be one of those girls. She'd avoided it thus far in her high school career, and no boy – no matter how cute he might be – was going to turn her into a passive, uninteresting Barbie. She attempted to keep that mantra in her head, but Reid had a way of turning her resolve to mush. He was completely charming, although he didn't seem to be aware of it. And that, in turn, made him even more charming. It was a losing battle. More often than not, they would take study breaks and end up chatting for an hour longer than the 15 minutes they had intended to set aside.

Once Reid discovered Katie knew a little about baseball, he was eager to discuss the subject, quizzing her and listening to her insights. Katie had watched lots of games with her dad over the years, so she was already aware of the basics and some of the more popular stats. Talking to Reid provided her with a different angle on the sport. Through their conversations, she was able to get inside a player's head and see the game in a different light. The more Reid talked, the more Katie realized how cerebral baseball was. It was a lot more than just throwing a ball and hitting a ball. There was a lot of mental game to go along with the physical. In fact, she quickly figured out that the mental aspect was more important than the muscle, and she began to see how smart Reid really was. While she'd never really thought of him as dumb, she knew he wouldn't be graduating with honors either. She was starting to realize there were different kinds of intelligence, and Reid hadn't missed out on all of them. His math might not have been good, but if there was a course on baseball history and strategy, he'd ace it. She had no doubts about that.

Looking back, Kate realized those study break conversations had formed the foundation for her future career. She didn't want to give him credit, but deep down, she knew Reid deserved some acknowledgment for her success. He'd broken her heart, but he'd also helped provide her with some of the tools she needed for a successful career in baseball management. For that, she supposed she should be grateful to Reid and his lackluster math skills. If not for their nights spent doing pre-calc homework and subsequently talking baseball, she doubted she would be sitting in major league general manager's office today.

This realization gave her a slight sense of obligation to hire Reid. Fortunately, he was also the best man for the job. She knew it was the right decision for the team, even if it meant opening a door to her past she'd never imagined going near again.

After phoning the communications department to begin drafting a press release regarding Reid's hiring pending his acceptance, Kate opened her e-mail and scanned the messages. Most of them immediately went into the trash. Next, she went to a popular sports web site to check out the latest transactions and rumors. News was slow at the moment; if only Reid or his agent would call to approve the contract, she could make the hiring official, and the Pioneers would make a splash in the press. Not only would there be plenty of analysis about the risk of taking on

Reid and his history, but he would be the youngest hitting coach in the game. The airtime would thrill James Scott. Kate glanced at the phone again, almost willing it to ring. She was anxious to publish the headline. A small part of her knew she also wanted to hear Reid's voice again, but if he called her "Katie," she might not be able to continue playing it cool around him.

Finally, as Kate was straightening up her desk and office, which she did at the end of each day, her phone rang, and her assistant relayed the one caller's name she'd been waiting to hear.

"Hey Kate," Reid said, after she picked up her extension. "The contract looks good. I'm in."

"I'm glad to hear that," Kate said. "Our communications folks have started doing a press release. Could I transfer you to them so they can include a quote or two from you?"

"Sure, but not until you agree to have dinner with me tonight," he said.

"I don't know how late I'll be here," Kate said despite the fact that she had been preparing to leave when he called. "You might have been the biggest thing on my to-do list, but you weren't the only thing."

Reid chuckled, and Kate blushed as she replayed her words in her head and realized how unintentionally suggestive her statement sounded.

"I understand," Reid said. "I'd be happy to wait until you're done at work. I don't like to eat alone and you're the only person I know in this city."

"Last I knew, Reid Benjamin made friends wherever he went."

"That may be true, and I'll have plenty of time to make new friends, but tonight, I'd like to have dinner with an old friend."

Kate sighed. He wasn't backing down. The communications department was waiting on his statement, and Reid was waiting on her acceptance of his invitation.

"Fine. You still like seafood, right?" she said. "I'll meet you at Splash around eight."

"Perfect," Reid said. "Now let me give my statement, so I can clean up in time for dinner."

She rolled her eyes at that comment. She'd seen Reid only a few hours earlier and he looked fine. She couldn't imagine any reason he'd need to clean up. But right now, she wasn't going to call him out on that. She punched a few buttons and talked to the communications director before connecting Reid to the department. She then finished the task of closing up for the evening and headed down to the communications department to sign-off on the press release.

By the time she climbed into her car, she had just enough time to drive across the city to Splash. Traffic required her concentration, but it wasn't enough to distract her from the myriad of emotions going on inside her. She couldn't decide how she really felt about this meeting. On one hand, she was interested in catching up with Reid. A lot had happened to him since they had last spent significant time together, and she was curious to see how it had changed him. Despite her inner protestations, she did still care about him on some level. On the other hand, she dreaded the old feelings this dinner might dredge up. She couldn't afford to go back to that emotional turmoil – especially not with her job on the line. Then again, she was going to be seeing him frequently now, so maybe it was best to start getting used to chasing those old feelings away.

Reid was already at the table when she entered the restaurant. He spotted her when she came in the front entrance and waved her over. As she approached, he stood and, instead of offering a handshake, pulled her into a hug. His embrace was warm and strong, just as she remembered. She was surprised at how familiar it felt after all these years. As she retreated from his grasp, she tried to shake off the nostalgia but Reid wasn't cooperating.

"It's so great to see you, Katie. I can't believe we're going to be working together after all these years."

"It's just Kate now," she corrected him as she took her seat. "And you'll be working FOR me."

Reid cocked an eyebrow and looked at her for a minute. He laughed lightly and finally nodded.

"You're right, I'll be working for you, but I'd like to think of it as working with you," he said. "You know, like when we used to study together. It started out with you tutoring me, but eventually, we were just studying together."

He had a point, but Kate didn't think calculus and Major League Baseball could be compared that easily. Then again, they were both situations in which each of them needed some sort of help from the other. She only hoped this time around would result in less hurt on her side of the deal. She planned to do everything in her power to guarantee that.

"That was different," Kate said. "You needed my help for awhile, and then you didn't. I still don't really understand why you kept coming over to study."

"Your mom made the best cookies in town, and I liked talking baseball with your dad," Reid said. "I could tell it made his day."

Kate smiled at the memory. Whenever Reid came over, he and her dad would spend the first several minutes hashing out the latest baseball headline, trade, or game. Kate had felt virtually invisible, but it had made her dad happy. Almost as happy as the day she told her father she'd gotten her first job in minor league baseball.

"It did," Kate agreed. "He really liked you."

"I liked him too," he said. "I liked your whole family, even your sisters."

Kate rolled her eyes, remembering all the study disruptions when her younger sisters thought they needed to show Reid their new dress or toy. Reid never seemed to mind. He would stop and pay attention to them every time, which only encouraged affections from the young girls. They were crushing hard on Reid, and they didn't make a secret of it. They would giggle and even flirt a little. Kate would watch with a mixture of amusement, annoyance, and jealousy. Yes, jealousy. As a teenager, Kate was incompetent when it came to flirting. She was afraid of looking stupid or foolish, so as she watched her sisters not only flirt, but flirt successfully with Reid, she was envious.

"They liked you more than anyone else in the house," Kate said. "They were your biggest fans."

"And here I always thought you were," Reid said, smiling at her.

Kate felt the heat creeping up her neck. She hoped it hadn't reached her cheeks as his comment silenced her. She didn't know how to respond. In truth, she had been a huge fan of his and that had been the problem. Her adoration of him had gotten in the way of her judgment, which cost her a lot in the end. She lifted her menu to study it, reading it a bit more intently than was necessary; she'd been to this restaurant hundreds of times. When the waitress arrived to take their order, she chose her usual - salmon, lightly seasoned, with steamed vegetables. Reid chose the daily special without even asking what it was. This highlighted another reason she and Reid hadn't worked out. She liked routine and predictability while he had always been more adventurous and spontaneous.

Once the menus were no longer between them, Kate had no choice but to look across the table into those green-speckled hazel eyes, which, in turn, seemed to be studying her.

"So how have you been?" he asked. "I mean, obviously, you're doing well, professionally, but what about the rest?"

"What else is there?"

"Well, are you married? Seeing anyone?"

Kate bristled a bit at the question. It was an innocent one and a common one, but one she never enjoyed hearing. And she definitely didn't feel like it was any of his business. He had relinquished that right years earlier.

Reid could tell his question bothered her, as her nostrils flared slightly and she pushed her long dark hair back over her shoulder. He didn't quite understand the hostility, but he was too distracted by her hair to dwell on that for long. Reid remembered how it had felt to run his fingers through those locks, and he had to restrain himself from reaching out to see if they were still as soft as ever. The color was basically the same, with a few auburn highlights added in.

"No and no," she replied. "I have my work and it keeps me busy. That's enough for me."

"But you deserve more," Reid said. "Someone deserves you too."

"Funny, you didn't seem to think so a few years ago," she spat back.

Reid sat up a little straighter, as if she'd actually reached out and slapped him with her hand instead of just with her words. He was surprised by the bitterness of them. He frowned as he studied her. They hadn't been in touch for a long time – each busy building their own careers. Obviously, she had done a better job of that than he had. Still, he couldn't imagine what he'd done or said to evoke that tone in her voice.

Kate hadn't meant for the words to come out like that. She probably shouldn't have said anything at all. She didn't want him to think she was still affected by him or that she ever thought about their past. But she was and she did. His memory crept up on her every now and then, but the frequency had slowed quite a bit in the last two years. She could already see that reversing. She would be seeing him practically every day for the next eight months, and those distinct eyes and that devastating smile were bound to keep her memories of him close to the surface. Granted, not all of those memories were bad ones, but the bad ones made even the good ones hurt a little.

"What's that supposed to mean?" he asked after a few moments of tense silence.

"Nevermind," Kate said. "It's been a long day, and I haven't slept much lately with the stress of this hitting coach search. I don't know what I'm saying."

She reached for her glass of wine and took a sip, silently praying he would let it go. She really wasn't in the mood to hash out their past – now or anytime in the near future. She was prepared to deal with the memories, but she wanted to deal with them on her own, without his interference.

Reid was tempted to push her but he decided against it. The ink was barely dry on his contract, and he wanted and needed this job. He also didn't want to upset her. He had never wanted to upset her, and sensing that he had once done just that bothered him. He wished he knew what he'd done but he could tell he wasn't getting any of those answers tonight. He decided to shift into a topic that would make her more comfortable.

"So, how's your family? I haven't been back home in a while. Do they still live there?"

Kate relaxed visibly as she smiled and filled him in on her family. Her parents were retired but still living in the same house. They spent much of their free time enjoying their grandchildren's company and activities, as all four of Kate's sisters lived within 30 minutes.

"I get to see them all when I'm in Arizona for spring training," Kate said. "Mom and Dad also come see me for a week or so each summer. Dad makes sure it's during a series he wants to see, of course. Mom likes baseball, too, but Dad's the fanatic, so she lets him choose."

"Is he still a Mets fan?"

Kate smiled, surprised he remembered that. Then again, Reid and her father had spent hours discussing baseball, so she shouldn't have been too shocked.

"Of course," she said. "He even bought a replica of your jersey after they signed you. He was so proud."

Reid smiled, but then his smile faded and he looked down at the table.

"Yeah, I'm guessing he's not so proud anymore."

"You'd be guessing wrong," Kate said, noting the sudden lack of confidence in Reid's handsome features. "I had a voicemail from him this morning. Three minutes of him ranting about the Mets letting you go. I'd say he's still one of your biggest fans. He'll be thrilled to know you're working for the Pioneers now, and I'm sure he'll be excited at the chance to see you when he visits this season. He'll probably even ask you to autograph that jersey."

Reid looked up at her again and although his full confidence wasn't back, his expression didn't seem quite so self-defeating.

"I'll sign anything for him. It'll be good to see him again. Your mom, too," he said. "What about your sisters? Do you see them very often?"

"Again, usually when I'm in Arizona for spring training and again during the winter holidays," she said. "With the kids now, they don't get many chances to come to Portland to see me. Maybe when the kids get a little older. The oldest one, Brody, is only five; he's starting to get into baseball, but Chelle doesn't think he's ready to sit through a whole game yet."

"I can't believe Chelle has a five-year-old," Reid said. "She's still 11 in my mind."

Kate laughed.

"She's even younger than that in my mind, but I know what you mean," she said. "Anyway, Brody is five, and he just got a new sister, Brielle. Cassie has a three-year-old boy, Sage. Melanie has one-year-old twin girls, Ilana and Isla. Samantha has one boy, Jacob. He's not quite one yet."

Reid shook his head in disbelief. He'd sent enough wedding gifts to realize people their age were at the married-with-children stage. He'd also attended several of his teammates' weddings over the years and saw many players' children during team functions. It still seemed like a strange reality to him. He just couldn't imagine spending his evenings helping with homework and his nights in bed with the same woman. He supposed he'd want it someday, but at the moment, marriage and parenthood sounded like a prison to him.

"Where are your parents living now?" Kate asked. "Last I knew, they'd moved to Tucson."

"They're still there. I don't think they'll ever leave Arizona, and they like the area. It took them a little while to get used to it, but my mom is in a few clubs, and my dad is big into his golf league."

"Do you see them often?"

"Not anymore," he said. "Just holidays, and even those are short visits."

It was sad, but true. Reid wasn't as close to his parents as he had once been. Sam and Kathy didn't like the headlines they read about their son – the non-athletic ones. They didn't care about his declining stats, but they were horrified and embarrassed by Reid's infamous drinking and womanizing. The tabloids exaggerated his activities, but they weren't entirely fictional. He enjoyed alcohol and women, and the New York media didn't miss a beat. They were always waiting outside clubs and had even parked themselves outside his apartment building on more than a few occasions. The women were never embarrassed to be photographed on his arm or leaving his building in the morning. In fact, he was sure some of them only went out with him for the media attention. But that didn't really bother Reid. After all, he always got what he wanted and needed out of the deal.

"I've been busy with baseball, and they don't really like New York," he said.

There was no way he would tell her how his relationship with his parents had crumbled. He wasn't proud of it, and he wanted to save some face with her. He was pretty sure Kate knew all about his reputation too, but he wasn't about to own up to it. She was already too aware of his career failures. That was enough.

"That's too bad," Kate said. "Well, maybe you can see them during spring training. We'll be right in their area."

"Yeah, maybe," he said.

He was pretty sure he wouldn't see them, but he wouldn't admit that to her.

They spent the rest of the dinner discussing the business of baseball – clearly a much more comfortable topic for both of them. By the time dessert arrived, they had made it through half of the Pioneers' lineup, discussing the strengths and weaknesses of each batter. Reid was already familiar with some of the guys, having faced them on the field or read about them, but he wanted Kate's input too. Not only was she his boss, but she knew the game. And he knew that. He trusted her analysis, and he trusted her.

As far as he could tell, she trusted his baseball skills as well, but beyond that, he wasn't sure. From across the table, he studied her demeanor. She was all business. She'd been pretty cold when he tried to get personal with her. He was aware their past wasn't perfect, but he was surprised that she still seemed to be affected by it. If he wanted her friendship back – and he did – he would have to earn it. And it didn't look like it would be an easy task.

Reid and Kate fought over the check when it arrived, but eventually she let him take it. He didn't seem to care that she could write it off as a business expense; he wasn't letting her pay. She should have remembered that from their past. They walked out together and she waited while he hailed a cab.

"I'll see you tomorrow at the press conference," he said.

"And Fan Fest," she reminded him. "Everyone's going to be excited to meet you."

"I'm looking forward to it too," he said, as a cab pulled up to the curb by him. "Well, there's my ride."

Before she realized what was happening, he was descending on her and she felt his lips graze her cheek gently. Kate shivered at the contact. When they parted, she stared at him with wide eyes. Reid appeared unaffected as he calmly thanked her for joining him at dinner and climbed into the cab. Kate was glad he didn't wait for a response from her because she wasn't sure she could have offered one. She blinked a few times, and then she turned and headed to her own car.

For the rest of the night, that simple kiss on the cheek played over and over in her head. She flushed when she thought about the feel of his lips on her skin. It had been quite innocent, yet her reaction had been anything but. Her body didn't seem to harbor the same resentment toward Reid as her head and heart did. That annoyed her. She gave herself a silent lecture about the price of letting Reid in again. As she tossed and turned, she wasn't sure her inner monologue did anything more than delay the sleep she desperately needed for the following day's events.

Chapter Three

Somehow, Kate managed to arrive at the ballpark early on Saturday. The sleepless night may have actually helped her on that front. Each time she managed to quiet her brain enough to doze off, she would awaken a short while later. She finally gave up on meaningful sleep at 5:30 and got up, heading for the shower to start her day.

Fan Fest was slated to begin at 10, but the previous year's event suggested fans would start lining up around eight. To avoid the crowds and give herself enough time to prepare for the day, she sat down at her desk a little before seven. She had a large cup of coffee nearby and she turned on her iPod, hoping the combination would help wake her up and get her brain going. An e-mail regarding the hiring had been sent to coaches and players in the organization before the press release had circulated. There were a few replies to that e-mail in her inbox, and she scanned them, pleased to see all responses were positive and a few were even enthusiastic. She also saw a few notes of congratulations from some of her colleagues in other organizations. She smiled as she began typing up notes for her speech. She felt good about hiring Reid, but the affirmation from trusted peers was encouraging and provided some extra fuel as she worked on composing a speech to introduce Reid at Fan Fest.

She was putting the final touches on her speech when her office phone rang. She answered, expecting to hear Mr. Scott's voice on the other end. But it wasn't the team owner.

"Hey Katie. You're in the office early. This is the only number I have for you, so I thought I'd give it a shot. I forgot to ask you last night – what time should I be there today?"

It took her a moment to shake off the shock of hearing Reid's voice on the other end and respond, but only a brief one.

"I've scheduled the announcement for 11," she said. "You should probably be here a little earlier than that. Feel free to park in the players' lot. I've given the guard there your name, so you'll be able to get in without any trouble."

"Sounds good, I'll head out now," Reid said. "See you in a little bit, Katie."

He hung up without another word, denying Kate the opportunity to remind him not to call her "Katie."

She shook her head and turned back to her computer to print out the short write-up introducing Reid to the media. After reading through it a few times, she took a break and shifted her eyes to the windows and the field below. In a few hours, there would be people milling about in the dugouts as part of the full ballpark tour. The outfield would be open for fans that wanted to play catch. The rest of the action would be in the main concourse that circled the ballpark – autograph sessions, question and answer segments with various players and coaches, and a few kids' games.

Kate turned back to her desk, reading over her agenda for the day and singing along softly to the Stephen Kellogg & the Sixers song coming out of her iPod speakers. She didn't realize she wasn't alone until she heard someone else singing along. She looked up and saw Reid standing in her doorway. She stopped singing immediately and even turned off her iPod.

"You still like that band, huh?" Reid asked. "It's a shame they're not together anymore. After you introduced me to their music, I've done pretty well at keeping up with them. Nothing can beat that first show we went to though."

She ignored his attempt to discuss their past and commented on his appearance instead. He was dressed in the same suit as the previous day, but with a deep red shirt this time instead of black.

"Wearing the team colors is a nice touch," she said, ignoring his mention of their past.

"Yeah, I'd like to say I planned it that way, but honestly, I just like this shirt," he said, smirking.

Kate could understand why. The shade complemented his coloring very nicely. Then again, she'd never seen Reid look unattractive. He had even managed to make school-issued heather gray gym clothes look hot. More than once during her high school days, she'd lingered in the gym entrance during his class, watching him run laps and smack volleyballs with athletic ease. She didn't notice she had studied him for so long until Reid cleared his throat.

"Are you ok, Katie?"

"Yeah, I guess I'm just spacey today," she said. "Yesterday was exhausting, and I didn't sleep well last night."

Reid laughed lightly. "With the time change and all the

excitement, I didn't think I'd be able to sleep either, but once I hit the pillow, I was out."

Of course he'd had no trouble sleeping. Kate shouldn't have expected any different, yet it bothered her quite a bit that she'd been so stressed and sleepless over their reunion, and he was unaffected by the whole thing. She wondered how he could be so at ease around her considering their history. Then again, awkward was her specialty, not Reid's.

Katie and Reid studied together that entire fall, all through winter and on into spring. Other girls at school were extremely jealous of Katie and all the time she got to spend with the star athlete. They did everything they could to make her school days miserable, whispering behind her back, completely ignoring her in the hallways, and spreading lies about her. Fortunately, Katie didn't care much what they thought. They'd never been her friends anyway so their opinions didn't matter.

Her best friend, Amy, remained a steady companion. The two had been friends since grade school when they'd been paired up for a project on Theodore Roosevelt. Amy had taken notice of all the time Katie and Reid spent together, and she regularly interrogated Katie about it. It was clear she was curious, not jealous. Amy usually preferred to study alone, but she'd joined Katie and Reid a few times and had spent significant time observing the two together.

"I don't know how you get anything done with that gorgeous creature sitting right there," Amy said to Katie one day. "I'd just be staring at him the whole time."

Katie shrugged. "I guess I don't really notice he's there most of the time."

Amy shot her friend a look of disbelief and then shook her head.

"You might be able to tell yourself that, but you can't fool me, Katie," she said. "I was sitting next to you at the game the day you started drooling over him. There's no way you've been able to hide your massive crush. You're not that good of an actress."

Katie made a face at Amy. "First of all, it was never a massive crush, just a little one, and I'm over it, so there's no acting involved. We're just study partners."

"You spend four nights a week together. Something is going

on."

"We're just studying."

"The whole time? No one has that much homework."

"We talk baseball sometimes. But that's it."

That wasn't a lie. Katie and Reid's conversations rarely veered from school or baseball, but occasionally they talked about other people in their school. She teased him about all the girls who fawned all over him – obnoxiously cheering for him from the stands (sometimes even when he hadn't had anything to do with the play), handing him their phone numbers and bringing him baked goods. Katie had witnessed a lot of these moments and couldn't help but smirk when Reid would dump the phone number in the nearest trash can or hand a plate of chocolate chip cookies to one of his teammates. He always waited until the girls were out of sight, of course. He may have been uninterested, but he wasn't a jerk.

"Why don't you like any of those other girls?" she asked him one night as they studied for spring mid-terms.

"Who said I don't?"

"Well, are you dating anyone?"

"No."

"Then that tells me you don't like them."

"They're nice girls. Pretty, too. But I'm just not interested in dating right now," Reid said. "I need to focus on school and baseball."

"You know they're all clamoring to get a prom invitation from you."

"Well, they aren't going to get one."

"You're not going to prom?" she asked.

She couldn't imagine the most popular guy in school skipping out on one of high school's biggest events.

"Oh, I'll probably go. Just not with any of them," he said. "I was actually thinking we should go together."

Katie looked up at him in surprise, her World War II study guide momentarily forgotten. He was still staring intently at his own worksheet, which made her wonder if he realized what he'd just said.

"You and me? Why would you want to go to prom with me?" she asked when he remained silent for several moments.

"Because we're friends and I like hanging out with you," Reid said. "Plus, I figure it's a good way to thank you for all your pre-calc help this year. I never would have passed on my own. I've brought my grade up to a 'B' since we started studying together. My other grades have improved too. I owe you big time."

He looked up from his study guide and met her gaze.

"So what do you think?" he asked.

It wasn't the invitation Katie had dreamed of, although she'd never admit to anyone that she had dreamed of it at all. She'd even finally convinced Amy that she had no feelings at all for Reid beyond studying, discussing baseball, and a casual friendship. But now, with this invitation on the table and his eyes piercing her, waiting for an answer, her heart was pounding and she was having a hard time thinking straight. Somehow she got it together long enough to answer his question.

"You don't owe me anything, but sure, I'll go to prom with you," she said, hoping she sounded casual.

There was no way she could have declined his invitation. She may have been in denial about her interest in Reid, but she wasn't stupid. Every girl in the school would have given up manicures for three months for the chance to be Reid Benjamin's prom date. She'd never even had a manicure, but she was already scheduling one in her head, along with a hair appointment and shopping date to prepare for what was sure to be a night she'd never forget. It didn't even matter to her that he had invited her as a friend and as a 'thank you' for her tutoring help. She was going to prom with Reid Benjamin. The fact mattered more than the reason.

It took considerable effort to keep her smile from splitting across her face and even more effort to keep from bragging about it in school. In fact, she didn't tell anyone for several days, until she asked Amy about prom dress shopping.

"I thought you weren't going," Amy said.

The girls had discussed prom a month earlier after Brady Berry had invited Amy. At that time, Katie stated quite vehemently that she wasn't interested in attending. Amy was disappointed, but she didn't push Katie. Obviously, she was pleasantly surprised to see her friend's change of heart – and more than a little curious about what had caused it.

"Well, I wasn't ... until Reid asked me to go with him," Katie said.

She had to bite her lip to keep from smiling, even as her best friend gasped and started shrieking excitedly. This was exactly why Katie had waited until they were away from school and inside her house. She didn't want to cause a scene, and she knew Amy would do just that when she heard the news.

"Reid Benjamin asked you to prom?!? When? How? I need details immediately."

Katie shrugged. "He asked me Monday night, but it wasn't a big deal. He just thought we should go together as thanks for me tutoring him."

"That's such a lame cover," Amy said. "He could give you a card as thanks for tutoring him. He's taking you to prom because he wants to. He likes you."

"Don't get all crazy," Katie said. "He's not interested in me. He's not interested in anyone, really. He told me he just wants to focus on baseball and school. That's why he's taking me. He knows I'll take it for what it is – going to prom as friends and nothing else."

Amy wasn't convinced. Despite Katie's ongoing denial of anything going on between her and Reid, Amy insisted the prom invitation was not as innocent as it seemed.

"Well, we'll make sure he sees more than a friend or math tutor on prom night," she said.

Katie tried to keep her prom plans quiet, but the word got out anyway. This generated interesting behavior from the girls in the school – glares from afar and absolute butt-kissing up close. Their jealousy could not have been more obvious or intense. It would have been annoying if Katie didn't find it so amusing. She wasn't fooled by any of the antics. She knew none of them were genuinely trying to be her friend, but she had a little fun with them anyway. She accepted a few lunch invitations and gave vague answers or simply smiled when the girls asked if Katie and Reid were dating.

Her calm demeanor at school was a far cry from how she felt as she got ready on the day of the dance. Katie had searched five stores, trying on gowns of all lengths and colors before she found the perfect one. It was an ice blue strapless gown with navy blue beading that sparkled and danced in an abstract pattern from the sweetheart neckline, along the curves-hugging bodice and continued all the way to the ankle-grazing hem. A slit up to her left thigh showed a hint of leg and made it easier to move around. Amy was speechless when Katie stepped out of the dressing room in it, and that's when she knew her shopping was done.

Her selection looked even better now with matching jewelry and shoes. With help from some professionals, her green eyes sparkled, her lips glistened with a soft shade of pinkish-peach, and her chestnut hair was currently half-pinned, creating a cascade of curls down to just below her shoulder blades.

It was a far cry from the girl Reid was used to seeing, and the look on his face when he got his first glimpse of her was priceless. Her father led Reid into the den where Katie was waiting, and for several moments, he just stood there, staring at her from halfway across the room.

"Wow," he said finally. "You look great."

She noticed that there was a bit of a catch in his voice. He cleared his throat a bit in attempt to cover it up, but she still heard it.

"Thanks," Katie said, smiling. "You do too."

It sounded like a copout response, but it was true. He stood before her in a black tux with an ice blue tie and vest. In his hands was a plastic box containing a cluster of white roses surrounded by tiny ice blue flowers and tied with a navy blue ribbon. Katie noticed his hands were shaking a little as he put the corsage on her wrist. She told herself that was because they had an audience – both sets of parents and all four of her sisters were watching their every move. It unnerved her a bit as well, but she somehow managed to remain deceptively calm on the exterior as they posed for a few photos and then headed out to his car.

They chatted nervously on the way to the restaurant, where they would be meeting some of his friends and their dates. Katie wished Amy and Brady could be there so she would have someone to talk to, but they had other plans so she would have to catch up with her friend later. In the meantime, she did her best to make conversation with the other girls while Reid talked baseball with the guys. She just didn't have much in common with the other girls, and they didn't seem very interested in talking to her. She didn't care except that it made dinner feel like it was dragging on. Every so often, Reid would turn and talk to her, and she caught him keeping an eye on her throughout the meal. She was relieved when they finally left and headed to the dance.

Inside the school, Katie and Reid waited in a long line to have their photo taken in front of a shiny silver curtain. The prom committee had selected a casino theme for the festivities, so the entire gym was decked out in silver, black, and red. Oversized playing cards and dice completed the look. It had all seemed pretty cool at the time, but when Kate looked back on those photos (before hiding them in a box in her closet), it looked pretty tacky. Then again, it was high school prom. Tacky was expected.

Once they were done with photos, Reid immediately shed his jacket. She walked beside him, chatting idly as they checked out all of the decorations and other couples trickling in. Many of their dinner companions were milling around as well, but they hadn't spoken to Reid and Katie since the restaurant. In fact, they were on the opposite side of the room. That was fine with her, but she couldn't help wondering if it bothered Reid.

"Your friends and their dates don't really like me, do they?" she asked him as they found a place to sit with their sodas.

"Do you care what they think?" he asked.

"No, but I don't want you to regret asking me to prom."

"I don't. I asked you because I wanted to, and I'm glad I did."

"Even if that means they ignore you all night?"

He shrugged. "Look, the guys don't have a problem with you. It's the girls, and they're just being petty and stupid. As soon as the music starts, the girls will go off to dance together, and the guys will talk to me again. It's fine."

Katie nodded, but she had a hard time believing he was really fine with the way the evening was going. Prom was one of their last hurrahs with high school friends, and she wanted him to have fun.

She momentarily forgot about Reid's friends when Amy and Brady walked up to them. Brady was on the soccer team and he knew Reid from a few classes. While the guys talked about post-graduation plans – college for Reid and the Army for Brady – Amy pulled Katie a little distance away so she could grill her about the evening so far.

"It's better now, but dinner sucked," Katie said quietly to Amy. "His friends' dates hate me, so they were kind of rude."

"Those girls are snobs, so who cares? You're here with Reid, and he's looking sharp."

Katie smiled and nodded in agreement. "He does look good, but he always does."

"Are you ready to admit you're still crushing on him?" Amy asked her.

"No," Katie said, but her smile betrayed her protest.

"It's okay if you are. He's hot. I might even have a crush on Reid if it wasn't for Brady," Amy said. "Having a crush on him is completely acceptable. Maybe now is the time to admit it to yourself and to him."

Katie shook her head back and forth. "No, I'm just going to enjoy tonight for what it is."

Amy sighed, and Katie braced herself for another lecture, but the boys ran out of things to talk about so they joined the girls' conversation, which shifted to school and the prom. Katie couldn't help but notice how comfortable Reid seemed with her friends. Maybe the four of them could hang out this summer before they went their separate directions. She knew she shouldn't let her mind go there, but she couldn't help it. Prom and Amy's insistence were going to her head.

Her nerves from the afternoon returned when Reid led her out to the floor for a slow dance. As she moved into his arms, she could sense the stares from people around them, which made her a bit uneasy. She didn't have time to dwell on the outsiders though. She was too focused on Reid and how it felt to be this close to him. During their study sessions, she had sat next to him several nights a week and they'd accidentally touched plenty of times, but this was different, new, and unexpected. She felt a little nervous and jumpy, yet at the same time, being here felt so comfortable and right.

Reid seemed completely relaxed, talking with her about his excitement for baseball camp, which would take him to North Carolina just a few days after graduation. Katie talked a little about her summer plans, which included working part-time in the ticket office at Chase Field until it was time to head off to Arizona State. They also talked about their friends, family, and other random things as they returned to the dance floor for each slow song. Reid boycotted the dance floor during the fast songs, so Katie talked or danced with Amy while Reid caught up with his friends.

As the night went on, Katie and Reid's dance conversations fell into a lull. She tried to tell herself it was because they were talked out, but she had a nagging feeling that wasn't it. Something had shifted between them. She noticed their hold on each other grew more relaxed and they'd moved closer to each other. By the time the last song was playing, there was little air between them and she was resting her head against his chest.

"Do you want to go to the after-party at Jake's?" he asked her softly.

She wasn't thrilled at the idea of being around his jock friends and their snob girlfriends, but she was even less thrilled at the idea of ending her night with Reid either. So she agreed, and an hour later, after they'd changed out of their formal clothing, she was following Reid through a crowd of their classmates in the basement of Jake's parents' house. It was no small basement, or small house for that matter. Jake's family was among the wealthiest in town, and the size of their home exhibited that notion.

"Too bad I didn't bring my suit," Katie said sarcastically as a half-dozen teenagers pushed past them to get to swimming pool and hot tub.

"We could go swimming without suits," Reid suggested with a straight face

His serious expression made Katie's face grow hot. And then he laughed.

"I'm kidding," he said, nudging her. "Come on, let's get something to drink and look around a little. Jake's house is pretty cool."

Katie nodded and followed him to the full buffet of food before they made the rounds. They watched people play Final Fantasy on Playstation 2 in one room, and they joined a group of people watching a marathon of *The Osbournes* on MTV in another room. The number of people made it all a bit chaotic, but Katie was only vaguely aware of what was going on around them. She was too distracted by Reid's presence at her side and the fact that they had been holding hands or touching in some way for most of the evening. It had started at the dance as a way to keep up with him in the crowd, and it had carried through the rest of the evening, sometimes at unnecessary times – like now. She tried not to think too much of it, but that was getting more difficult as the night wore on and his touch grew more familiar and addictive. She didn't want to pull away, even though her brain was doing everything in its power to convince her she should move away from him if she wanted to keep from falling harder for him.

After two episodes of Ozzy, Sharon, Jack, and Kelly, Reid helped Katie up off the floor and led her outside. The pool and hot tub were full as they passed, continuing on through the expansive grounds surrounding the house. Several yards away from the pool, they found a bench in the garden. They could still hear the laughter, chatter, and splashes from the pool, but it wasn't loud enough to be a distraction. The darkness and some scattered landscaping also afforded them some privacy from the view of their peers.

"This has been a really fun night," Reid said, after they sat down.

"Yeah, it has," Katie agreed. "I'm glad you invited me."

"I'm glad too," he said. "Sorry my friends' girls tried to ruin it."

"They tried, but they didn't. I don't care what they think of me. In a few months, I probably won't even remember any of them."

Reid smiled and nodded. "That's what I like about you, well, besides the fact that you can talk baseball with me all night without your eyes glazing over. I like that you don't really care what other people think of you. You don't care that you're not popular."

It was probably Reid's attempt at a compliment, but Katie heard it a bit differently. She was well aware of her social status at the school, but hearing Reid say it sort of bothered her.

"Gee, thanks for the reminder," she said.

Her tone was defensive, and Reid straightened a little.

"I didn't mean it that way," he said. "I mean, I didn't mean it in a bad way."

"Yeah, well, what is 'popular' anyway?" Katie asked, but her tone betrayed her attempt at apathy. "By definition, shouldn't it mean everyone likes you? Because I don't think the so-called 'popular' people really live up to that definition. There are plenty of people who don't like them and don't want to be them. I know I don't."

"I know, I know, and I agree completely," Reid said, squeezing her hand. "I shouldn't have said anything. Sometimes I just can't talk the way I want to."

They were both quiet for a few moments. She felt like her entire evening had unraveled. The magic of being with Reid on the dance floor. The warm feeling of his hand covering hers. All of her romantic notions about Reid were quickly disappearing during this conversation, and she felt like she was crashing back to reality. He fidgeted next to her, obviously trying to think of how to repair his words. Meanwhile, she was silently fuming, feeling embarrassed and confused about what was happening.

"Katie, I think you missed the point in all of that," he said finally. "I said I like you."

She turned her head to study him. Surely, he couldn't mean that the way her heart was hearing it.

"Yeah, I know you like me," she replied, trying to right her emotions. "We're friends."

Reid shook his head and laughed a little.

"Why are you laughing?" she asked.

"Because you aren't listening to me. Katie, I took you to prom tonight. We danced all night. And now I'm sitting here, holding your hand, telling you I like you. What part of that says 'friends' to you?"

Katie swallowed hard and continued to study him, trying to process his words. Should she let her heart take them and swoon with happiness? Or should she let her head take the lead and attempt to analyze if there was a different meaning to his words?

He didn't give her time to sort out that dilemma though because he leaned in and kissed her. Katie was so surprised by his action she didn't respond to his kiss at first. Reid started to pull away, misreading her lack of reaction. She didn't let him go though. She put her free hand behind his head and kept him close, pressing her lips to his again. This one, with both of them in the game, lasted much longer and packed even more sensations.

Finally, she let him go, and they both pulled back, staring at each other. Katie felt dizzy and off-balance. Reid just looked stunned. He opened his mouth to say something, but before he could get the words out, they heard shouting coming from behind them. They both looked over their shoulders to see Jake standing in the pool area, loudly announcing that the party was over. Katie glanced at her watch and saw that it was after 4 a.m. and then she looked back at Reid, who still hadn't moved. She hoped he would finish whatever he'd been about to say. She hoped he'd kiss her again, but none of that happened.

"I guess it's time to go," he said, standing up and reaching for her hand.

Katie followed him back to the house and through the party. It might have been her imagination, but his grip on her hand felt different as they thanked Jake's parents for hosting and headed back out to Reid's car. She waited for him to say something on the ride home, but he drove in silence. When he stopped in front of her house, Katie opened the door and turned to look back at him, giving him an opening to say something.

"I guess I'll see you at school," he said.

That wasn't exactly what she'd been expecting him to say, but she went with it.

"Yeah, big calc test," Katie said. "Do you want to come over to study tomorrow?"

If he came over, maybe they'd have a chance to talk. Or kiss again.

"No, I think I've got this one, but thanks. See you Monday."

Her heart sank at the flat tone of his voice. He didn't sound like same guy who had chatted with her so easily all evening. Despite her inexperience with guys, she had a feeling that wasn't a good sign.

Katie got out of the car without another word. She heard his car pull away from the curb before she even reached the front steps. She locked the door behind her, awoke her sleeping parents to tell them she was home, and then climbed into her bed. She should have been exhausted, but she couldn't sleep. That kiss had awakened her body, and Reid's behavior after the kiss had sent her mind racing. She couldn't figure out what had caused him to go from hot to cold in a matter of moments. She could only assume it had something to do with the kiss. Admittedly, she wasn't very experienced in that realm. She had only kissed three guys before Reid. None of them had ever complained though, and she certainly had no complaints about the kiss with Reid. It didn't make any sense.

The next few weeks provided nothing in the way of answers or clarity. Reid seemed to be ignoring her in the hallways. Their study sessions halted. When their prom photos arrived, she gave him his copies and his only response was "thanks." It was as if they didn't know each other at all.

Without solid answers from Reid, Katie drew her own conclusions. She could only assume Reid had been playing some kind of game with her. Maybe it had even been a bet among his circle of friends, which they were likely all laughing about now.

Embarrassed by what had happened, Katie didn't tell anyone – not even Amy – about the events at Jake's house. Somehow, despite Amy's best efforts to pry, Katie was able to keep her kiss with Reid a complete secret. She covered questions about why he wasn't talking to her with a story about how he got mad when she called his friends lame at the prom after-party. Thankfully, Amy bought it and let the subject go. Katie didn't want to talk about what really happened with Reid. No one could ever know how foolish she'd been. She was completely crushed, but she made every effort not to show it.

Katie was more relieved to see graduation day than she'd previously expected. Part of her was sad she likely wouldn't see Reid again. But by the same token, it meant the end of awkward hallway encounters and the subsequent sick feeling in her stomach. And a larger part of her took comfort in that. She was ready to put high school – and Reid Benjamin – behind her.

It had been a long time since that first kiss, but Kate's vulnerability to Reid hadn't ended with graduation. If it had, she wouldn't have given him the chance to break her heart a second time. Nor would she be so affected as he stood in front of her now, more than a decade later. The only difference was that her wall against him and other men was much higher now. She just had to figure out how to keep it that way.

For starters, she needed to stop gawking over every outfit he wore. They were just clothes, even if they looked extraordinarily good on him.

"Well, I'm glad you're rested. This is a big day," she said.

She walked around her desk and handed him a sheet of paper. As he read it over, she gave him a verbal rundown of his itinerary for the day.

"First, we'll have the press conference. Then I'm going to have you sit in on one of the Q and A sessions. Feel free to mill around and do whatever you want for the rest of the event. After Fan Fest is over, I've scheduled a cocktail event so some of the players and coaches to meet you and talk with you."

Reid blinked a few times as he listened to the day she had planned out for him.

"Wow, you aren't easing me in."

"I wasn't aware you needed easing in."

He grinned. "Aw, you do still know me, Katie."

"That's another thing. My name is Kate now. Not Katie."

"But I like Katie better."

"Do you like it better than having a job?"

"Oh, lighten up, Kate," Reid said, reaching out and pinching her cheek playfully. "I'll try to remember to call you that, but I can't help it if I fall back into old habits."

She pulled away from his touch as though she'd been burned. But when she spoke, her voice was ice cold.

"Since you brought it up, calling me 'Katie' had better be the only old habit you struggle with here," she said. "I know you've had trouble with alcohol recently, but I hope that's changed. I won't stand for any embarrassment of this organization."

Reid's smile fell and he nodded solemnly. "Yeah, I saw that part of my contract."

"I thought it was necessary."

"I understand. And I'll behave. You have my word."

"Good. I hope it's worth more than it used to be."

Surprise and curiosity registered on his face at her remark. Kate could tell Reid was contemplating her words. She wondered how it was possible that he had forgotten the times he had let her down and hurt her. Yet the expression on his face told her he didn't feel like he deserved her bitterness.

James Scott entered the room, interrupting their conversation. He didn't knock, but his imposing presence didn't require warning. The Pioneers' owner stood just a shade over 6'5", but his linebacker-esque shoulders made him look taller. His jet-black hair was always perfectly styled, and he dressed like he had stepped out of the pages of *Golf Digest*. The irony was that he wasn't much of a golfer. He played in the occasional charity event and joined some of the players for a round or two during road trips, but baseball was his focus. Growing up in the Dallas suburbs, James Scott had spent many childhood summers accompanying his grandfather, father, and uncles to Arlington Stadium. He had been in the stands for the first Texas Rangers game ever and many milestones since, including Kenny Rogers' perfect game, which he liked to bring up in conversation at least five times each season. The man was a true baseball fan, and he preferred to keep his mind on the sport in which his money and passion was invested. Most of his fortune had come from a trust fund, which he wisely invested in stocks and some real estate. Eventually, this afforded him the opportunity to be principal owner of a Major League Baseball franchise. He expected his venture to feed his fortune as well as his competitive nature.

Kate was not at all surprised to see the owner show up in her office that morning. Clearly, he was anxious to meet the newest member of his staff – a hire he'd been waiting for longer than he thought was appropriate.

"Mr. Benjamin," James said, extending his hand. "It's nice to finally meet you. I've been following your career for some time, and it's great to have you in the Pioneers family. Don't let Kate intimidate you. She's a tough one, but she has a softer side too."

"Trust me, I know," Reid said, as he turned to shake the older man's hand. "I'm excited at the chance to work with her. She knows her baseball."

"That's exactly why I hired her," James said. "I've met men who know less about the game than she does."

"Me too," Reid said. "I've even played against some of them."

The two men shared a laugh and started chatting about some of their shared acquaintances.

Kate left them to their conversation and went back to her desk so she could read more e-mails and scan the latest transactions before her presence was required downstairs at Fan Fest. Now that the hitting coach situation was resolved, she had time to look at their rosters and see where they might need some extra options, such as catcher. Their current backstop was hitting a respectable .250, picking off sixty percent of would be base stealers and handling their pitching staff with ease, but Ben Ramirez couldn't catch 162 games. Their backup from the previous season had been shipped off to Tampa Bay as part of a trade for a new bullpen arm, and she wasn't completely comfortable with the leading catcher in their minor league system. He had a ton of upside, but he'd only recently converted from first base to catching. Kate and her staff believed he needed a little more time behind the dish in the minors before breaking into the big leagues. Catchers always developed slower than other position players, so they needed to be patient with this one.

As the time for the press conference drew nearer, Kate made a few notes to check on the availability and cost of a few players before closing her notebook. She looked up and was suddenly aware that she was now alone in her office. Reid and James had wandered out of her office at some point while she was distracted by batting averages and on base percentages. She was impressed she'd been able to focus on her work even with Reid in the room, to the point of not even noticing whether or not he was there. It made her feel better about the prospect of working with him.

With her phone and folder of notes in hand, Kate headed down to the lower level of the ballpark. The aforementioned men were already mingling with some of the reporters who had begun filtering into the media room. The space was used almost daily during the regular season, but it had been fairly quiet over the winter. Kate approached James and Reid, subtly urging them to take their seats at the long table at the front of the room. She couldn't help but notice how perfect Reid looked in his grey suit and deep red shirt with the team logo in a grid-like pattern behind him. He looked like he belonged, and judging by the smile on his face as James Scott introduced him, it appeared he felt like he belonged already as well.

Kate fought to pull her gaze from Reid and turned her attention to the reporters. With the official introduction complete, the assembled gallery began asking questions of James and Reid. Predictably, the first reporter questioned Reid's ability to coach considering his own failures at the plate. Reid seemed to expect it, and he explained how he had worked with several young hitters at the University of North Carolina.

"Sometimes knowing what you need to do and being able to do it are two different things," Reid said. "I may not have the ability to hit at a big league level, but I have plenty of knowledge about it. I've seen a lot of pitchers and a lot of hitters. I know I can help the Pioneers improve their already impressive offense."

The next few questions surrounded Reid's impressions of the Pioneers, as a team and an organization. Reid spoke diplomatically about the Mets, the organization that had launched his career, before expressing his excitement about being in Portland and starting a new chapter of his life in baseball.

"You were only released a few days ago. How can you be sure another team won't want you in their outfield?" a reporter asked. "How would you react if that opportunity came up?"

Several recorders beeped as Reid took his time answering the question. His pause was a bit unsettling, and it caused Kate to turn and look at him.

"I don't think that's going to be an issue," Reid said. "But even if it does, I've made a commitment to the Pioneers. James and Kate can trust that I will stand by my commitment. That's who I am."

Kate and James fielded a few questions about other organizational matters before the press conference ended. Reid followed the front office folks back out into the hallway and into a staff elevator. Inside, it seemed like they let out a collective breath.

"That went pretty well," James said. "I'm going to check out a few of the autograph lines. Reid, I'll see you at the cocktail hour later. I know a few of the other partners are anxious to meet you. Enjoy the day, and don't let Kate wear you out."

Reid laughed a little, and Kate blushed when she realized where Reid's mind had taken that comment. The owner, of course, was unaware of their history and thought nothing of Reid's chuckles. He simply waved before stepping off the elevator a few moments later, turning quickly to the left.

"If he only knew," Reid said softly.

Kate heard Reid's comment, but chose to ignore it as they exited the elevator and walked in the opposite direction. Silently, she led him down the wide corridor. She was pleased to see a line at the cash register in the team gift shop. They continued on into a small conference room, where a few dozen fans sat in rows of chairs, facing two of the Pioneers' young outfielders. Kate introduced Reid to the players, and once the session had started, she quietly left to monitor some of the other Fan Fest activities.

For the most part, she was just relieved to be away from Reid. She'd spent more time with him in the past 24 hours than she ever thought she would again. The effects of his presence were going to be unsettling at best and disastrous at worst. She hoped she would get used to it over time so they could both do their jobs without their history interfering. She didn't have time to dwell on the past; her job required her to look at the future.

After a lap through the Fan Fest stations, Kate returned to her office. The upper level offices were silent, except for the humming from the heat vents as she sat back down at her desk. She decided to keep the silence and left her iPod off as she opened the trade wire web site and her notes. She began to peruse the listings for catchers who might be available to split duties with Ramirez. There were a few free agents with potential, and with camp starting in a few weeks, they might be willing to take lower dollars just to have work. It was a workable option, but Kate would prefer to work out some sort of trade for a catcher. The Pioneers had some decent chips in the farm system that might be attractive enough to another club. She wrote down a few names as well as their key stats and began assigning numbers to prioritize the list. After looking over the list, she picked up the phone to call Ed Sampson, the GM in possession of her first choice. Even though it was Saturday, GMs were never really off-duty. He answered on the third ring, and while he didn't laugh at her initial offer, he didn't accept it either.

"You'll have to do better than that if you want Jamison," Ed said.

He named two minor leaguers and it was Kate's turn to scoff. He wanted two of the top prospects in the game. She had labeled the two as untouchable, which basically meant they were staying put unless she could swap them for a big fish. The catcher she was asking about was a medium-sized fish at best.

"You and I both know that's not happening," she said.

"Well, I had to try," Ed said.

"Same here," Kate said. "I knew prying Jamison away would be a long shot, but I had to at least make an attempt."

"Yep, I get it, and I appreciate the interest," he said. "Good luck finding a catcher. There aren't a lot of great options out there. Some good defense, but shaky offense. Then again, maybe your new hitting coach can find a gem in there somewhere."

"Yeah, maybe," Kate said.

"That was a good pick-up, by the way," he said. "The guy's had it rough lately, but I think he's still got some good in him."

"I do too, obviously," Kate said. "Thanks for the vote of confidence though."

She hung up with Ed and made a few more calls, but no one else was willing to deal with her at the moment either. Each of them made a comment on her hire of Reid Benjamin, which wasn't surprising but was definitely encouraging. Maybe the Mets had given up on Reid, but it was clear other GMs still saw him as somewhat of a threat. She was anxious to see how that would pan out in the weeks and months ahead.

As she hung up with the fourth GM she'd called, her stomach growled. She looked at the clock and realized it was almost two. She still didn't have an answer to their catching dilemma, but she needed to get something to eat. She should probably check in on Fan Fest as well.

She shut down her computer and locked up her office before heading down to the main concourse, which was alive with people decked out in Pioneers gear milling between stations, chatting about the players they'd just seen and those they hoped to see. Kate had tried to convince all players to attend Fan Fest, but it wasn't required, and some of them had other off-season obligations. Fortunately, many of the players in her organization understood the importance of interacting with fans, and they genuinely seemed to enjoy it. She bought a sandwich at a concession stand and ate it while she continued her rounds. As she passed an autograph table, she caught a glimpse of Ian Davis posing for a playful photo with a teenage boy. The youngster's grin could not have been bigger, and the fans right behind him in line were laughing and enjoying the moment as well. At the next table, Justin Tanner was talking to a young girl who declared very loudly that she wanted to play baseball like him instead of softball. Kate continued on, eventually making her way to the lower levels where the fans were lined up to take a few pitches in the batting cages. Kids and adults alike were patiently waiting for their turn to feel like a big leaguer, even if only for just a few moments.

It was nice to see the ballpark occupied again. Pioneer Stadium was a gorgeous facility – the newest in the nation but designed with tradition and old school charm. She loved coming here every day. Even during the off-season, it was a beautiful place to work. It was even more special on days like today when the optimism and excitement about the team were likely the highest they'd be all season. There is nothing quite like the start of a new season. Everyone is undefeated and still a contender for the World Series. Sure, on paper there are always favorites, but in the time leading up to Opening Day, it feels like anything is possible and everyone has a chance. That optimism would begin to fade after game one, when only half of the teams in the leagues could still claim to be undefeated and the grind of a full season began to wear on everyone in the business. But for now, there was still hope.

Kate didn't even try to contain her own smile as she took it all in. Days like today made the stressful offseason worth it, and they reminded her why she chose this career path. Being a GM required long hours, a thick skin, and a knowledge of stats and data that sometimes made her head hurt. Some would say she'd given up a lot for her job – romance, a family, and a home life – but, as she constantly stated, she wasn't interested in those things anyway. Occasionally when she saw her sister's children or kids at the ballpark, there were brief moments of wondering what her own children would be like. Then she remembered that her lifestyle didn't even allow for a pet. Plants weren't likely to survive her schedule either, so children were definitely out of the question.

Chapter Four

Kate was so lost in her thoughts she didn't notice she was no longer standing alone. Well, she hadn't technically been alone since she left her office, but she'd viewed everything from the perimeter, keeping to herself. She heard a throat clear a few feet away, and she shouldn't have been surprised to look over to find Reid at her side. She should have sensed his proximity, but she didn't, and she wondered how long he'd been standing there.

"Seems like a pretty good turnout," he commented. "I'm used to New York crowds, but this is decent."

She probably should have been slightly offended by his comparison, but she wasn't. She was well-acquainted with the differences in fan counts among various franchises. She'd seen the good, the bad, and the ugly during her time in the business. The Pioneer fan base was steadily growing, but it was difficult with a new team, especially since Seattle was just three hours away. Many in the Pacific Northwest had adopted the Mariners when they were enfranchised in 1977. It was tough to break four decades of loyalty. Kate understood that and had encouraged stakeholders to be patient in drawing fans to the ballpark. Slowly, the Pioneers were attracting new fans and those seeking a team closer to home. Attendance went up a little with each passing season, and that's all Kate could ask for at the moment.

"Maybe someday we'll have New York crowds," Kate said optimistically.

"That might be expecting a bit much given the population difference," Reid said.

"Good point, but you can't blame a girl for dreaming," Kate said.

"It's good to dream," he agreed. "There are some great fans here anyway. I've had a lot of fun today."

"I'm glad to hear that," she said, smiling proudly. "I like to think we have the best fans in the majors."

"They're certainly the friendliest I've encountered in awhile,"

Reid said. "None of them have cussed me out yet, so that's a point in their favor."

Even though he'd tried to drown out the fan criticism while he was with the Mets, Reid had still heard plenty. It was hard to miss when it was being yelled from nearly every corner of the stadium. And avoiding fans while he was out in the city was practically impossible. Everyone knew who he was. Funny, that's what he thought he wanted in his childhood dreams of being a ballplayer. But the reality had turned out to be more of a nightmare. On some level, he knew he deserved the shouts and boos. He hadn't lived up to anyone's expectations, not even his own. He never expected to be an instant All-Star, but he believed he had the talent to be a serviceable if not reliable player for the Mets. He'd worked hard through college and the minors to build his skills, and although it felt like a long road, he'd believed it would all pay off when he finally got the call-up. At first, he was right. Everything was going just as he planned, but then it all changed. All of a sudden, he couldn't get hits to fall in, and then the strikeouts became the standard outcome for his at bats. He still didn't know where he'd gone wrong, and now it was too late to fix it. At least for himself.

In his new role, however, he had the opportunity to help other players maximize their offensive talents. He only hoped he didn't fail at that too. After spending the morning with Pioneers fans and a few of the players, he was beginning to feel the pressure. These were good people with high hopes. He wanted to help those hitters give the fans something to cheer about well into October. He would give them his best and hope it was enough. He owed them that.

If he was being completely honest, he knew he owed it to Kate too. He couldn't afford to let her down after she'd taken a huge gamble and hired him. When she offered him the job, he momentarily thought she was doing him a favor, extending a kind gesture to an old friend. But their conversation that morning seemed to indicate otherwise. Her words and tone made it abundantly clear that she still had some anger toward him and his past behavior, but she'd pushed past it for the good of the organization. She'd done this for the team, not for him. Because of her, he now had a new opportunity to impact the game he'd loved all his life. He needed to make sure she didn't regret her decision. Maybe he'd manage to earn her respect again in the process.

"You're not in New York anymore," Kate said. "You'll find the fans here are pretty patient and forgiving. Just look at how they've taken to Derek Beaman."

Reid cocked his head in thought. He knew the Beaman story well, and it was one to which he could relate.

Derek Beaman had been a top draft pick by the Houston Astros after one season of college ball thanks to a killer left-handed delivery that made opposing hitters whiff and scouts drool. His minor league career had started off promising. He breezed through A and AA ball and was named minor league pitcher of the year in the Astros organization.

By the age of 21, Derek was already in AAA, and after a rough first month, he quickly found his stride and was leading the league in strikeouts and ERA by July. While the message boards buzzed about when he would be called up, he collapsed on the mound in the middle of a game holding his left arm. He needed surgery. Season-ending surgery. It could not have happened at a worse time for the young pitcher. At the very best, his career was put on hold. At worst, he might not return to baseball at all. Doctors couldn't guarantee anything.

The surgery went well and everyone was hopeful Derek would be on track to rejoin the team sometime in the new season. Things took an unexpected turn during his rehabilitation when Derek got hooked on painkillers. Badly. And when the painkillers weren't strong enough, he sought out other drugs. He was arrested twice, and the second time knocked him out of Major League Baseball. It seemed his career was over before it really ever started.

Derek's life was on a downward spiral. His baseball dream was over, and a relapse chased his wife from their home, taking their infant daughter with her. If not for his older brother, Derek might have landed in the obituary section before his 24th birthday, but Mike Beaman took the young addict in and straightened him out. With some tough love and more than a few arguments, Derek found sobriety and returned to Major League Baseball.

Kate had taken plenty of heat for her signing of Derek Beaman. He submitted to random, regular, and frequent drug tests. But even with those stipulations in his contract, the media had still berated Kate. Opposing fans taunted and poked at Derek's drug use often. Pioneer fans had been wary at first, but he'd worked hard and given them some good innings. If the length of his autograph line was any indication, the fans were starting to warm up to him. If the fans could embrace a guy with that kind of history, maybe they would accept Reid too.

"Sports fans love a good comeback," Kate said.

"It makes for the best story," Reid agreed.

"When it comes to you, I don't care about the story, I just expect your best effort," Kate said.

"And that's exactly what I'm going to give you," Reid said.

"I know you will," Kate said, nodding. "You're a hard worker."

Reid smiled a little. "Did you just give me a compliment?"

Kate blushed. And then she frowned. "No, I just stated a fact."

"Funny. It sounded like a compliment to me," he said.

She didn't have a retort for that. Even with all that had happened and all the years that had passed, Reid still had a way of making her feel completely inept at speaking. Feeling flustered, she looked at her watch.

"It's almost time to shut down," she said, changing the subject. "The cocktail event isn't until five. You're free to do whatever you like until then."

"I was going to look around at the facilities some more, but I don't want to get in the way of the fans, so I guess I'll do that another day," he said. "Maybe we could hang out for a while."

"I need to go back to my office. I have plenty of work to do," she said.

"It's Saturday."

"You know baseball doesn't stop for the weekends."

"No, but the season hasn't even started yet, and I'm willing to bet you've already put in way more than your due this week."

"We have a lot of holes in the roster. I need to find a catcher who can hit. And it wouldn't hurt to find a few bullpen arms we can store in AAA just in case."

"A few hours won't hurt. You can pick it up tomorrow, right?" Reid said. "If you want, I'll even come in and look at names with you. Maybe I can offer some insight."

"No, thank you. I know you mean well, but it's my job, and I'll handle it," Kate said. "You probably need to start sorting out your move anyway."

"Yeah, I guess," he said. "But the offer stands. I'm here to help you. As I recall, you once offered to help me when I felt a little in over my head."

"That was pre-calc. Much different from managing a Major League Baseball team," Kate said.

"You just don't want to have to repay me with a date like I did back in the day," Reid said in a teasing tone.

Kate shot him a fiery look, and Reid drew back a little.

"Even if we could date, which we can't, what makes you think I would even consider it?" she asked.

"Geez, Kate. I was just teasing," he said. "What did I do to deserve that kind of anger?"

"You really don't want me to get started," she said. "And, frankly, neither do I."

She practically spat those words just in case her glare didn't convey her displeasure.

"Wow," he said. "I don't know what I did, Kate, but -,"

James Scott walked up then, and Kate was relieved at the owner's sense of timing. She was not interested in continuing this conversation, which felt a lot more like a confrontation.

"Reid, my man," he said. "I just realized I didn't talk to you about your living situation. I own some properties around town. Let me know if I can help you find a place to set up."

Kate was glad James wasn't particularly perceptive, as he seemed completely oblivious to the tension between Kate and Reid.

"That would be great," Reid said, turning his attention to the team owner.

James nodded, and the two men arranged a time to meet up so Reid could see a few Scott Properties before he returned to New York.

Kate only vaguely heard any of it. She was still fired up over the brief jaunt down memory lane Reid had initiated. She knew it was foolish to hope they could work together without ever discussing their past, but she planned to do everything in her power to avoid it. She didn't want to rehash it. She knew it wouldn't fix anything. Clearly, he didn't see that he'd done anything hurtful and she didn't see the point in telling him. An apology wouldn't do any good after all these years. And it was entirely possible he wouldn't offer one anyway. That thought made her even angrier. She needed to get away from Reid.

She quietly excused herself from the men and decided to take another trip through the festivities as they wound down. It helped her wind down a little too. Fans were all smiles as she passed them on their way to the exits. Their happiness reminded her she had a job to do. Refocusing on her work, she was able to shove Reid Benjamin to the back of her mind. She could feel her whole body relaxing a little as she took in the crowd.

Kate managed to steer clear of Reid for the rest of the afternoon as she returned to her office to look through some more stat pages and possible pick-ups for the team. The natural light in the office began to dim and she realized she should probably close it up for the day. Only one thing stood between her and home.

By the time she arrived at the cocktail event, Reid was deep in conversation with three of the Pioneers players. She was relieved she didn't have to make any introductions. Then again, she should have known that would be unnecessary. Reid had always been a social person and making friends was easy for him. He didn't need any guidance in that realm.

She went to the bar and ordered a glass of white wine. When she turned, Don Carroll was at her side.

"Well, you finally did it. I thought we'd head to Arizona with no hitting coach," the manager said.

"Come on now, Don. When have I ever left you ill-equipped to do your job?" she asked.

Don gave her a look. "Do I have to mention Sean Weaver?"

A ballplayer-turned-manager, Don had been in several organizations before joining the Pioneers. He didn't pull any punches and always let Kate know how he felt about her personnel decisions. Sometimes it seemed he was trying to tell her how to do her job, but by now, Kate was used to it. A lot of men in the business thought they knew better than she did. She had done her best to show she was perfectly capable of evaluating and hiring talent, but it didn't always work out as she had planned.

"Are you kidding me? You're still mad about that?" she asked. "It's been three years, and he was my first free agent pick-up. I'm sorry he wasn't Jered or Jeff. He's not even related to them, but I honestly thought he was going to be serviceable in the bullpen."

"Well, you were wrong. He wasn't even serviceable as a bat boy," he said.

"That's a little harsh," Kate said.

She could understand the manager's frustration, and knew she deserved to bear the brunt of it. She'd signed Weaver based on one scout's opinion and he'd never lived up to the hype. Every now and then, he'd throw a scoreless inning, but it was more common for him to give up three home runs in less than an inning. She'd never heard the Pioneers fans "boo" as loudly as they had when he came out of the bullpen. They were a forgiving and patient bunch, but by July, they'd seen enough of him. Unfortunately, they had to endure a few more months of him as Kate couldn't afford to release him and no one in AAA was ready to take on his role. It was her worst signing to date, and she had hoped she'd lived it down by now, but apparently the manager wasn't ready to forgive her yet.

"You know what was harsh? Having to march him out there every few days when the rest of the bullpen was gassed. He was a last resort, but I still used him way more than I wanted to," Don ranted.

"I know, and I'm sorry," she said. "I made it up to you the next season when I brought Jace Brigham over though, right?"

The mention of the young phenom she'd spirited away from the Giants brought a smile to Carroll's wrinkled face.

"That's what I thought," Kate said, smirking. "See, I've gotten better at my job."

"Well, I'm anxious to see what Benjamin can do for our boys," Don said. "I've always liked him as a player, but I know he's had some struggles. Hopefully those are behind him. Especially the off-field stuff. We don't need any of that."

"I wouldn't have hired him if I thought that would be a problem," she said.

She saw a hint of doubt on Don's face, and she felt an urge to set his worry at ease.

"Listen, I've known Reid for a very long time. I know what he's made of and what kind of person he really is," Kate said. "Reid Benjamin will give you the best he's got. And, trust me – that's really something special."

"Another compliment? This must be my lucky day."

Until she heard his voice, Kate didn't realize Reid had come up behind her while she was talking to Don. She wondered how long he'd been standing there. Obviously long enough to hear her last comment.

"Don't get too used to it," she said to him.

"No kidding. She doesn't throw out compliments too often," Don chimed in. "She's a tough boss, Benjamin. I hope you're ready for her."

"Oh, Kate and I go way back," Reid said, smirking at Kate. "I'm more than ready for what she throws at me."

Kate wanted to slap that smirk off his face. And she certainly didn't appreciate the suggestive nature of his tone. Beyond the irritation of being reminded once again of their history, she didn't want the manager or anyone else in the organization to think she hired Reid for any reason other than his baseball skills. She'd worked hard to disprove the rampant theories that women were too emotional to make logic-based decisions. If her history with Reid ever came out, many would assume she'd hired him for other skills, and she was quite certain that all of her efforts would be for naught. Her reputation was on the line. If Reid screwed that up for her, the sliver of compassion she had for him would completely disappear. She would never be able to forgive him.

While she silently fumed, the two men next to her were sharing a good laugh. They'd shifted the conversation from her, thankfully, to baseball stories and ballplayers with whom they'd both worked. She hoped Don had missed Reid's insinuation or chalked it up as typical male banter. She finished her glass of wine and decided she definitely needed another. The cocktail hour still had plenty of hour left. She would need some liquid help to get through it.

When she turned back with her new glass of wine, Don was no longer at the table, but Reid was still there. Waiting for her, apparently.

"Feeling a little calmer now?" he asked. "I thought smoke might come out of your ears a few minutes ago."

"Reid, we need to be really careful with what we say about our past," she said, keeping her voice low. "I don't want people to think that's why I hired you. And I hope you don't either."

"People hire old friends all the time. It's not that big of a deal," he said.

She gave him a look of disbelief. "Our history is a little more complex than that, unless you've forgotten."

It took a lot of effort for Reid to keep a straight face. He hadn't forgotten, but it amused him that she seemed to think he had. It was even more entertaining to see how much that irritated her.

"Whatever," Kate said, clearly buying his act. "It was a long time ago, and I really want it to stay there. My job is on the line here, Reid, and so is yours."

"Alright, alright," Reid said, chuckling and giving her that winning smile. "I'll keep it quiet. I know how to behave when I have to."

"I'll believe that when I see it," Kate said.

Reid just grinned as she walked off to talk to some of the Pioneers players. She made it clear she did not want him to follow, so he stayed put. He didn't want to annoy Kate, but he had a feeling he wouldn't be able to avoid that. He'd never been good with his words – particularly where she was involved – but it seemed he was going to have to take extra care when he was speaking to her. He hadn't yet started his job, but he wanted to keep it. He wanted to succeed at something. Something besides upsetting Kate. But that was going to be a challenge. Everything he said seemed to fire her up. And sadly, not in a good way.

He'd much rather see the good fire in Kate. Reid had vivid memories of how passionate she could be. He hadn't thought about those occasions in quite a while, but now they flashed through his mind like a highlight reel, and he watched her across the room, comparing her to the girl in his head. It was a pretty sharp contrast – hot and sexy in his mind, cool and all business in person. Part of him wanted to know if the woman in his mind still existed. She didn't show any signs of it at the moment. Then again, she had always been fairly guarded, but when she let that guard down – hang on. Kate had let him see her true self a few times, and those were the memories flowing through his mind right now. They were incredible and so was she, in ways no one else in this room knew. But Reid did. He knew it very well. He wouldn't mind knowing it again, but there was no way Kate would let him in again. Not with the apparent anger she harbored toward him.

He tried to imagine what he'd done to earn such ire, but his mind couldn't quite get there. He preferred to focus on the good times. Plus, the last time he'd seen her had been right before he hit a rough time in his life – and the bottle. That might be playing a factor in his recall. He didn't like remembering those days, so maybe he'd also managed to erase a few memories of Kate and whatever he'd done to hurt her. He didn't know if she'd ever tell him what he did, and he wasn't sure he wanted to know either. He had enough failures to try and fix at the moment without adding another.

Ten days later, Reid was officially a Portland resident. He'd wasted no time selecting one of the Scott Properties to call home, and it only took him a few days to settle things in New York. He decided to hold onto his condo, although he let his former Mets teammates know it was available for sublease if they knew anyone who was interested. Packing didn't take him long either. The only things he needed were clothes and a few personal items he had kept with him even through all his minor league moves.

The only delays in his move had come in the form of people calling to congratulate him on his new job. College coaches and teammates, Mets colleagues, and younger players he'd helped – everyone was eager to share their excitement over his new position. It was touching and encouraging that so many people believed he could do it, and although he was fairly sure of his skills, the votes of confidence certainly helped.

The encouragement from friends almost made up for the silence from his parents. He'd called them when he left Portland but got their answering machine. Oddly enough, the Benjamins still had one of those, but Reid wasn't sure they checked it very often. If they did, they didn't return his calls. He didn't really blame them though. His parents had slowly been distancing themselves from him over the past few years, and his on-field failures had nothing to do with it. He simply wasn't the man they'd raised him to be. Thanks to the New York media, his drunken escapades and constant carousel of female companions were well-documented. The final straw, as far as he could tell, had been the night he assaulted a photographer. Reid had been leaving a night club, where he'd gone to soothe his broken ego following a particularly terrible game in which he'd struck out four times and committed two fielding errors. After a few drinks and wordless conversations with a few beautiful women, he was feeling a lot better. The photographer was waiting outside to get a shot and wasn't leaving without a good one. Reid should have ignored the photographer's rude and snide comments, but the alcohol had robbed him of that capability. Instead of a great snapshot of the Mets' big signing failure, the photographer left with a broken nose and grounds for a lawsuit that would net him more cash than the photo would have.

Reid settled out of court, but the publicity kept him in the media for weeks.

Reid had done more than disappoint his parents; he'd embarrassed them. Thus, he hadn't seen Sam or Kathy in more than a year. He was so ashamed, he hadn't even returned to Arizona for the holidays, opting to mail gifts instead. But he still tried to check in with them every few weeks. Even if they weren't claiming him at the moment, they would always be his family, and he hoped someday he'd be able to make them proud again. Maybe this new job would be a step in that direction.

The cross-country drive gave him plenty of time to think about his new responsibilities. Transitioning from player to coach wouldn't be terribly difficult given his time volunteering at UNC. Working with professional athletes would present different challenges than working with college athletes, but he was up for it. He also used the driving time and the Bluetooth in his Mercedes GL-Class to call each Pioneers player with whom he would be working. He'd met several of them in whirlwind fashion during Fan Fest and the cocktail party, but he wanted to make sure he introduced himself to each player and got a sense of their goals for the season. He let them all know the hours he planned to be at the ballpark in the coming week so they could stop by and start working with him before the start of spring training.

Nearly every player took him up on his offer of extra work. He thought he'd only spend a few hours a day at the ballpark, but he quickly realized he needed to be there nearly all day, and he didn't mind one bit. His work ranked higher in priority and interest than unpacking and setting up his new house. That could wait. The batting cages felt more like home anyway, and he didn't mind spending almost all of his waking hours there. It seemed more important to get settled in the ballpark than in his new condo. He developed a quick appreciation and knowledge of the players who came in to work with him. Their work ethic was impressive, and he was excited about the potential in all the young men.

He shouldn't have been so surprised at the collection of talent. Kate had been the one to bring them all here. She was smart. She didn't make major mistakes – at least not in baseball. He'd followed her career casually over the years, and he'd done a little nightly research on her since he'd joined the organization. She'd had a few signings flop, but every GM did. To her credit, Kate's miscues hadn't been too expensive and none had hurt the team long-term. She was doing a great job in her role, and he was confident her success would translate to the field sooner rather than later.

He hadn't seen her since his return to Portland. Every day when he went to the ballpark, he resisted the urge to stop into her office. He only hesitated because he remembered the way they left off at the cocktail party, and he was not keen on upsetting her further. His goal was to win her over again. He'd done it more than once in the past without much effort, but clearly it would be a more formidable task this time around. He needed to start by earning back her trust, and he figured the best way to do that was to avoid bringing up the past – which he seemed to want to do every time he saw her – and just get to work. So that's what he did.

Kate may not have laid eyes on him yet, but she was well aware of Reid's return. His vehicle was unmistakable in the employee garage – a black Mercedes SUV with vanity plates that read "REID 17" could only belong to one person. The manager and players were eager to inform her of his presence as well, and she was glad to hear their excitement. It seemed Reid was already hard at work. She shouldn't have expected anything else, but it pleased her nonetheless. It was good to know that although many things about Reid had changed over the years, his baseball drive and work ethic had remained the same.

She was hard at work too, filling roster holes as efficiently and effectively as she could. The calendars now said February, which meant pitchers and catchers would report to spring training in less than two weeks.

She'd finally found a free agent catcher to campaign for their back-up role. Carson Slater was a late-round draft pick straight out of high school. He only played two seasons in the Mets' minor league system before enlisting in the Navy. After two years of active duty, he was now in the inactive reserves and eager to take another swing at a baseball career. Kate had sent a scout to see Carson in his hometown a few weeks earlier and the report was encouraging enough to sign him to a low-risk contract. During a brief phone call in which Kate welcomed him to the organization, the young catcher revealed he had worked out a few times with Reid Benjamin when they were both Mets prospects.

"He was already a big deal, and no one even knew who I was,

but he was willing to talk to me about my swing," Carson said. "One day, he stayed with me at the field until way past dark. I'm sure he had better places to be, but he never complained and he didn't leave until he felt like I really got it."

"I'm sure he'll be glad to see you again in Arizona," Kate said. "And if you make it to Portland sooner, he's been holding batting cage hours pretty regularly."

"Yes ma'am. I've already told my wife I'm heading out tomorrow," Carson said. "Second chances like this don't come along too often. I don't plan to take it lightly."

His words echoed through her mind for the rest of the afternoon. Several phone calls later, they were still with her. He was absolutely right. Second chances were rare, and to be honest, she didn't usually believe in them. Sometimes, those decisions paid off, but more often than not, they didn't. Her short history of second chances fell in the latter category, which was why it was so upsetting that he was now back in her life again. Reid's reappearance may be helping her out professionally, but it was doing nothing for her personally. Nothing positive anyway.

Despite her best efforts to wear herself out with work and exercise before she went home, lately her mind still had enough power at the end of each day to replay memories of Reid. As she tried to go to sleep, she was bombarded with thoughts and images of study nights and senior prom. If her brain – and history with Reid – stopped there, she might have been able to function just fine. But there was more. Plenty more.

When she headed off to college, Katie threw herself into her life at Arizona State University. She'd spent all summer wallowing over Reid and his sudden disappearance. But once she arrived on campus, she told herself that was over. College was going to open new doors and help her close the old ones. She filled her academic schedule, joined a few key student organizations, and quickly made new friends.

Her dating life took off too. Maybe it helped that she wasn't so focused on one guy. Well, that wasn't entirely true. It's just that now she was more focused on forgetting him. And Katie found no shortage of distractions.

In the fall, she dated a football player who was sweet and handsome but didn't have a lot to say. She was fine with that for a few steamy months, but she grew bored and moved on. By spring, she'd connected with a guy in her sports marketing class. He didn't play any sports, but he was plenty knowledgeable. Basketball was his favorite, and when they weren't locking lips, they were trading sports tidbits and theories. Neither romance lasted longer than a semester, but Katie had no regrets. They did a lot to build her confidence, her relationship experiences, and her bank of sports knowledge. She dated a few more guys for briefer periods of time, and it wasn't lost on her that she deliberately avoided baseball players. One trip down that road had been enough for her.

Her most serious relationship started in the spring of her sophomore year. She met Casey Brock in the most cliché place on campus — the library. They both needed the same finance journal for a class and had waited until the very last minute to seek it out. She saw him walking away with it as she approached and frantically pleaded with him to let her use it first even though they both knew there wasn't enough time for each of them to read it before the library closed. The journal couldn't leave the library, and a paper on the article was due the following day. He could have been a jerk and walked away without a word, but he didn't. She was relieved when he offered to share it with her. They sat side-by-side on a couch in the corner, each holding a side of the journal, reading it and taking the notes they'd need for their respective short papers. After they finished the reading, he asked her to get a cup of coffee. Since she'd need the caffeine to get through the rest of her homework — and he was pretty nice to look at — she agreed. They spent the next three hours talking and laughing, and she barely had enough time to finish her paper, read for her marketing course, and shower before heading to class. There was no sleep for her that night, but she didn't mind. Casey had been good company, and it turned out to be the start of something really great.

Katie and Casey were virtually inseparable over the next several months. He was charming, funny, and incredibly smart, and she was completely in love with him by the end of the semester. He visited her over spring break — meeting her entire family in the process. But he didn't seem daunted by it at all. For her birthday, he gave her the baseball book she'd been eying for months. It was better than any jewelry or flowers, and it showed how well he knew and understood her. He was incredibly thoughtful and made her feel as though she was the most special girl in the world.

More than all of that, he was patient with her on the physical side of their relationship. She was still a virgin, which surprised many of her friends and earned her plenty of teasing. She took it all in stride, confident in her resolve to wait for the right guy and situation. She was pretty sure it would eventually happen with Casey, but only in good time, much to his dismay and frustration. Casey didn't break up with her over it like the other guys had, but he definitely wasn't thrilled by her holdout. He didn't quit trying either. Each time they were together, he got a little further than the last, but she always stopped him before all the clothes came off. She knew once that happened, there would be no turning back. She wasn't ready to go there just yet.

Summer break was their first lengthy separation since they'd met. He had landed a great internship in Chicago and she returned to her hometown for an internship with the Diamondbacks. Her position in community relations was kind of dull at times, but it provided her with experience in MLB, opportunities to network within the league, and – best of all – free admission to games.

Being home was an interesting transition though. In her absence, Katie no longer had a true bedroom. Chelle, the next oldest, had inherited it when Katie left for college. As a concession, her parents designated the basement as Katie's territory when she was home. It had a couch that converted into a bed, an entire entertainment set-up, a bathroom, and even a refrigerator. It was almost like having an apartment. Even better, the other girls were not permitted to enter that area, so it became a sanctuary of sorts. She'd gotten used to having lots of freedom at college, so she was grateful her parents seemed to understand her need for privacy and did their best to accommodate that. She loved her family, but as soon as dinner was over, she was ready for some solo time. Her sisters' nightly arguments over clothes, TV, and anything else they could fight about were just too much.

Casey called regularly, and their conversations always brightened her day. She missed him a lot though, and it didn't help that Amy, her only friend from high school, had left a few weeks prior to spend the remainder of the summer traveling through Europe with Brady. Katie didn't have anyone to hang out with, and it made the summer feel really long. And lonely.

On her way home from work one night in July, she stopped to rent a movie. She still hadn't seen the new *Pirates of the Caribbean* movie even though it'd been out for months. A night with Johnny Depp and some of her mom's homemade party mix sounded perfect. She was waiting in line with her selection when she heard someone say her name. It'd been almost two years since she'd last heard that voice, but she still knew immediately who it belonged to before she turned to look at him.

"Hey Katie," Reid said. "I've been trying to get your attention for like five minutes. I felt like an idiot."

Katie stared at him for several moments.

He should feel like an idiot, but not because he's calling out my name with no answer.

"I haven't seen you in a while," Reid said. "How are you?"

She was still just staring at him. He seemed taller now, but she wasn't actually sure he'd grown in height. He had put on some weight and muscle, so that made him slightly more imposing than he had been in high school. But that wasn't what had her speechless. She was a combination of stunned and angry that he was speaking to her. She hadn't seen him since graduation, and he hadn't spoken to her since prom. And, now, all of a sudden, he was acting like they were old friends.

"Are you still at ASU?" he asked.

She nodded, the first acknowledgement she'd given him since he approached her.

"How do you like it?" he asked.

"I like it just fine," she said, breaking her silence.

"Glad to hear it," he said. "North Carolina is awesome. I'm on the baseball team, of course. I was going to play in a summer league, but with my dad and all, I figured I better come home for a few months instead."

That got her attention.

"What's wrong with your dad?" she asked.

"Oh, you didn't hear?" he asked. "I figured everyone knew by now. He had a heart attack this past spring."

"I'm so sorry to hear that," Katie said. "How is he?"

Katie had always sincerely liked his parents. Even after Reid disappeared, Sam and Kathy had been friendly to her.

"Thanks," Reid said. "He's doing better. He keeps telling me I should be out playing baseball instead of bumming around here, but I would have felt bad not being here while he's recovering, you know?"

She nodded, trying to imagine herself in Reid's situation. She would have made the same choice.

"Anyway, he insisted I get out of the house tonight but none of my friends are around, so I thought I'd just get a movie," he said. "I wanted that one, but I think you got the last copy."

He was pointing at the selection in her hand and Katie looked down as though she'd forgotten what she rented.

"Oh," she said. "Sorry."

"No problem," he said, smiling. "But maybe we could watch it together. It'd be fun to catch up."

Katie didn't immediately respond. Part of her was still a little angry about the way he'd treated her after prom – kissing her and then acting like he didn't even know her. But it had been more than two years. She rationalized that she should just be over it. And above all, it was Reid. Standing there with that smile that still made her feel warm inside. She couldn't stay mad at him. But did she really want to spend time with him? What was there to catch up on? Part of her still wanted answers about prom, but another part of her wasn't sure she should open up those wounds again. Maybe it was time to put it all behind her.

"Sure, why not," she said, shrugging.

Reid insisted on paying for the movie rental as well as a few sodas. He followed Katie back to her parents' house, where he was instantly welcomed and invited to join them for dinner. Naturally, Reid accepted the invitation and helped himself to two servings of meatloaf and mashed potatoes while he visited with the Marks family. He shared bits about his college experiences while listening intently as each of the younger girls clamored to fill them in on what they deemed big life events. Katie didn't get a word in, but that was fine. She was content just studying Reid, listening to his stories, and trying to determine why he was here tonight after avoiding her for so long. She was no closer to an answer as they left the dinner table and escaped to the basement with their movie, sodas and a Tupperware full of her mom's party mix.

"I should be full, but I've missed this stuff so I'll make room," Reid said as they settled in on the bed.

Katie never bothered to fold the bed back into a couch each morning. It seemed like a waste of time. It was more comfortable this way, most nights anyway, since she usually fell asleep watching reruns of *Law & Order*.

She was thankful she had at least taken the time to make her bed that morning and that there was no dirty laundry strewn about the room. As it was, the setting was awkward enough. She hadn't seen Reid in two years, and now she was alone with him on a bed in a darkened basement.

Anyone else could see where this could lead, but Katie had no clue. When she stopped at Blockbuster that night, she never imagined she'd barely watch half of the movie she'd waited months to see. There was something about being near Reid now. Time had done nothing to diminish his effect on her. Even with Johnny Depp on the screen, she was all too aware of the boy next to her. And of how he'd grown since she last saw him. She stole a few glances at him, noticing the hint of stubble on his chin and the definition of muscles in the arm that lay beside hers.

They were only about 30 minutes into the movie when Reid looked over at her. She could feel him studying her but didn't acknowledge it for several moments. Then he asked her if she remembered prom night.

"Parts of it," she lied.

"Do you remember the best part?" he asked.

"Which part was that?"

He answered by leaning over and kissing her. It was far from the tentative gesture on prom night. They weren't shy teenagers anymore. They were both more experienced and wasted no time showing off what they had learned since their first kiss.

Katie was certainly enjoying Reid's show. His kisses were the perfect mix of soft and demanding as his tongue coaxed hers into an easy and sensual dance. His hands slid over her like they already knew every curve and were still hungry to explore them. She responded with her own sense of eagerness as his actions set off a series of sensations in her she'd never experienced before. At least not this quickly. Or this intensely. It all came on so fast, her head was spinning and her body was tingling. She arched against his touch and wrapped one of her legs around his, pressing closer. She moved against him without even realizing what she was doing. But Reid knew exactly what he was doing, and he was clear about what he wanted. He used his lips and hands to convince her she wanted it too. Not that she needed much convincing. Almost from the first touch, Katie was all in.

She didn't put up any effort to stop him even though she had plenty of opportunities to do so. Reid pulled his lips from hers to remove her clothing and to let her take his off. Her mouth was free while his traveled over the rest of her body, producing bursts of pure bliss wherever they landed. He whispered a faint apology for delay as he searched for his pants and the square package tucked away in one of the pockets. This left her several moments to change her mind to put a stop to the path they were on. But she didn't. "Stop" never entered her mind. In fact, she whimpered with longing when he pulled away to search for protection and it seemed to be taking so long even though it was probably less than a minute.

Katie probably should have been nervous, self-conscious, or scared. This was the first time she'd ever been naked with a man, and as she watched him fumble a bit with the condom, she realized he was about to be inside her. But she didn't experience even a hint of trepidation. The passion Reid had ignited drowned out any negative emotions that might have tried to surface.

When he returned to her, she eagerly pulled him close, desperately wanting to feel his skin against hers. Reid seemed to want it just as badly. He wasted no time settling between her legs, and her body seemed to be a perfect fit for his. She experienced only a fleeting moment of discomfort as he eased into her. Reid gave her a few seconds to adjust before he slid out and then back in. At first, she just lay there, unsure of what to do, but then he whispered for her to move with him and she instinctively lifted her hips against his. He groaned in response, which encouraged her to match his rhythm. As their pace went from slow and easy to hot and frantic, she pressed her fingers into his muscled back and let out soft cries mingled with his name.

Between kisses, she looked up into his eyes, noticing that they looked darker than usual. In the soft light from her small lamp, she thought she saw a little green in them, but then his eyes were closed again and her study of him was forgotten as her body began to tremble uncontrollably. She'd never been here before, but she was pretty sure she was on track for something really amazing. Her eyes opened wide and she arched her back as the most decadent sensations coursed through her until she finally came undone. He wasn't far behind, and she thought she could still feel his body shaking as he collapsed on top of her and then beside her.

When their bodies were still again, they lay there for several moments, silent except for their ragged breathing. Katie could hear her heart pounding, and it seemed so loud she wouldn't be surprised if he could hear it too. As her mind cleared and her thoughts returned, she remembered Casey and immediately felt guilty.

How could I do this? Casey has been good to me. He's waited months for me. And for what? So I could completely forget about him and give my virginity to someone else? A guy I haven't spoken to in almost two years?

Katie turned her head and looked at the guilty party. Well, the other guilty party. His face was relaxed in sleep. The only movement was the gentle flutter of his closed eyelids. She watched him for a moment, trying to figure out how he'd managed to get to her like this. In the span of a few short hours, he'd somehow made her forget his post-prom actions, her boyfriend, and her long-held desire to wait for the right moment and person – and there was no reason for her to believe Reid was that person. Her mind was a mess of thoughts and emotions, and he was sleeping like nothing in the world had changed.

She woke him up a short while later and sent him home. Her parents were cool, but they wouldn't be too thrilled to discover Reid had spent the night. Katie bit her lip and watched him as he dressed. She wanted to ask him all the questions swirling in her brain, but she didn't. She simply pulled on a robe, walked him to the door, and said goodnight.

Later the next day, Katie made one of the toughest phone calls of her young life. Her heart was heavy with guilt as she told Casey her feelings for him had changed. She blamed the distance and having a lot of time to think. She didn't burden him with any further information. He was crushed enough. He didn't need to know about Reid. It wouldn't do him any good. She hated herself as she hung up. She had always thought people who broke up over the phone were cowards, but in this case, it couldn't be helped. She had no way to get to Chicago to see him face-to-face, and she couldn't delay the break-up until September.

Her guilt lingered, but it seemed to go away whenever she was with Reid. Which was a lot. Over the next few months, they were together several nights a week. Sometimes they would go to the ballpark, but more often than not, they spent their evenings in her basement bedroom. On those nights, they didn't even pretend they were going to watch movies. They never really discussed why any of it was happening; they just got lost in each other.

Katie didn't have any problem with that arrangement. But as the summer was coming to a close, and Reid was getting ready to return to Durham, she knew they needed to have that dreaded conversation. She asked him about a long distance relationship.

"I don't like labels, but I also don't want to lose you," Reid told her, touching her cheek in a way that made her weak in the knees every time. "Let's stay in touch and see what happens."

So she settled for phone calls and texts, where they talked about their daily lives and planned future visits. In the fall, she went to North Carolina every month. His schedule didn't allow him time to get away, but she was happy to travel to him. It cost her nearly every extra dime she'd earned at her summer job, but she kept telling herself it was worth it. And when she was with Reid, it felt worth it. The distance was getting tougher though, and even though she tried pretending she was okay with it all, she wasn't. And by December, it was starting to show.

"What is wrong with you?"

Katie looked up at her roommate, Jill. They had met freshman year, bonding over mutual disgust for their roommates at the time. By the end of the year, they were best friends and had lived together ever since, first in the dorms, now in an apartment, which was surprisingly cheaper than campus life. Jill was an education major and was still dating her high school sweetheart, who was at college in Alabama. Jill was the only one who knew about Katie's summer affair, and although she told Katie she was surprised, she didn't judge her. She'd been very supportive of Katie and Reid's long distance relationship, even though she had yet to meet the guy.

At the moment, the girls were taking a break from studying for finals and watching *A Walk To Remember*.

"You have never been the kind of girl who stares at her phone all day?" she asked. "It's like you're not even noticing Shane West is on the screen. You picked out this movie because you said he's your favorite."

"He is," Katie said. "And I'm not that kind of girl, but I haven't heard from Reid all week."

"I'm sure he's just busy," Jill said. "That happens with Nick and me sometimes. Guys lose track of how many days go by between calls."

"Reid's not like that though," Katie replied defensively. "He always calls at least twice a week."

"Well, maybe something came up this week," Jill said, shrugging. "And you were just with him last weekend, so maybe he had a lot to catch up on."

"Yeah, like another girl," Katie said.

"Okay, now I know this isn't you," Jill said. "You were never insecure with Casey. Come on, Katie. Give Reid a little bit of credit. And a little more time. If you say he always calls, then he'll call."

Katie shrugged and pushed her phone aside, attempting to focus on the movie. But her thoughts wouldn't leave her alone. She wasn't sure why she was so worried about Reid cheating on her. Maybe it was because of what she'd done with him over the summer. She still felt guilty for her actions, and she wondered if that feeling would ever go away. For the rest of the weekend, she went over and over it in her head and finally convinced herself that her own misconduct was the reason she was so insecure about Reid.

Those feelings floated away when he finally did call Sunday night. Hearing his voice changed her mood from nervous to happy. But her relief lasted only for a few moments after she answered. As they exchanged stories about their week, she noticed a difference in his voice. She finally asked him if he was tired.

"Yeah, a little," he said. "But, Katie, I've been thinking..."

Her heart sank a little. Those words never led to something good.

"I don't think this distance is working for me," he continued. "You deserve so much better, and I just can't give it to you right now."

"Why don't you let me decide what I deserve?" Katie pleaded.

"Because I care too much about you," Reid said. "My life's busy now, and it's only going to get worse when baseball season comes around. And you have a lot of things you need to do. You can't be flying out to see me all the time. It's just not right."

"I guess you have a point," Katie said. "Is this what you really want?"

"No, but I think it's what's best for both of us right now," Reid said.

"It's pretty arrogant of you to think you know what's best for me," Katie said. "But clearly, you've already made up your mind, so I guess this is it."

"I'm sorry, Katie," Reid said. "I'm really sorry."

He hung up, and she stared at her phone, which flashed with the time of the call. They had only been on the phone for ten minutes – their shortest conversation ever – but it'd been long enough to break her heart.

She set the phone down beside her on the bed. Lying on her back, she just stared at the ceiling until it became blurry. Finals were a bit of a blur too, but somehow she survived all of them. Returning home for Christmas break, she offered only vague answers when her parents asked about Reid until they eventually stopped asking. She felt foolish, hurt, and embarrassed, and she didn't want anyone to know the truth about what had happened.

It still made Kate angry – among other things – to think about that time in her life.

She'd given Reid a second chance. He'd taken her virginity and broken her heart. That's when she learned that second chances only brought pain.

Okay, so that wasn't completely true.

She couldn't deny that Reid had given her plenty of pleasure as well. First times were supposed to be awkward, but it wasn't with him. And it only got better after that. Those nights were some of the most blissful she'd ever experienced. He had set the bar very high, and she wasn't sure if it was just because he was first or if he was really that good. But of all the men she'd been with since then, none compared to Reid.

No one had ever hurt her like he had either. She'd cried for days, wallowed for weeks, and stayed bitter for months. The college break-up felt like repeat of the post-prom avoidance. And then some. It seemed each heartbreak at his hands took a little longer to remedy. Clearly, with Reid, she couldn't have that kind of pleasure without equal parts pain.

And that wasn't a price she was prepared to pay again. Keeping distance between them was best.

Chapter Five

Reid's resolve broke first.

After two weeks of glancing at the administrative elevators on his way to the cages, he finally gave in and went up to the general manager's office. Kate's secretary said she was on the phone, so he agreed to wait even though there was no promise of when she might be free. He wasn't in any hurry.

His batting appointments had begun dwindling as the players took advantage of their few last days with family before heading to Arizona. The slowdown had given Reid a little more time to get settled. He'd unpacked and purchased some furniture. Only the basics though. A bedroom set, a couch, a coffee table, and a TV would get him by. At the moment, his TV was only hooked up to a Blu-ray player. He figured there was no need to get cable until he got back from spring training. If at all. He probably wouldn't need it. Once the season was in full swing, he didn't expect to spend a lot of time at the house except for sleep. On the occasions he was home, awake, and not working, he figured he could find other forms of entertainment.

He hadn't yet explored the Portland nightlife scene. It wasn't likely to be as lively as New York's, but he was certain he could find some women to keep him company. His affinity for female companionship probably made him look like a womanizer to outsiders, but that was an unfair assumption. He worked in a male-dominated profession. He spent countless hours with other men, so he preferred to spend his precious free time in the company of the fairer sex. Their softness and sensuality helped provide balance in his life. And, even though it didn't appear to be the case, he was actually quite picky about the type of women he dated. Sure, they were all attractive, but he was also drawn to the strong, independent type. Uncovering their softer side was always thrilling, and they rarely asked more of him than he was willing to give.

Lately, he'd been thinking a lot about the days when Kate had kept him company. Or rather the nights. Admittedly, he mostly only recalled the physical aspect of their relationship. He'd tried to remember other things but failed, and that made him wonder if there had been anything else. Surely, there had been. Kate wouldn't have been with him if there wasn't something more. But he couldn't drum up many memories of her in which she wasn't naked. Attention to unpleasant events and conversations had never been one of his strengths, and apparently he had blocked out any bad that had happened between them. Kate seemed to have done the opposite.

After 20 minutes of waiting, Reid was granted entrance to Kate's office. She was seated on the couch with her laptop in front of her, dressed in jeans and a button-down blouse in deep purple. Even with the formal top, it was the most casual he'd seen her look since he'd arrived in Portland. The Kate before him was a stark contrast from the Kate he'd seen at Fan Fest and the cocktail event, but she looked as good as ever.

"What can I do for you, Reid?" she asked, without looking up from the computer screen.

"I was hoping you might join me for lunch," he said.

She looked up and just stared at him for a moment. He couldn't read her expression, but her response didn't surprise him.

"I'll have to pass," she said. "I don't have time for lunch today."

"You work too hard," he said. "Then again, you always have."

"I have to work hard, Reid," she said. "This business is tough. And being a woman in this business is even tougher."

He wondered why she chose to go on the defensive instead of accepting his compliment. He took another swing at turning the conversation around.

"Probably true, but you're not just any woman; you're Katie ... sorry, Kate Marks," he said. "You don't have to work as hard at this as the average woman would."

"I appreciate the kind words, but I disagree," she said. "I do have to work hard. And I don't mind it one bit. I love my job."

"That's great, but I hope someday you love more than that," he said.

"Are you really giving me advice on priorities?" she asked. "You?"

He sighed. He hadn't meant for this to become another confrontation between them. It seemed they couldn't have a regular conversation without the tension rising.

"Is this going to happen every time we talk?" he asked.

"What?" she asked.

"Me making a harmless comment and you getting upset with me," Reid said. "Look, Kate, I'm sorry if I did something to you in our past that makes you hate me, but we're working together now, and I want us to be friends again. I don't want these arguments to get in the way of that. What can I do to make you hate me less?"

"I don't hate you, Reid," she said. "You wouldn't be standing in my office right now if I hated you."

"But you don't think much of me either, do you?"

"I think you're a gifted athlete with a lot to offer as a coach."

"Is that all?"

"That's all that matters to me."

It was Reid's turn to stare blankly. He'd lost the respect of a lot of people in recent years. Adding Kate to the list shouldn't have affected him. But it did.

"Wow. Okay then. Sorry I bothered," he said. "See you in Arizona."

Kate saw the hurt flicker in his eyes before he turned to go. She sighed as the door closed behind him.

When her secretary told her he was there to see her, she'd braced herself for his presence. Even though she hadn't seen him in more than two weeks, his invasion of her mind and dreams had been enough to rattle her. And put her on the defensive, apparently. She couldn't hear his words for what they were. Her comprehension remained clouded by her past experiences with him. Or rather her past vulnerability to him. She was determined not to let him get close to her again. For her, the only way to do that was to start pushing him away the minute he walked in. And that wasn't as easy to do as she made it look. Her anger with him had resurfaced upon his return, but the resulting dreams had reignited her attraction to him. The polarizing feelings made her head hurt sometimes, and she had a history of giving into attraction when it came to Reid. She couldn't let that happen now. When he asked about lunch, she had to turn him down even though she was hungry and this was one of her lighter days at work. She had resolved not to spend any unnecessary one-on-one time with him. It was the only way to combat those eyes, that mouth, that body, and how good they all looked up close. Not to mention how good he was at using that mouth and body on her. The thought alone made her shiver, and she blinked a few times, trying to clear her mind.

It didn't work.

She got up to walk around her office. Her stomach growled, and she was glad it waited until Reid was gone or he might have insisted on her taking a lunch break. Instead, she had her secretary order takeout from her usual place and sat back down on the couch with her laptop. She had a few more personnel items to take care of and then she needed to finalize her travel plans for Arizona. It was time to work.

That was Kate's mantra over the next few weeks, and there was plenty of work to be done as the team got ready for the season. She needed to stay focused.

This was especially necessary every time she walked through the practice fields and spotted Reid working with the players. She paused to watch him a few times, noticing his patient, easy approach. He seemed really comfortable as he worked on hitting drills and watched batters swing. The younger men listened eagerly when Reid stepped in to talk to them about each part of their swing to correct or tweak it. Once, Reid looked up to find her watching. She expected him to call out to her or give her a smile, but he merely nodded. She nodded back and continued on to the next field to check out the pitchers.

Reid was aware of Kate's presence every time she walked through the practice fields. It took all of his will not to acknowledge her. But one day he couldn't help himself, and he looked up to find her watching him work. He couldn't read her expression, and he remained puzzled as she turned to go without saying a word. He watched as she walked away. For longer than he intended to.

"Hey Coach B, you like Miss Marks?"

Reid turned to find Carson Slater watching him with an amused smile. He'd enjoyed the opportunity to reunite with the young catcher. While the kid was a little rusty with the bat after so much time away from the game, he'd made some progress in the last few weeks. But bat speed wasn't exactly on Carson's mind at the moment. It wasn't on Reid's either, and apparently he hadn't done a good job of hiding it.

"She's my boss," Reid said, trying to shrug it off.

"Yeah, but it looks like you'd like to be her boss, if you know what I mean," Carson said.

"If that's supposed to be suggestive, it's terrible," Reid said. "I hope you're better at calling a game than you are at dirty talk. And I feel sorry for your wife."

"My wife has no complaints," Carson said, confidently.

"Good, now let's make sure your manager doesn't have any either. Back to hitting," Reid said.

"Fine," Carson said, settling back into his batting stance. "But you should be doing some hitting of your own this season."

Reid rolled his eyes but didn't offer any verbal response to Carson's challenge. Fortunately, he didn't give Reid any more trouble.

They both knew Carson didn't have time to be messing around. The season was just weeks away, and the young catcher needed every bit of that time if he was going to be ready to take pitches in his first ever major league baseball game. Reid was nervous and excited for Carson. A major league debut was a once-in-a-lifetime event. If Carson was like every other player Reid had encountered, he knew Carson had dreamed about that day. Reid wanted to make sure he was well-prepared for a debut worth remembering.

After giving Carson some things to work on, Reid moved on to the other players awaiting his help. Opening Day wasn't too far down the road, and he hoped his players were ready for it. So far, he felt like he was doing a good job, and no one was telling him any different, so he was going with it. The players were listening to him and making the adjustments he suggested. Sometimes those adjustments worked right away. Other times, he had to talk the players into sticking with it, telling them it would take more time for it to click.

His days were always busy, and they were about to get longer with spring training games about to begin. As it was, when he returned to his hotel room each night, he was too exhausted to do much more than order in food and watch a movie or college basketball. In spring trainings past, he regularly hit the bars and clubs, but even if he wasn't being mindful of the clause in his contract, he didn't have the energy now. He had vastly underestimated the amount of work his coaches had done when he was a player. He made a mental note to make sure to say some extra thanks next time he saw some of them.

Reid thought a lot about his old teammates and coaches these days. It was strange leading spring training drills and workouts instead of participating in them. At times, he longed to participate. He missed the feel of a good run, the smack talk in the batting cages, and a full day of fielding drills. He missed feeling completely worn out after a long day at the fields. It was a different kind of tired than what he was feeling now. He was proud of his role as a coach, but it didn't give him the same sense of exhilaration and accomplishment. He suspected that might come in time, but he doubted he'd ever get over his desire to be on the field again. Even though he was committed to his responsibilities as a hitting coach, he hoped it was a temporary stop en route back to playing.

He also hoped this year would help him work through some of the things that had taken him off of his game.

Athletically, he worked out every morning. Long before his players were even out of bed, Reid was already at the field. He ran laps, lifted weights, and took some swings in the cage with a pitching machine. There wasn't much he could do to test his fielding skills, but he tried to take every measure possible to keep his body in top physical form. Or rather get it back there. At the close of the most recent season, he'd taken some time off. A lot of time. Too much time. Instead of working out, he'd been going out. Getting released might have been the wake up call he needed to get serious again. He sought additional motivation as he watched young players every day who were working hard and were more than happy to be playing in the league he'd been in only months earlier.

Personally, he'd also made some significant lifestyle changes. Since his release, he had slowed down on the alcohol considerably. And the women, too. He'd met a few beauties in Arizona who gave him a nighttime workout, but the frequency was far lower than usual for him. At first, that hadn't been intentional. He simply hadn't had the time or energy for either. Fortunately, that meant he hadn't had time to miss them either. The players he coached were all the company he needed right now. As long as he stayed busy, he could stay focused on doing what he needed to do to get back on track and get his life back on the path he'd charted out years earlier.

One evening, as he was leaving the fields, already thinking about the pizza he was going to order, he heard someone calling his name. He turned to see Derek Beaman running toward him. Derek was a pitcher, and since American League pitchers only took a few at bats a season, Reid hadn't had a chance to work with him just yet, but he knew who the kid was.

"Coach B, can I talk to you for a minute?" Derek asked, a bit out of breath once he caught up with Reid.

"Sure, Beaman, what's up?" Reid replied.

"Do you have dinner plans?" Derek asked.

"I was just going to get a pizza and take it to my hotel room," Reid said.

"Mind if I join you?" Derek asked.

"I suppose not," Reid said. "But wouldn't you rather hang out with the other players?"

"The guys I usually hang with are hitting the club tonight, and I don't think that's a good idea for me," Derek said. "You know?"

Reid did know. Derek's history of drug use meant he was tested frequently. He couldn't afford a slip-up of any kind. Going to a club with the guys might seem harmless, but Reid knew it could easily open a door to a whole mess of mistakes for Derek. Costly mistakes.

He nodded at the younger man.

"Yeah, I know what you mean. Let's go find some food."

The men abandoned the pizza plan and stopped at a chain steakhouse instead. Dusty, sweaty, and still in their baseball clothes, Reid and Derek looked a little out of place. But this town was used to baseball players and fans taking over in February and March, so there weren't too many stares.

When they sat down, Reid looked at the beer menu, but then glanced at Derek. The kid had come out with him to avoid alcohol. Reid didn't need a beer that bad, so he stuck with water. The waitress who took their order eyed both men with interest, but Reid decided she was a little young for him, and Derek barely seemed to notice her. Reid found that interesting – he would have behaved completely different at Derek's age – but he didn't comment on it.

Throughout the meal, the men discussed baseball. Reid was impressed by Derek's optimism and high expectations for himself. He also had plenty of complimentary words about his peers, explaining what he thought he could learn from each of the other men – even the rookie. Derek asked Reid about some of his experiences playing, and the two ended up swapping minor league stories and laughing long after the waitress had brought the check, which Reid quickly picked up.

"I make good money too, I can get it," Derek said.

"Don't worry about it," Reid said. "You can pay next time."

A little while later, Reid dropped Derek off at the building where he shared a small temporary apartment with three other guys.

"Thanks for having dinner with me tonight," Derek said. "I know you have a history too. Kind of like mine."

"We've all got a history, Derek," Reid said. "Maybe you and I should hang out now and then. You can help me stay out of trouble."

Derek laughed. "I think Miss Marks meant for you to keep me out of trouble."

"Miss Marks? What does she have to do with this?" Reid asked.

"She was at the fields this morning when the other guys were talking about going out. They were giving me kind of a hard time about not wanting to go. They mean well, but they don't get how hard it is," Derek said. "Anyway, Miss Marks came up to me later and said I should track you down and try and hang out with you. She said she thought we'd get along real well. Guess she knew what she was talking about."

"Katie usually does," Reid said, smiling a little.

Even when she made no sense to him, Reid had to admit Kate had always been smart about her words. She knew what to say and how to say it. That had been his downfall, so it was something he'd always admired in her.

"Katie? I've ever heard anyone call her that," Derek said, bringing Reid out of his thoughts.

"And you probably won't again," Reid said. "In fact, you better not tell her I called her that. We're old friends, and I used to call her Katie. She isn't very fond of it now, I guess. I should probably follow your lead and stick with Miss Marks."

Derek laughed. "Yeah, that's probably a safe bet. No need to piss off your boss."

"No doubt," Reid said, chuckling.

I've done enough of that already.

"See you tomorrow, Coach B," Derek said as he closed the car door and headed inside the apartment building.

As he drove back to his hotel, Reid thought about Derek's words. He was surprised Kate had told Derek to spend time with him, considering their last conversation when she said he was a terrible person. Okay, so she didn't say those exact words, but she might as well have. She'd said he was a good athlete and that was all that mattered. If you added in the way she spoke to him, it was clear she didn't hold him in high esteem. So then why was she encouraging a young player to hang out with him? Especially a young player with such a troubled past? If she thought so little of him, why would she entrust such a high-risk investment to his company? It didn't make any sense.

His attempts to analyze the whole situation kept him up later than usual that night. As a result, he overslept the next morning and woke up too late to get in a workout. He felt a little out of sorts as he grabbed a quick breakfast and washed it down with a cup of coffee on his way to the ball fields.

Several players were already stretching when he walked up.

"You're late, Coach B," Carson said.

"I'm not late," Reid said. "I'm just not early for once."

"Yeah, that's late for you," Carson replied. "It's all good. I'm sure she was worth it."

Reid laughed and shook his head. Carson's assumption was amusing because it wasn't correct, but it wasn't completely wrong either. Indeed, a woman had kept him up late. Unfortunately, the distraction was completely of a mental nature instead of what Carson was imagining.

"Don't you worry about that right now," Reid said. "Let's get to work. Come on, I'll run with you guys since I was 'late' this morning."

Running with the team actually helped Reid clear his head a little. He also joined them for jumping jacks, push-ups, and sit-ups. By the time they started hitting drills, his mind was solely on baseball and the work he needed to do for the day.

He spent extra time with Carson until they broke for lunch. Then, he took his spot in the dugout at the main diamond for that afternoon's first game of the spring. It was a perfect Arizona day – clear and sunny with a game time temperature in the mid-80s.

There was no better weather for baseball, in his opinion.

It didn't take him long to spot Kate in the stands. Once again, she was dressed casually – jeans and a polo shirt that was somehow perfectly cut for her figure without being inappropriate. Her hair was pulled back in a way that was simple and professional all at once. There was nothing about her look that should have made her stand out and yet Reid had found her in seconds. He was careful not to stare at her for too long this time. He didn't need to be called out by his players again. Or worse, any of the other coaches. That didn't keep him from glancing in her direction often during the game. His eyes were drawn to her. Fortunately, no one caught him – especially Kate. She didn't seem to be the least bit aware of him, and that bothered him more than he wanted to admit.

After the game, his ego was soothed a bit when he found her waiting for him near the clubhouse.

"I wanted to thank you for spending time with Derek Beaman last night," Kate said. "I'm sure you had different plans for your evening, but I appreciate you helping out one of our players."

"No big deal. I had a good time with him. He's a good kid," Reid said. "But I was surprised you referred him to me."

"Why?"

"I got the impression you don't have a very high opinion of me."

"I told you I think you're a very gifted athlete."

"But you didn't say anything about me as a person."

"I don't think I know you well enough to have an opinion on that.

"Are you kidding me?! You know me better than anyone else here."

"You're wrong. I used to know you. But I don't anymore."

"Come on, Katie."

"And every time you call me Katie, you just prove you don't know me anymore either."

Reid started to reply, but Kate put her hand up to stop him. She had a lot more to say.

"Look, maybe I'm not sure about the person you are anymore, Reid. But I knew you once, and I believe you can be a good resource and mentor for all of our players, including Derek," she said. "When I heard the other players badgering him about going out to the club, I was impressed that he stood his ground and politely rejected their invitations. I also knew that their offer might be tempting if he left the field with no other plans. You are a little older than he is, but you've experienced some of the same things as he has, so I encouraged him to talk to you. I'm glad he did, and I'm glad you two had a good time."

"We did," Reid agreed. "I'm just curious about why you would send a young player with his kind of history to me when you're obviously not too fond of some of the choices I've made in my past."

"I think you should stop worrying about my opinion of you. I'm not sure why it matters so much to you."

"It matters because you're my boss. And you used to be my friend."

"Well, now I'm just your boss, so just do the job I hired you to do."

"You know I'll do my job."

"Show me."

Kate could feel Reid's stare on her back as she walked away from him. She was surprised she'd been able to keep her composure during the conversation. It was meant to be a short one – she just wanted to thank him for helping Derek, and he was supposed to nod and continue on with his day. She should have known better. There was no such thing as a short conversation between them. That just wasn't their style. Instead, they always had to dig deeper, pull out their defenses, and go a few rounds before one of them walked away. It was emotionally exhausting, and Kate wondered how she would endure a whole season of this without exploding or melting down. It was going to be one or the other. She could sense that for sure. She only hoped that whichever route she chose, she went through it in private and was able to continue functioning in her job until and after it occurred.

She joined the other front office staff members in the meeting room for a quick post-game discussion. There wasn't any urgent business, but it was good to touch base and share opinions about the team. In the coming days, they would begin to make the first rounds of cuts – deciding which players would stay in major league camp and which would be sent over to minor league camp. Each round of cuts got progressively harder, and she knew it was possible some players would be released by the end of spring training. Those decisions were always difficult. The business of baseball could be very emotionally trying. Kate hated being the one to destroy or delay someone's childhood dream, and yet she knew she'd played that role many times. Even though she'd only been a GM for a few years, she'd already had dozens of exit conversations with players. The sadness on the faces of the young men was often enough to break hear heart. Some seemed to see it coming, while others were caught completely off-guard. Disappointment was universal, even when they tried to act tough and hide it from her. Those conversations routinely tested her resolve to avoid being described as heartless or overly emotional. It was a difficult balancing act, but she did her best to offer compassion and sympathy to the players while remaining professional with her words and the way she treated them upon exit. And she always held back her tears until after the player was gone and the door was closed. She wondered if any of the other GMs went through this. In a way, she hoped they did. She hoped she wasn't alone in her emotional tests. She hoped there were other GMs who saw their players as actual people with real feelings rather than just commodities to be used up and tossed aside.

Maybe I should ask Reid about that.

Once upon a time, Reid had enhanced her baseball knowledge by providing valuable insight from a player's perspective. He had experienced a lot since then and his perspective was undoubtedly broader. She suspected she could benefit from a serious talk with him about what he'd seen and felt so far in his time as a player. But as she thought about talking baseball with him now, she smirked and shook her head. She and Reid couldn't even exchange a simple "thank you" without it turning into a heated discussion. There was no way she could talk to him about more meaningful topics.

After the quick meeting, she headed back to her hotel, eager for a workout, a nice dinner, and some wine as she watched mindless TV. It was her favorite way to end these Arizona days because once the regular season started, evenings would no longer belong to her.

The Marks family swarmed the Pioneers' spring training ballpark a week later. Families were a familiar sight at the spring training fields, but this family was a little larger than most.

Ron and Sharon, along with their four daughters, four sons-in-law, and six grandchildren took up a good portion of two rows in one section. But their presence seemed much larger. The kids were all under the age of five, and, even though they were well-behaved, they were a handful. When the adults weren't tending to the little ones, they were catching up with each other. The family connection was easy to spot too. The elders had gray hair and the sons-in-law and grandchildren varied in their colorations, but each of the daughters had hair in the same shade of brown. It was quite the spectacle.

As Reid stepped out of the clubhouse, he heard his name being called. He looked in the direction of the vaguely familiar voice and saw an older man standing at the edge of the section waving a Mets jersey. It had been nearly 10 years since he'd seen Ron Marks, but he hadn't changed a bit. Even though he'd barely glanced at the jersey, Reid knew it would bear his number and last name. Without hesitation, he jogged over to the stands.

"Reid Benjamin," Ron said. "I can't believe it."

"You can't believe what?" Reid asked.

"It wasn't that long ago, you were doing math homework in our living room," Ron said. "Now you're in the big leagues - first as a player and now as a coach. Crazy how quickly things change."

"It was quite a while ago," Reid said. "But, yeah, it's good to be working with Kate again."

"You two always did make a good team," Ron said.

"We did," Reid agreed, smiling. "We'll be a good one again, I think."

"I hope so," Ron said. "It would be fun to see the Pioneers in the postseason."

"That's the goal. It's what everyone's after," Reid said. "We could do it too. Kate's assembled a fine team here. The talent definitely has the potential to go far if we can put it all together."

"That's always the key, isn't it?" Ron said. "Anyway, I know you have a job to do, so I won't keep you from it. Especially since I know your boss can be pretty tough."

The men exchanged a smile.

"But will you sign this jersey for me before you go?" Ron asked.

"Of course," Reid said. "I'll sign anything for you. Your family's always been good to me."

"I still think you should be playing ball," Ron said. "You're a talented young man."

"I appreciate that, sir," Reid said. "I'm sure I'll play again someday, but for now, I'm helping other players find their best. I think it's a good opportunity for me. Might even help me when I return to playing."

"Well, I wish the best for you, Reid," Ron said. "You've always been a good kid."

Reid laughed. "Funny, that's probably not how people would describe me these days."

"And how many of those people know the real you?" Ron asked.

Reid looked at him thoughtfully for a few moments. It was a hard question. Direct. Exactly what he should have expected from Kate's father. She was a lot like him in that sense. It was a good question though too, and Reid didn't quite know how to answer it. He was pretty sure he didn't need to. His silence pretty much said it all. He finished signing the jersey and handed it back to Ron.

"It was good to see you again," Reid said. "Say 'hi' to the family for me."

"You should join us all for dinner tonight," Ron said. "Then you can say 'hi' to them yourself."

"Are you sure? I wouldn't want to impose on family time," Reid said.

He had a feeling Kate wouldn't appreciate his attendance, but he wasn't going to say that.

"You could never impose, Reid," Ron said. "We'd love to see you and catch up. Please, join us."

Reid considered the offer only briefly before accepting. He was looking forward to catching up with the Marks family, and it sure beat dinner alone in his hotel room. Ron gave him the details, and Reid waved to the rest of the family before jogging back to the players.

As Reid watched players stretch and warm up for the game, Ron's words kept going through his head. How many people did know the real him? That was hard to say. Sometimes it seemed no one did, and he couldn't decide if that was a circumstance of his decisions or if he'd created the distance on purpose. He had never thought of himself as anything but genuine and real, but maybe he needed to rethink that. He was rethinking a lot of things lately, so it certainly fit the theme.

Reid abandoned his self-evaluation once the game started. He needed to focus on what the offense was doing and see where they needed to make adjustments. There had been a lot of strikeouts in the first week of games, and he still hadn't remedied that problem. He couldn't decide if it was just a slow start or if the batters were really having that much trouble reading the pitches. They looked a little better today and managed a 7-6 win over the Cleveland Indians, but there were still some issues to correct. He made some notes during the game and stayed after to talk to a few of the players about what he'd seen and what he wanted them to work on.

The game had been over for two hours when he was finally showered and on his way to meet the Marks family. He found the restaurant and the large group pretty easily.

"Sorry I'm late," he said, noticing half-consumed drinks and appetizers scattered throughout the table.

"That's just fine, Reid," Sharon said. "We saved you a seat, and you can still order. We're in no rush."

"Yeah, we know your boss pretty well. She's not very easy to please, so we figured you were hard at work," Ron said with a wink. "We're glad you joined us though."

"Thanks," Reid said, sitting down next to Kate.

Her sisters all smiled at him and introduced their husbands and children. He nodded and tried to remember all the names as they went around. Through it all, Kate said nothing. It was obvious to him that she was not okay with his presence. But to her credit, she didn't comment or make an issue of it. He was grateful, and he hoped they could enjoy a nice meal without an argument. He had always liked the Marks family. He spent a lot of time at their house his senior year of high school and that one summer during college. They had always made him feel welcome. At time, he felt like part of their family – something he appreciated right now. His own family had shut him out, but it seemed the Markses didn't care about any of his mistakes. They accepted him for who he was, and he needed that. He wanted a family like that. He supposed that was part of his draw to Kate – he adored her family. But, really, he knew that was only part of it. There was more about her that appealed to him. So much more.

Sitting next to her over dinner was the closest he'd been to her in a while, but he was still drawn to her in a way that was simultaneously intriguing and terrifying. He had felt the familiar the pull between them from the moment he walked into her office for that interview. It was the same pull he'd felt all those years ago when they studied together. It had compelled him enough to ask her to prom. He still had no regrets about prom or any of the other time he'd spent with her. There was a connection between them he never could quite understand or deny. Time should have diminished the connection. But it was definitely still there – as intriguing and terrifying as ever. He wondered if she felt it too. Every time she brushed her hair back, he caught a whiff of her perfume. That might have contributed to the pull he was feeling. The scent was subtle, yet sexy. *Appropriate for her*, he thought. He wanted to lean closer and smell more of it, but he knew that would be too much. She was tolerating his presence – even if she hadn't even acknowledged him since he sat down – and he didn't want to push her boundaries any more than he already had. Because of the setting, she couldn't pull away – at least not physically – but he knew if he pushed her too far, he'd only make her uncomfortable, and that was the exact opposite of what he wanted.

Kate was dismayed, but not surprised, when her dad told her he'd invited Reid to join them for dinner. Her parents had always adored Reid. Of course they did. The Reid they knew was a hard-working student and a talented baseball player. They didn't know about the Reid who had broken their daughter's heart – multiple times. She'd never shared those events with them, so she supposed their affection for him and their inclusion of him in family dinner was partly her fault.

When he hadn't arrived before they placed their order, she hoped Reid had changed his mind or would fail to show. She should have known better. Any hope she had of an evening without Reid was dashed the moment she saw him in the doorway to the party room, which her large family had commandeered for the evening. The size of their group and their intent to make it a long meal made the party room the best place for them. It was a large room, but once Reid arrived, it felt very small.

Even more unsettling than his arrival was the instant level of comfort he had with her family – not just her parents, but also her sisters, brothers-in-law, nephews, and nieces. He asked her sisters about their kids and their jobs. Sports were an easy topic to discuss with the other men. There was never a lull or awkward silence in the conversation.

To an outsider, Reid probably looked like the fifth son-in-law. A glance at Ron and Sharon told Kate her parents certainly wouldn't mind if that was the case. They listened to Reid's stories with unabashed interest, eager to catch up with him like an old friend. Her mother gave her more than one wink and nod, which Kate knew was not-so-subtle code for "you should date him." She'd seen it enough over the past several years to read it a mile away. She had always done her best to ignore it, and she intended to continue those efforts now. She gave her mother a subtle shake of the head every time she winked. At least she hoped it was subtle enough that Reid didn't catch it.

Thankfully, he didn't seem to notice. He was too caught up in sharing baseball stories. His major league experiences may not have been successful, but the way he spoke seemed to convey that he didn't view his entire professional career as a failure. The confidence and joy in his words were unmistakable, and if she had dared to look at him, she suspected she might see the boyish sparkle in his eyes to confirm her theory. He loved baseball, and even though it hadn't worked out as he had planned, it was clear he still found the same joy in the sport that he'd felt before he was playing it for a paycheck. For Kate, this realization was as saddening as it was encouraging. She was glad he enjoyed his work, but it also made her feel a bit of sympathy for him that he was no longer playing the game.

Ah. There was that pesky sympathy again. She kept telling herself he didn't deserve any pity from her, but that didn't stop her from feeling it. And that brought on the annoyance that seemed to surface every time Reid was around. He sparked plenty of other emotions as well, but annoyance was the only one she cared to acknowledge. The other emotions would only take her back to a place she never wanted to go again. A place she couldn't go again if she wanted to keep her sanity. And she needed her sanity if she was going to do her job.

When the evening finally came to an end, Kate hugged all of her family members as they loaded into their cars. It was just "goodnight" for now. They would be around for a few more days, and she'd spend time with them at and between games. It would make her days more hectic than usual, but she didn't mind. It was good to have time with her family. Her career didn't allow for much of that, so she tried to take advantage of opportunities like this whenever she could.

As the cars pulled away, she turned to walk back to her own car only to find Reid standing a few feet behind her. Waiting for her.

"I think this is the longest we've gone without arguing," Reid said.

"The evening's not over yet," Kate said.

"That's true, it's not," Reid said. "Do you want to go get a drink or something?"

"I don't think that's a good idea."

"Why not?"

"Because you just said we've gone the whole evening without arguing. Let's quit while we're ahead."

"Come on, Kate. We still have a lot of catching up to do. Maybe you can tell me why you're so angry with me."

"Now that is definitely not a good idea."

"I think it is. It's time to get it out there. How can we work together if the past is always hanging there between us?"

"If you don't know what you did, I don't see how me telling you is going to fix it," she said. "I'm not interested in rehashing our past. As you said in our interview, I'm not interested in falling back, I want to move forward."

"And how's that working out for you?" Reid asked. "You can hardly look at me anymore. And you don't talk to me unless you have to. Tell me again how you're moving forward."

Kate glared at him and unlocked her car, getting in.

"That's it? You're just going to leave?" Reid said.

"We've broken our no-argument streak, so my job here is done," Kate said. "Goodnight Reid."

She pulled away from the curb and Reid sighed. And then he cursed at himself. He probably shouldn't have asked her to get a drink. She was right when she said that wasn't a good idea. And he definitely shouldn't have mentioned talking about their past. That clearly wasn't a good idea. Her reaction told him as much. But he really did want to repair whatever was broken between them so they could be friends again. Maybe they'd never be as close as they once were, but he could really use a good friend. He hadn't had one of those in a long time. He'd formed plenty of relationships throughout his career, and they were all valuable to him. But given the turn his life had taken in recent years, it was clear he needed another kind of friend. Someone with whom he could be real. Someone who wouldn't use him. Someone he could trust. Someone who wouldn't be afraid to call him out when he messed up. Kate had been that person for him once. He wanted her to be that person again, but confronting her about the past obviously wasn't the way to get her back. It only made her shut down. He needed to get her to open up. He'd have to try another strategy. Fortunately, he had plenty of time left to figure it out. There was a whole season ahead of them.

Chapter Six

Kate didn't see Reid for the next few days, but she certainly heard about him. Her family was as in love with him as ever. Maybe even more than they were before.

Her brothers-in-law were in complete awe of the fact that they had dinner with a major league ballplayer. Never mind that they regularly shared holidays with Kate. Spending time with an MLB GM didn't seem to impress them as much as a few hours with Reid Benjamin. The controversy surrounding Reid's career didn't seem to bother them a bit. The men were clearly excited about their encounter with the ballplayer, and they continued to bring Reid up in conversation way too much for Kate's comfort.

"He really used to hang out at your house?" asked Dean, husband to Cassie, Kate's second youngest sister.

"Yep, he came over to study with Kate all the time," Cassie said.

"Studying, yeah ... I'm sure," said Abe, husband to the youngest, Samantha.

"We were," Kate said, vehemently. "We were just studying."

"They went to prom together too," Samantha said.

"Yeah, they looked amazing together," said Melanie. "I still have that picture somewhere."

"There was really never anything else?" Abe asked, looking at Kate.

Kate shook her head. "Nope. Just studying."

"Maybe we'll have to ask him about that," Abe said.

"I'm sure he'll answer the same way," Kate replied.

Abe didn't look convinced. Neither did any of the other guys. Kate wasn't all that convinced either. She wasn't sure how Reid would answer questions about their history. And she didn't really want to wonder about it. She was just grateful when her brothers-in-law dropped the subject in favor of discussion about a recent trade made by the Yankees.

But she didn't escape the mention of Reid that easily. Her

parents enjoyed talking about him too. Their affection for Reid hadn't waned a bit over the years. Ron and Sharon constantly chattered on about how much Reid had changed – he seemed taller, older, and more mature. Kate didn't agree with the last part, but she didn't say that to them. She might have her own grievances about Reid, but her parents didn't need to know about those. She had been elusive in her explanations of their breakup and estrangement in the past. While they were still enamored with Reid, Ron and Sharon also expressed some concern about him – but not about his career or reputation. More than once, they brought up Reid's comment about how he hadn't seen his parents in "a while." He'd been vague about it, but her parents seemed to sense "a while" meant longer than just a few months.

"Sam and Kathy don't live that far from here," Ron said. "They really haven't been here to see him yet?"

"Not that I'm aware of," Kate said.

"I don't understand that," Ron said. "Why wouldn't they come see him?"

"Maybe they're busy," Kate said.

"We're busy too, but we take every chance we have to see you," Sharon said.

"I know, and I'm glad you do, but maybe the Benjamins are different," Kate said.

"Something just seemed off when he was talking about them," Sharon said. "Did they have a falling out? I know he's made some mistakes, but ... he's still a good kid."

Kate wasn't surprised her parents still worshipped Reid. They'd always been very forgiving and open-minded. Reid's parents were certainly more conservative and guarded.

"It's none of our business, Mom," Kate said.

"I thought Reid was your friend. Doesn't that make it your business?" Sharon asked.

Kate sighed. "Reid and I aren't friends like we used to be. And even if we were, his relationship with his parents wouldn't be any of my business."

"Don't you care about his happiness?" Sharon asked.

"Right now, I really only care about his role as a hitting coach," Kate said.

"That's cold, Kate," Ron said. "And that's not like you."

"It's business, Dad," Kate said. "My relationship with Reid is strictly professional."

Ron shook his head. "Kate, I know this industry is tough sometimes, but I hope you never forget that the players and your staff are also people. And I especially hope you never forget where you came from – which happens to be the same place as Reid. Think about that, Kate."

Kate didn't know how to respond to her father's lecture on ethics. And he wasn't the only one who had something to say about her relationship with Reid. Chelle pulled Kate aside while the others were busy with the kids, who were clamoring for autographs from the players.

"So, what's it like being around Reid again?" Chelle asked.

Kate shrugged. "It's fine. No big deal."

"Really? I think it'd be weird seeing him after all you two have been through," Chelle said.

"I don't know what you're talking about," Kate said. "We were study partners. That's it."

Chelle walked around to look Kate in the eye.

"I found your diary when I got your room. I know about prom," Chelle said. "And I know what happened that one summer too."

Kate studied her sister for a few moments, trying to determine what exactly Chelle knew about that summer.

"I was young, but I knew what sex was and I knew what it sounded like. I definitely heard sex coming from our basement that summer. Sounded like it was pretty good too."

Kate turned red and hushed her sister, who just laughed in response.

"Don't worry. I haven't told anyone. I liked having a secret."

"It was supposed to be my secret."

"Well, it's mine too. So you can be honest about all of this with me. I know something went wrong after that summer, even if you never said. What's it like seeing him after all that?"

Kate was quiet for a few moments. She felt a mixture of embarrassment, annoyance, and relief that her sister knew about her history with Reid. The relief part was odd, but for the first time since his return, Kate had someone with whom she could discuss her feelings about Reid's sudden return to her life. It kind of felt like a weight had been lifted, even though she didn't know what to do with that weight now. As Chelle stood waiting for an answer,

Kate was having trouble finding words.

"I don't know," she said finally.

"You seemed really tense at dinner the other night," Chelle said. "You didn't even talk to him."

"Everyone else was talking to him anyway," Kate said.

"But he was waiting for you to talk to him," Chelle said.

"What are you talking about?" Kate asked.

"You forget how much psychology I studied before I decided to stay home with the kids," Chelle said. "I watched both of you during dinner."

"And?"

"And I saw the way he kept looking at you."

"What way?"

"Like he wanted you to talk to him, acknowledge him ... anything."

"I think I've acknowledged him plenty by giving him a job."

"I think he wants more than that."

"Well, I don't."

Chelle gave her sister a look.

"I don't. I really don't," Kate repeated. "He's invited me to dinner and tried to get me to hang out, but I just can't go there."

"Why not?"

"Because he hurt me, and he doesn't seem to realize it. More than that, he doesn't seem to have a clue what he did to hurt me."

"Maybe if you clear the air, you can work on getting over that hurt."

"Who says I'm not over it?"

Chelle gave her a look and Kate shrugged.

"I don't see the point in talking about it. What's done is done. Besides, he doesn't even think what he did was wrong."

"I wish you could hear yourself. In one breath, you're saying you can't let Reid in because he hurt you. And in the next, you're saying it's all in the past. Which is it, Kate?"

"Whether I'm over it or not doesn't really matter. I just don't care to re-live it."

"Maybe you don't want to, but maybe you need to. If he really doesn't understand what he did to hurt you, you should tell him. He seems like a good guy, Kate. I think he'd try and make it right. Maybe he deserves another chance."

Kate rolled her eyes. "What makes you think he even wants

another chance?"

"It sounds like that's what he's trying to do. But, honestly, I'm more interested in whether or not you want another chance with him," Chelle said.

"I don't," Kate said. "I've told you over and over I'm not interested in a relationship."

"You have your work, I know," Chelle said in an annoyed tone. "Your work is important and time consuming, and you're really good at it. But I think someday you'll regret making work your life."

"It's my life, so it'll be my regret," Kate said, shrugging.

"But you're my sister, and I want you to be happy."

"I don't see what Reid has to do with that."

"He's made you happy before."

"He also hurt me pretty bad before. I can't go down that road again. He's had two chances. That's more than enough."

"Aren't you a baseball woman? What happened to three strikes?" Chelle asked.

"Baseballs are thicker than my heart," Kate said, turning to go.

"But clearly not as thick as your head," Chelle said, her voice fading as Kate walked away.

Chelle broached the subject of Reid a few more times during their stay, but Kate shut it down as quickly as she could. She'd said enough to her sister already. More than enough. Chelle was convinced Reid and Kate had unfinished business, and that her sister needed to address it. As far as Kate was concerned, it would have to remain unfinished. She wasn't keen on re-opening those wounds.

As the countdown until their return to Portland entered single digits, Kate stayed busy making roster decisions for the Pioneers and each of their farm teams. She felt good about the teams they would put on the field at each level. She was particularly pleased with the major league squad. The pitching still presented some worries, but the offense was looking strong. Some of that was due to the work done by veterans over the winter and some was due to new acquisitions. She was certain Reid deserved some of the credit as well, although she wasn't about to approach him and offer that praise.

In fact, Kate did her best to steer clear of Reid for the rest of spring training. She was in her office most of the time, making phone calls and dealing with business. She walked through the practice fields daily and was at almost all of the home games. But she kept her distance from the hitting coach, and he stayed away from her as well. Either he was too busy or he got the message from their last conversation. She hoped it was the latter, but that proved not to be the case as he sat down next to her when they boarded the team plane back to Portland.

"Hey Boss. How am I doing so far?" Reid asked, smiling at her.

In addition to his signature grin, Reid was also wearing dark grey slacks and a deep blue polo shirt. Every stitch flattered his physique, and it took all of Kate's willpower not to just stare at him.

"The offense looks really good," she said. "The hitters look comfortable at the plate, and they seem to be seeing the ball well."

"So you think I'm doing a good job then?" he asked.

"It's hard to tell how much credit you deserve just yet," she said. "The season hasn't even started."

"Wow. You're tough," he said.

She shrugged. "I prefer to think of it as honest. Besides, the players deserve some credit too. They work hard."

"Yeah, I guess I see your point," he said. "I just hope you'll give me a fair chance to impress you at some point this season."

"I gave you a job, Reid. I think that counts as a fair chance," she said.

"I'd like to think I earned the job a little," Reid said.

Kate didn't respond and she felt Reid studying her as she pretended to read her roster notes.

"You really don't like me, do you?" he asked after a few silent beats.

"It doesn't matter if I like you or not."

"It does to me. How do I know that won't affect your professional evaluation of me?"

"Clearly, I know how to separate business decisions and personal feelings or you wouldn't be here right now. Just do your job. That's enough for me."

"It's not enough for me. I want us to be friends again, Kate."

"We haven't been friends for a long time, Reid."

"I know, and now I want to change that. I'm willing to do

anything."

"Your job is to improve the offense. That's the only reason you're here."

Silence followed.

She kept her eyes on the document in front of her.

"Look at me, Kate."

She wanted to ignore him and stand her ground, but she decided it would give her protest more credit if she made eye contact with him and was able to stay strong. She turned her head slowly, meeting his gaze. She should have known this would weaken her resolve. Those eyes were too much for her. They'd always been too much for her. Those light brown circles with flecks of green were so powerful, especially when they sparkled. They were pretty flat at the moment, filled with curiosity and a little bit of hurt. But they still affected her. She felt her stomach flip flop.

"I have been racking my brain, trying to figure out why you're so angry with me," he said. "Our past is a little up and down, but I can assure you I never set out to hurt you. I would never do that. I guess I did though, and I'm sorry for that."

"If you don't know what you did, then there's no reason for you to apologize."

"Obviously there is. I hurt you, and I don't want you to still feel hurt by me. I want to make things right with you."

"I don't know if that's possible."

"There has to be a way, Kate. Please."

"Why are you so hung up on this? Why can't you just go about your work and ignore me?"

"Trust me. I wish I knew the answer to that. All I know is I've been trying to ignore you for the past three weeks and it didn't work."

"It worked for me."

He sighed and shook his head. "If you say so."

Feeling defeated, Reid got up and moved to another open seat. After three weeks of trying to devise a way to talk to her without arguing, he had decided to go with the honest approach. No jokes. No baiting. No sarcasm. Just honesty. But it didn't work any better than his previous attempts. If anything, it might have made things worse. When she finally looked into his eyes, there was anger and annoyance, but he was pretty sure he saw a little hurt there too. He had cut her deep. Far deeper than he'd been aware. As far as he could recall, his only crime had been breaking up with her over the phone. It was definitely not his proudest moment, but at the time he believed it was the right decision for both of them. He vaguely remembered that call, blaming their break-up on distance. There should have been no reason for her to take it personally. So what if distance was only part of the picture? She didn't need to know the rest of it. No one did.

That summer Reid spent with Katie during college had been amazing. One of his favorites to date. He'd been with a few girls before Katie and more since her, but the sex with her still stood out as the best he'd ever had. He should have known that would be the case though given the electricity he'd felt the first time he kissed her.

When he asked her to prom, he knew he liked her, but the invitation was supposed to be platonic. He enjoyed her company and thought they'd have a good time together. He definitely hadn't planned to kiss her, but after their evening together, it felt right. Until it was over and he realized something had shifted between them, unlocking a whole new level of emotions he wasn't ready to deal with. So he avoided her until he left town. He'd seen the confusion in her eyes when he passed her in the hall, and that made him feel guilty as hell, but the guilt wasn't enough for him to confront all of the other things he'd felt.

The first night he slept with her was also unplanned, and it brought back all of those emotions from prom night – with even more intensity. They were still scary, but he couldn't stay away from her this time. And it seemed she couldn't get enough of him either. That summer was a blur of kisses, bare skin, and more orgasms than he could count – although now he wished he had. He was pretty sure he hadn't outdone that number in such a short span of time since then.

When it was time to go back to school, he told her didn't want to commit to a relationship with a label. But if he was being honest with himself, he knew he was already in one. He was completely devoted to Katie. He thought about her every morning and every night and plenty of times in between. He texted her as often as his phone plan would allow, and he looked forward to their regular calls. They never lacked for conversation. He was beyond smitten with her, and it was starting to take over his life. His studies started suffering but not nearly as much as his baseball game. When a teammate confronted him about his slow bat and bad fly ball routes, Reid instantly knew what he had to do. Katie was slated to come see him, so he figured he'd break up with her then. But then she arrived, and every time he looked at her, he only wanted to kiss her and take her to bed. Needless to say, they didn't do a lot of talking that weekend. He thought maybe they'd be able to work through it. Katie still wasn't pressuring him for any kind of label, so he decided maybe he could keep it casual and try and refocus on his game.

Then he came home from class on Monday and found his roommate dead. The autopsy said Tony had taken a lethal concoction of pills.

It hadn't been an accident. But Reid was alone in that knowledge.

While he waited for emergency personnel to arrive, Reid found the note. Tony's handwriting and grammar weren't the best, but the message was clear. His high school girlfriend – a girl he'd planned on marrying after graduation – had cheated on him and was pregnant with the other man's baby. Tony said he couldn't live without her and he also couldn't stay with her and raise that child, so he took the only route he saw available. Reid shook his head as he read the note. He had seen Tony and his girl just a few weeks earlier. He'd talked to Tony that morning before class. There had been no indication anything was wrong.

Before the paramedics entered the dorm room, Reid tucked the letter in his pocket and later destroyed it. He knew it was wrong of him to tamper with the scene, but he felt like he was doing the right thing for Tony's family. Somehow, he decided it would be easier for his friend's loved ones to accept his death if they believed it was accidental.

While he may have eased the suffering of his roommate's family, Tony's death had left a huge impact on Reid. He suddenly realized how much power a girl could have over a guy, and he didn't want to be that guy. He couldn't afford to be that guy.

In the week that followed, Reid put off calling Katie. He'd never had to break up with anyone. All of his relationships had been casual and fleeting. A few of the girls got upset when he drifted away, but it never really bothered him. Katie was not like those girls. She was special, and he had to handle this differently.

When he finally called her Sunday, he knew he couldn't delay it any longer. He broke up with her almost immediately after she answered the phone. There was just no point in dragging it out. He was still a little numb in his grief over Tony, so Reid didn't hear any hurt in Katie's voice. His memory told him she'd agreed and that the split was amicable.

Reid shut out a lot of people after that. He didn't hang out with teammates outside of practice. He declined invitations to parties. He went home for Christmas break but spent most of his free time at the gym or in his room. His parents had never been of the touchy-feely nature, so they didn't ask a lot of questions. They assumed Reid just needed a break to recharge after the fall semester. They knew Tony had died, but they didn't know any other details. They also didn't know Reid had been the one to find him.

When Reid returned to campus for the second semester, Reid tried to focus on his studies and baseball. Those two things would carry him beyond Durham, and he felt like they were the only two things within his power. They also required enough of his time and energy that he didn't have much left for other activities.

Except drinking.

Reid had been pretty responsible about alcohol until that point, but after Tony's death, he started drinking regularly. At first it was just a beer or two each night. But when that buzz didn't work, he switched to hard liquor – usually the cheapest whisky he could find. He rarely got completely drunk. He drank just enough to block the memories of the afternoon he found Tony so he could sleep. Somehow, the drinking did little to affect Reid's grades or game. He still didn't know how he managed to graduate with honors and one of the highest batting averages in the conference.

Then he was drafted by the New York Mets. It was everything he'd ever wanted, and the smile on his face in the photos from graduation day and signing day was bright enough to mask all the sadness and hurt Reid had been working so hard to hide for months. He was ready for a new start. Getting out of Durham and that dorm room was the key to moving on.

Immediately after graduation, Reid headed to rookie league. He put in long days of workouts, drills, and games, and the coaches praised his work on a regular basis. He bonded with his teammates, relieved to have a fresh start. His new friends knew nothing about his college roommate, and he didn't offer any information either. He wasn't trying to forget Tony, but he figured not talking about him would help him erase the memories of the afternoon of his death.

It didn't.

The images continued to haunt Reid in his sleep on a regular basis, unless he had a few drinks before going to bed. It helped quiet his thoughts and put him in a state of sleep that didn't allow dreams.

Women also provided plenty of distraction for his brain. Even in the small town where he was playing baseball, there were enough options for sex. Occasionally, he would go home with someone he met at the local bar and let her exhaust his body to the point that his mind shut off too. But those nights were limited by design. He needed to avoid complications. Even though he never promised the women anything more than one night, some of them tried to get more out of him anyway. A few had deployed some interesting strategies – trying to skip birth control or claiming fake pregnancies – but Reid was smart enough to see through them, and he kept them all at arm's length. It made him look like a jerk, but he couldn't worry about that. He had a career to think about, and he wasn't about to let a woman destroy it.

Alcohol was decidedly less complicated than women. Liquor continued to be his go-to through the minor leagues and into the majors. When times got rough or the memories of Tony returned, he hit the bottle. Obviously, there was also the occasional woman, and he'd gotten better at avoiding the clingy, manipulative type. He didn't think he had a problem with either of his vices. He continued to play well on the field, and no woman got her hooks into him for very long. He figured he was coping with everything pretty well.

But then he got called up. Suddenly, Reid's every move was put under the microscope of the major leagues, and the scrutiny threatened to chip away at the protective shield he'd spent years building.

His debut was magnificent. He was hitting well and fielding well, and he felt like all of his hard work was finally paying off. Driving to the ballpark each day gave him an unparalleled thrill, and his heart surged every time he took the field. Then, inexplicably, his performance started declining. He was doing the same things he'd always done, but the results were not there. He tried making adjustments in his swing, but nothing was working. Frustration was rising and his batting average was declining.

Reid's hitting coach and teammates had tried to stay positive and kept telling him he'd start hitting if he'd just relax. That was a good idea in theory, but putting it into practice proved difficult. Reid could not shake the pressure he felt each time it was his turn to bat. And each time he struck out or hit into an easy out, Reid fumed all the way back to the dugout. Pretty soon, Reid's teammates stopped talking to him during games. Their silence and avoidance was probably a result of his bursts of anger, but in Reid's mind, it was a display of disappointment. And he couldn't blame them. The Mets had bought into the promise of big talent, and he hadn't delivered.

His release hadn't been a big surprise to him, but it had been painful nonetheless. Even now, a few months later, it still stung. The Mets had given up on him, and no other team had shown any interest either. He'd fallen so far from where he thought he'd be, and he didn't have anyone to blame but himself.

Reid let out a long breath and looked around the plane. Half the players were sleeping, and the rest were either playing poker or watching movies on portable devices. They all seemed relaxed and happy. And why shouldn't they be? They were major league ballplayers. They were getting paid to play a game they loved. Reid envied them. He had been one of them only a year earlier. He wondered if he'd ever be one of them again or if he'd have to settle for the diluted joy he felt in his role as a hitting coach.

His gaze paused on Kate. Her eyes were glued to her laptop. Outside of dinner with her family, Reid hadn't seen her in a non-working moment yet. Even when she was at the games or walking through the practice fields, she wore a very serious expression. She always appeared to be in business mode. He wondered if she ever took time to relax. He wondered if she even knew how anymore.

With a smile, he thought about how he wouldn't mind reminding her. His memory flooded with visions of her lying beside him in bed, completely sated after an intense bout of lovemaking. Indeed, he knew how to help her relax. He knew how to kiss her in a way that made her forget about everything else. He knew the places that were the most sensitive to his touch and his lips. He could almost hear her cries and gasps of pleasure as he recalled his thorough exploration of her body.

His smile fell as he remembered her words and the bite of her tone when she spoke to him. She had no interest in a jaunt down memory lane or a reconnection. They were merely business acquaintances now. If she didn't even care to be friends with him, there was no way she'd let him get her into bed again. But that wouldn't stop him from thinking about it, and at this point, he wasn't sure he could stop those thoughts if he tried.

Kate glanced up from her work to find Reid staring at her. She couldn't read his expression, so she wasn't sure what he was thinking. She decided she was better off not knowing. He was probably still trying to figure out how they could be friends again. She wished he'd give up on that. To be honest, they had never truly been friends. Their interaction began because of her crush on him, and it had played out to create even more complications than she would have imagined. Electric kisses, amazing sex, and all kinds of feelings she'd never really vocalized. To him or anyone else. It was one thing to have feelings, and it was another thing to share them. Vocalizing how she felt about him made it more real. And left her open to being hurt. Not that she hadn't been hurt, but she always imagined it would have been a hundred times worse if Reid had known how much she truly cared for him. Or how much he had hurt her. And she never wanted him to know how much power he'd had over her. Their recent conversations had undone her plan a little, and she cursed herself for that. She wanted him to think she was indifferent to him. Instead, he was beginning to get an idea of how much he had hurt her. He still didn't see the whole picture though, and Kate hoped returning to Portland and starting the regular season would distract him from his efforts and give her the space she needed to regroup and shut him out again.

Now, with his gaze on her, it was hard to think about shutting him out. Those eyes were just too compelling. For a few moments, she just looked back at him. Whatever expression she wore was effective. He finally looked away, but not before giving her a small smile that sent a warm jolt down her spine. She quickly looked back at her computer screen, trying to shake the sensation and refocus on her work.

When the plane landed, Kate braced herself for yet another tense conversation with Reid. Instead, he walked by her without a word and boarded the bus that would take him and several of the players back to their vehicles at the ballpark. Kate gathered her bags and waited for a cab, relieved she wouldn't have to stave off Reid anymore that night. She was tired and ready to be home again.

Kate loved the modern, two-story home she'd purchased shortly after starting her job with the Pioneers. Full of craftsman charm, it was the best of old-world style and modern conveniences, and she'd decorated in classic, muted colors to highlight the gorgeous woodwork throughout.

The first floor was wide open and arranged in a way that felt cozy despite the expansive square footage. When Kate entered from the two-car garage, she walked into a kitchen equipped with top-level appliances that didn't get nearly enough use. Kate was a decent cook, but she didn't have a lot of time to explore those talents. A year earlier, she'd added a deck, which was accessible from the kitchen, and she hoped to find time to use it more in the near future. The living room was just a few steps away, with large windows overlooking the side yard, which was lined with a fence and trees. It was a gorgeous view, particularly in the winter when Kate enjoyed a glass of wine on the plush sectional couch in front of the fireplace while watching Christmas movies on the Hallmark Channel. At the front of the house was a welcoming porch with a wide front door that opened to the foyer, which divided the living room and formal dining room. The latter held a solid oak table big enough to comfortably seat twelve. Kate had only used it twice since she moved in, but she kept it set with her favorite china and stemware. On the left side of the foyer, next to the living room entryway, was an oak staircase leading to the second floor, which was home to two guest rooms, a bathroom, and Kate's master suite. Her bedroom, painted in a grayish purple and decorated with floral artwork, was decidedly feminine and a sharp contrast to her business persona. The floors were the same oak that ran through the rest of the house, and a plush dark purple throw rug provided padding each night as she climbed under a dark purple comforter on a queen-sized iron frame bed. The adjoining five-piece bathroom was done in the same color scheme, and her spa tub got plenty of use year-round. There were touches of indulgence throughout, but the overall theme of the home was simplicity and comfort. To her, it was perfect. Best of all, it was all hers. She'd never felt more adult or more successful than the day she signed the papers on her home and unlocked the door for the first time.

She didn't get to spend as much time in her home during the season, but that was actually a blessing in disguise. She found that when she was home for any extended length of time, loneliness would begin to creep in. Even with a good movie or music turned on, the house felt too quiet and too big. That's when she would become acutely aware of her singlehood. Her home seemed to be missing something or someone. But those feelings were fleeting, and she always managed to chase them away. She knew there were worse emotions in the world. She had experienced them plenty in her life. She would take isolated and lonely over hurt and betrayed any day. And every day for the rest of her life. She was fine alone. Better than fine, even. She was convinced of that. Or at least she would continue trying to convince herself of that.

She kept busy with work during the baseball season, and indulged in as much travel as her schedule would allow. Each year, between the last game and winter meetings, she would visit some new, exciting destination. Usually, she chose one that required a few bikinis, but every now and then, she'd go somewhere with rich history and culture so she could truly get lost in another world. Wherever she went, she always made a conscious effort to leave work behind – except in the case of emergencies – so she could truly clear her head. This made it easier to jump back into work when she returned.

Kate could certainly use that kind of clarity now. She hadn't managed to find time for a vacation over the winter, and it was catching up with her. A trip now was out of the question, so she sank into a tub full of lavender-scented bubbles instead. In addition to washing off the travel dirt, she hoped the aromatherapy would help her unwind and find sleep easily. Her mind was so cluttered, even more so than usual, and she suspected it would stay that way for the length of Reid's employment with the Pioneers. Particularly if he insisted on bringing up their past every time they talked. Dodging his questions and resisting his charms for an entire season would be exhausting if not impossible. She was already worn out, and there was still plenty of season ahead.

Chapter Seven

Opening Day is a holiday for every baseball fan. Even bigger than Christmas Day for some. It signifies the end of a long, cold winter and the beginning of what many hope to be a long and happy season. The first game in April serves as a fresh start for every club and a milestone for every rookie. On this day, the sun seems to shine a little brighter, the air feels clearer, and there's an undeniable jolt of energy and optimism for everyone associated with the game of baseball.

All of those sentiments were particularly true for Opening Day in Portland. The festivities were spectacular and the fans were loud, but for Reid, it all felt a little subdued. He couldn't decide if it was because of the change in scenery or the change in his role. As Reid stood along the first base line with the other coaches watching the players run onto the field for introductions, he thought back to his own first Opening Day in the majors. It'd only been two years ago, but he felt so much further removed from that momentous day. He certainly felt as though he'd aged more than two years since then. Disappointments and trials always seemed to make gaps in time seem larger than they were. But even all that had happened in the interim couldn't completely erase his memories of Opening Day and how he'd felt when he ran onto the field for his first April at Citi Field – optimism, pride, and pure joy. He still had those emotions on this day, but they were significantly more muted. He brought his attention back to the Pioneers' ceremony, and he couldn't help but smile at the rookies. Their enthusiasm and zeal was readily apparent, even though a few of them were trying to look like calm, seasoned pros. Maybe some of the fans were fooled, but not Reid. He saw the real emotions on their faces, and it helped him forget his pity party and enjoy the rest of Opening Day.

Once the fanfare was over, it was time for the first pitch and the first relevant game of the new season. For the Pioneers, the season began on a high note. Zach Sutter, Portland's ace, went seven innings, giving up just three runs and striking out ten. The offense drew seven walks and put together a few solid innings. It all culminated in a respectable 7-5 victory over the Boston Red Sox.

Boston took the rest of the series, but Portland bounced back to take two of three from the Los Angeles Angels of Anaheim to close out the opening home stand. This helped rejuvenate the energy of the team and the fans as the Pioneers hit the road for stops in Kansas City, Arlington, and Houston.

Reid had forgotten how rough the first few weeks of a new season were. Even with all the excitement and adrenaline, the adjustment to life on the go was a challenge. Spring training was designed to prepare them for playing every day, but it always felt different when the games mattered. To the casual spectator, it probably looked like just a few hours of work, but any ballplayer could tell you there was much more to it. The games might only be three hours long – give or take – but that was only part of an athlete's day. Workouts, batting practice, and post-game press often meant at least 10 hours spent at the ballpark. And with more on the line, there was an increased demand on physical and mental energy.

The first few road trips added to the challenge of transitioning to a new season. Between time zone changes, hotels, late flights, and finding time for food, Reid always felt a little off-balance until he got a few trips under his belt. Major league travel was much better than his minor league days of buses and cheap hotels, but it was still grueling and hard on the body. From Reid's perspective, adjusting to a new season was harder as a player, but he was learning it definitely wasn't a picnic as a coach either.

As he coped with the schedule and worked with his hitters, Reid had very little time to worry about Kate. He didn't see much of her either and he was pretty certain that wasn't a coincidence. He knew there were demands on her time, but after their conversation on the team's plane, he suspected she was doing everything in her power to avoid him. He finally caught up with her in the lobby of the team's hotel in Minneapolis. He was just returning from the ballpark, and she looked like she was headed out as she was wearing a short, curve-hugging black dress with bright red heels. He'd seen her dressed up before, obviously, but it still stopped him in his tracks. She'd always been gorgeous, but the years had been kind to her. She looked incredible.

"Wow," he said. "Hot date?"

"Hopefully," Kate said. "Blind date. So I don't really know if he's hot."

"Well, he definitely won't be disappointed when he sees you," Reid said. "I know I said it already, but – wow. You look really beautiful."

Her face developed a reddish tint, but Reid was pretty sure it was a blush this time, not anger. It was a more pleasant shade on her.

"Thank you."

"You're welcome."

They looked at each other for a few moments without saying a word. It was a tense silence, but the tension was different. For once, it wasn't angry. It was more curious and uncertain.

"Well, I should get going," she said finally.

"Have a good time."

"You have a good night too."

It was the first truly civil conversation they'd had since his interview. Reid was impressed and pleased. He was also strangely jealous of the man waiting to meet Kate. He had been planning to stay in and relax, but now he decided he should go out instead. He didn't want to sit in his room and dwell on the unknown man who was lucky enough to be in Kate's company for the evening. He didn't have a right to think or feel anything about the situation, so he needed a distraction to keep his mind busy.

After depositing his bag in his hotel room and re-checking his hair, he headed out to hit up his favorite bar in the Twin Cities. He was looking up the number of a cab company when he saw Derek Beaman sitting alone in the hotel bar staring at an amber-colored beverage. Reid approached him slowly.

"Derek," he said. "You okay, kid?"

"I don't know. I don't know why I ordered this."

Reid wasn't sure what was in the glass, but he was certain Derek should not drink it.

"Do you want it?" Reid asked, trying not to sound judgmental.

"I don't know. I thought I did. Obviously I ordered it. But then the bartender put it in front of me, and now I'm not sure."

"And why did you order it?"

"I just want to be numb for a little while."

"Is this about the game? You had a rough night, but it happens to everyone."

"It's not that."

"Then what happened?"

"Keely. She's dating someone. I saw it on Facebook. Fucking Facebook."

He knew from past conversations that Keely was Derek's ex-wife. The ex part only became legal recently too, if Reid recalled correctly.

Reid sighed and sat down. "That sucks. I'm sorry, Derek."

Derek shook his head and reached toward the drink. He was just tracing the rim of the glass with his finger, but Reid still knew the young man could go a step further at any moment.

"I know I messed up, but she was my everything, Coach B. She was my world, and I threw it all away. I deserved to lose her. I know that. But I'm trying to make it right. Make my life better again. I thought if I proved I wasn't a waste, she might come back," Derek said. "But if she's not coming back, what's the point of any of this? What's the point of staying sober? What's the point of living? I don't know if I want to live without her."

Derek's words cut through him, and Reid went rigid. They sounded familiar, except this time they were spoken instead of just written on college ruled notebook paper. Tony's lifeless face flashed through Reid's mind and he sucked in a breath. He couldn't let Derek go down that road, so he tried to think about what he would have said to Tony if he'd had the opportunity. He'd gone over his words in his head a million times, and now he had a chance to actually have that conversation – even if it was with Derek and not Tony.

"What else is important to you besides Keely?" he asked.

"Nothing. Nothing else matters."

"There must be something. Or someone. Think about it for a minute."

Derek sat in silence for several moments and Reid just waited.

"My daughter, I guess," Derek said finally. "And baseball. And my parents and brother."

Reid nodded. "That's a pretty good list. That's more than a lot of people have."

Derek's face scrunched up in thought.

"You should focus on them," Reid said. "Build a relationship with your daughter, keep working on your career, and stay in touch with your family. They'll get you through this a lot better than that drink will."

Derek looked back at the still full glass.

"I promise you the booze will not help," Reid said. "In fact, that drink could cost you everything you just listed. Are you ready to risk that?"

Derek didn't say anything. When he pushed the drink aside and stood up, Reid felt the tension leave his body.

"Good job, now let's go get some food," Reid said to Derek.

"Sure. I still owe you dinner anyway," Derek said.

Reid started to argue, but decided against it. Maybe it would make Derek feel better to pick up the bill.

"You're on," Reid said, patting Derek's shoulder.

While they ate, the men exchanged more minor league stories and laughs. There seemed to be an endless supply of both, and by the end of the night, Derek seemed to be feeling better. Reid was feeling pretty good too. Not only had he helped a young player in a time of need, but the evening was good for him too. It was the distraction both men needed to keep from thinking – or drinking – about the women in their respective pasts.

Kate didn't usually let friends set her up, but in a recent e-mail, Jill mentioned her husband had a high school friend living in Minneapolis, and Kate gave in. Midwest guys were supposed to be nice, and the e-mail came at just the right time. In recent weeks, Kate had decided it might be time to start dating again.

She hadn't had any kind of relationship in three years. Not since Jonathan. They had met at Winter Meetings and immediately hit it off. He was a ballplayer turned big league scout. He was handsome, charming, and very smart. It broke her self-imposed rule about dating former baseball players, but she hadn't felt that kind of instant connection with someone in a long time, so she jumped on the chance to explore it.

Their relationship started off hotter than an August day in Texas. After Winter Meetings, she spent several days and nights in his company and his bed, where she was quickly reminded of the perks of sex with an athlete. He'd been out of the game for a few years, but his body was still in prime shape. Much better than most of the bankers, lawyers, and accountants she'd dated in recent years. She lost a lot of sleep in those first few weeks, but she didn't regret a moment of it. She knew things would change as the season got closer, but Kate figured since he was in the business, Jonathan would understand the demands on her time and energy. And he did, but that didn't make their relationship any easier. They saw each other monthly and talked via phone and Skype almost daily. But at some point, they realized it wasn't enough. They both wanted and needed more physical contact, and it was impossible to make that happen without one of them making a career change. Since neither of them was interested in doing that, they called it quits after eight fragmented months.

The split gave Kate increased doubts about her romantic future. If she couldn't make it work with someone who could relate to her schedule, how could she make it work with anyone else? She gave up trying to find the answer or a relationship.

She wasn't even completely sure she wanted anything serious now, and she made sure Jill understood she was only looking for dates.

"Dates are a good start. Especially for you," Jill said. "But don't be so closed off to something long-term."

"I'm not ... I just don't know how anything long-term would work with my schedule," Kate said.

"You know, someday your work excuse will get old. And so will you."

"Hey! You're older than I am."

"Yes, and I'm married with a 5-year-old and a 2-year-old. What's your point?"

"My point is that we all have different goals. You've always wanted the husband, house, and kids."

"You used to want that too."

"Yeah, well, I own a house and I'm in a job I love."

"That's great, and I'm proud of you, Kate, but someday those things will seem cold and insignificant. You'll wish you had a family."

"I do have a family. A rather large one, if you'll recall."

"How can I forget? I went to one Thanksgiving at your house, and I had a headache after just a few hours."

The girls laughed together as they recalled Jill's introduction to the Marks' menagerie. As an only child, Jill had been completely unprepared for the level of noise and chaos in Kate's house. She was so overwhelmed that she insisted on complete silence as the girls drove back to campus a few days later.

"Really, Kate," Jill said, bringing them back to the present. "I hope you give Neal a chance. And any other guy you might meet too. You're more than just a great GM, you're also a woman. And a pretty fantastic one at that. I think you could make some guy very happy."

"I appreciate that, but my career is very demanding. I just don't know how much I have to offer right now."

"All I'm asking is that you enjoy dating and leave yourself open to the possibility of something more."

"I can do that."

Kate didn't think that was promising too much, and the idea didn't completely scare her. She just honestly didn't know if she was ready for any kind of relationship. Mostly she just wanted to meet someone who could help her forget about Reid, even if only briefly. Running into him in the hotel lobby had been a bit unsettling although she had enjoyed his reaction and compliment. It flattered her that he still found her attractive. But she reminded herself that his opinion of her appearance shouldn't matter anymore. He'd had his chance. Two chances in fact, and he'd blown both of them. She was ready to let someone else have a chance.

As far as she could tell, Neal Bruton might be just that person. They had spoken on the phone twice since Jill shared Kate's number with Neal two weeks earlier. Their phone conversations, although brief, hadn't been nearly as awkward as she thought they might be. He was intelligent, funny, and easy to talk to, and she was looking forward to putting a face with his kind voice. Looks weren't everything, but attraction was important, and Kate had no idea what he looked like. Jill wasn't much help either. The only thing she could offer was that he looked "like a good Midwest boy."

When she spotted Neal outside the restaurant, she wasn't the least bit disappointed. He looked to be about 5'10" with a build that backed his claim that he played league hockey and was a casual runner. His dark hair was cut short, in a way that looked low maintenance yet not too juvenile. When she approached him and introduced herself, his dark brown eyes seemed to light up.

"Hi," he said, looking her over. "Jill told me you were pretty, but she undersold you. You're gorgeous."

The compliment warmed her.

"Thank you," Kate said, smiling. "And you're just as handsome as she said you were."

Neal grinned and took her hand, leading her inside. They were seated quickly, and he advised her on his favorite menu items. Conversation flowed just as easily as it had on the phone, and as the meal went on, Kate felt very relaxed.

Neal was smart and very easy going. He had a good sense of humor, and his laugh was unique but charming. Kate was surprised and grateful that he wasn't a huge baseball fan. He enjoyed catching a game now and then, but he claimed he couldn't even name five players on the Twins' roster let alone any other MLB team. He saved that passion for hockey, a sport Kate admitted she knew very little about. It was kind of refreshing to talk to someone about something other than baseball. Every guy she'd previously dated had been in awe of her profession, which often made dates feel like extended workdays. She'd even had a few guys ask for free tickets and player autographs. It was nice to know she wouldn't have to worry about that with Neal.

He was a breath of fresh air in a lot of ways. He was polite to the wait staff. He was athletic without being a complete meathead. Most significantly, he listened as much as he talked. That was new for Kate. She was used to men who liked hearing the sound of their own voice and didn't seem to absorb anything she said. Neal was different. He leaned in, nodding and asking appropriate questions as Kate told him about growing up in Arizona with four sisters and the challenge of working in a male-dominated field.

"It took me a little while to get used to the banter and humor men use to communicate," Kate admitted. "I grew up with all girls, so I was used to tears, hugs, and compliments. Men don't do that."

"They definitely don't," Neal agreed, chuckling.

"At first, I was confused about why they were so mean to each other. It's still weird to me, but I eventually figured it out. They show their affection and respect by picking on each other."

"Yeah, there's a difference between insults and teasing."

"The difference used to be subtle, but now I recognize it more easily."

"And do you ever join in their style of banter?"

"Sometimes. I try anyway. I have to if I want to fit in. But it still feels awkward to me. It just doesn't come naturally, I guess."

"Well, that's because you're a woman."

"Yes, but sometimes I think they forget that."

"I don't know how that's possible, but I promise I won't."

Kate blushed at his words. She liked his subtle yet honest flirting style.

"So, how did you know you wanted to work in baseball?" he asked.

"I grew up watching baseball with my dad, and then I went to a lot of baseball games in high school. Mostly because I had a crush on one of the players."

He laughed. "Of course. I should have guessed."

"I know. It's so cliché. And I really I didn't want to be that girl, but somehow I was," she said. "I was already into the game, but this guy helped me see it from a player's perspective, and I realized how cerebral it was. I originally wanted to be in sports marketing, but I somehow found my way into the GM office. I still can't believe it sometimes."

"It seems like it'd be a high stress job."

"It is sometimes. I was really intimidated at first, so afraid of making a mistake."

"Everyone makes mistakes in their job."

"Yes, but my every move is scrutinized – by the team owner, the media, the fans. It's like I have thousands of bosses sometimes. But I've kind of gotten over that. And I haven't made too many mistakes, so I think I've settled in pretty well."

When it was his turn, Neal shared stories from his childhood in the Minneapolis suburbs and his job as an air traffic control specialist. Kate was more intrigued by his job than he was by hers.

"I still don't really know how I got into it," Neal said. "I've just always been intrigued by weather and weather patterns. I thought about meteorology, but that required a lot of school, and jobs aren't that easy to come by. I talked to a college advisor, and he suggested this. So I finished my science degree and then went to air traffic control school."

"That's still a lot of school," Kate said.

"Yeah, but I didn't mind it. I was really into what I was studying, so it didn't feel like work."

"I guess that's a sign you've found your calling."

"I guess so. There are definitely stressful days, but overall, I enjoy my work. I don't wake up dreading it."

"Same here. I think we're lucky in that."

"I think so too. I can't imagine what my days would be like if I hated my job," he said.

She was a bit unprepared when he shifted gears, although she suspected the topic would come up eventually.

"So do you date a lot?" he asked.

"Not really," she replied. "With my schedule, it's hard to meet guys who aren't in the business. And when I date guys in the business, it feels like work never ends."

"I can see that."

"What about you? Do you date a lot?"

"A lot of the guys in my hockey league are attached. They try to set me up with their girls' friends, but none of them have really worked out."

"Why do you think that is?"

"Well, my friends say it's because I'm too picky, but I just think it's because I'm not in a rush. I know what I want and I'm fine with waiting until I find it."

"So what is it you want?"

Neal laughed a little. "Everyone asks that, and I'm not sure how to describe it. I guess I'll just know it when I find it."

"And what if you don't?"

"Don't find it?"

"Well, I meant what if you don't know it when you find it, but I suppose you could also consider how you would feel if you don't find it."

"Why wouldn't I find it?" He seemed curious, not offended.

"I don't know," she said, shrugging. "I'm just not sure I subscribe to that theory that there's someone for everyone."

"Why not?"

"Because it sounds too easy. Too perfect. And life isn't easy or perfect."

He was quiet for a few moments, apparently thinking over her words.

"You make a good point," Neal said. "I didn't mean to imply that I think finding love is easy. Obviously it's not, or I wouldn't still be single. I just think it's worth waiting for the real thing. I have been accused of being a hopeless romantic. I haven't decided if I like that label or not."

Kate shrugged. "I've been told I'm jaded. And I probably am."

"Maybe I can change your mind," he said, smiling and reaching for her hand.

"We'll see," Kate said, smiling back at him.

As he put her in a cab back to her hotel a little while later, Neal kissed her cheek and told her he wanted to see her again. He didn't pressure her for a concrete date and seemed satisfied when she said, "I'd like that."

And she meant it. The date had been a complete success – far better than she'd expected. For a few hours, she was able to forget she was a baseball executive. More importantly, she was able to forget about Reid.

When Reid went to the ballpark the next day, he was still thinking about his evening with Derek. Seeing the young pitcher with that drink and hearing the sadness in his voice had struck a major chord, and it had been on his mind most of the night. He still hadn't decided what he should do next or if he should keep it to himself. On one hand, the situation was diffused. Derek seemed fine by the end of the evening, and he wasn't sure it had been a big enough deal to alert management. On the other hand, he wondered if Kate should be aware of the young man's emotional state. With Derek's history, it might be a good idea to be careful with him.

While he was still pondering his decision, he spotted the young man in question headed out to the field to play catch with Zach Sutter. Reid called out to him, and Derek signaled to the other pitcher that he'd join him in a minute.

"How's your day going?" Reid asked.

"Not bad. I'm better than when you found me last night."

"Glad to hear it. A good night's sleep can help. One day at a time, like I told you."

Derek nodded. "Yeah, I know."

"I hope you know you can talk to me anytime. If you're thinking about drinking or using or just feeling down, you have my number – use it. No matter what time it is."

"Thanks Coach. Are you going to tell Miss Marks about last night?"

"I haven't decided yet. How would you feel about me doing that?"

Derek shrugged. "I suppose she has a right to know. But I feel like I got it under control. I don't want her to worry I'm going to relapse. And I definitely don't want anyone else thinking I'm mental or something."

"You're not mental. Let's just clear that up right away," Reid said. "Second, I'll refrain from telling her for now. Unless I see it becomes a more serious issue. I just want to look out for you, Derek. I've known other guys like you, and I don't want to see you go down like they did."

Derek nodded. "Thanks. I promise I'll get it together."

"Just fake it 'til you make it if you have to. And let's plan on getting some good pizza next week in Chicago."

Derek grinned and nodded before jogging out to the outfield where Sutter was waiting.

Feeling good about the discussion, Reid continued on toward the clubhouse to see if Carson Slater was ready for a quick batting cage session. The young catcher hadn't seen a ton of playing time yet, but as the season went on, he was likely to get a few more turns behind the dish to rest the starting catcher. Carson's offense was still a concern for everyone involved – except Reid. He wasn't worried about Carson at all. He'd been watching Carson in batting practice and the few at bats he'd gotten to take. The catcher's batting average wasn't anything impressive, but Reid saw progress. He knew it was only a matter of time before Carson really started hitting. Still, he agreed to some extra cage sessions in attempt to ease everyone else's concerns.

When he found Carson, he didn't look the least bit concerned. In fact, he was whistling as he finished tying his shoes. Reid didn't recognize the tune, but it sounded like it was off-key. Carson looked up and the whistling stopped, but only because his face split into an ear-to-ear grin.

"Hey Coach B!" Carson exclaimed.

"Wow, you're really excited about this batting cage session," Reid said.

"Well, I'm always excited about that," Carson said, smiling. "But today, there's another reason I'm happy."

Reid studied Carson, waiting for him to reveal what had gotten into him. The guy was practically shaking with excitement. If he'd been a dog, Reid was pretty sure his tail would be wagging.

"I'm gonna be a dad!" Carson said, unable to drag out the silence or mystery for very long.

"Congratulations. Your first?"

"Yeah. Due in December. We weren't really trying, but we

weren't really preventing either, if you know what I mean. And it just happened. I can't wait."

"Good going. That'll be perfect time. You'll get to spend time with the kid before baseball starts up again."

"Right. Like I said, we weren't planning on this, but I think it's perfect timing. This feels like my year."

Reid couldn't resist agreeing with Carson's optimism.

"It sure seems to be," he said. "Let's get to work so we can see what else we can make happen in the Year of Carson."

It didn't seem possible for Carson's smile to be any bigger, but Reid's comment seemed to cause just that. The two men headed down to the batting cage. Together, they did some arm stretches and then Reid set up the machine to let Carson take some swings. While he was hitting, Reid carefully studied his form. There was nothing wrong with it. In fact, Reid was impressed with the young man's swing considering he'd been away from the game for an extended period of time. It gave Reid hope that maybe a little time away from playing wouldn't hurt him either. Maybe it would even be good for him. While he was helping other players, maybe he would end up helping himself.

After a little while, Carson put the bat down to take a break.

"You know, I was reading about you online a few days ago, Coach B," Carson said. "Don't take this the wrong way, but you used to be a really good player. Everyone thought you were going to be an All-Star. What happened to you?"

"That's a good question," Reid said. "I've thought about it a lot, but I still don't really know what went wrong. I just stopped being able to hit. And once that got in my head, the rest of my game went downhill too."

"Do you want to play again?"

"Of course. A true ballplayer never stops wanting to be in the game. You should know that better than anyone."

Carson nodded. "So then why are you here? Why aren't you trying to play?"

"No one wanted me to play this year."

"So you're giving up?"

"No. Not at all."

"So then what are you doing to try and get back in it?"

"I keep up with workouts so I'm still in shape. But right now, I'm really focused on you and your teammates. I want you guys to do well."

"Right, but hopefully you find time to work on your game too. Why don't you take a few swings right now? You can use my bat."

Reid hesitated, but Carson was insistent, so he stood and took the bat. As he climbed into the cage, Carson went to the other end to set up the pitching machine. Reid took a few practice swings with the bat, getting a feel for the weight and nodding to Carson when he was ready. He missed badly on the first five balls and was about ready to tell Carson to turn it off. But as he stood up straight, he looked at Carson and three other players who had gathered to watch their coach. He realized he wouldn't let them quit after just five swings, so he couldn't allow himself to either. He got into his stance again and focused.

Swing. Miss.

Swing. Foul.

Swing. Dribbler.

Swing. Crack.

The ball zoomed to the back of the cage.

Reid was surprised by the sound the ball made when it came off his bat. He hadn't heard that sound with such proximity in a long time. He was still staring down at the bat when the next pitch breezed by him. He got into stance again, and out of the next ten pitches, he hit seven of them solidly. As Carson turned the machine off, Reid straightened. He heard clapping and turned to see the other players applauding him.

"OK, OK, enough of this," Reid said, feeling more than a little flustered by all of the attention. "That was really fun, but this is your work time. Who's next?"

He stepped out of the cage and resumed his post near the machine so a few of the other hitters could take some swings. As he watched them, he kept thinking about those few moments when he'd had a bat in his hands. It felt amazing. He knew he missed playing, but those feelings were now amplified after that cage session. But he meant what he said to Carson – he was committed to helping the Pioneers for now, and he was going to make good on his promise.

The morning after her date with Neal, Kate was still thinking about him and how much she had enjoyed his company. She was pretty sure she broke every code in the dating world when she texted him to suggest lunch. It would be at least another month before she had a chance to get to the Twin Cities again, and she wanted to make sure she saw Neal at least once more during this stay. He responded quickly and suggested a cafe for their meeting. Apparently he was equally as eager to see her, so Kate didn't really care about breaking dating rules. Maybe it was time to make her own rules. Following everyone else's guidelines hadn't created much success for her in the past, so why not try something different? She didn't figure she had much to lose with Neal anyway. If she blew it, she'd be gone in 24 hours anyway and she'd never have to see him again. If it worked, well, then they'd both find a way to see each other. Either way, her heart wouldn't get broken. It couldn't get broken. Neal was safe. And, for now, that's exactly what she needed.

The cafe he had recommended was charming and unique. It was also really busy, which she took as a positive sign. Their 40-minute wait seemed to fly by as they chatted, and when they were finally seated, she saw why the place was so popular. The menu was overwhelming. It wasn't that there was a large selection, but the dishes were so unique she wanted to try everything. As a compromise, she and Neal each chose a different dish and shared their selections. Both entrees were delicious, and while she rarely indulged in dessert, she agreed when he suggested ordering the piece of chocolate cake with salted caramel icing Kate had noticed when they walked in.

The food and atmosphere were great, but it was the conversation Kate enjoyed the most. Neal was funny, thoughtful, and smart. He told some fascinating stories about his job and even a few about Jill's husband. Kate looked forward to the next time she saw Nick so she could ask him about them. Kate was so caught up in Neal's stories that she lost track of time. By the time he asked for the check, she glanced at her watch and saw that it was after two.

"Oh no! I'm going to be late for the game," she said.

"I'm sorry. I shouldn't have kept you," Neal said. "I had no idea."

"It's fine. I should have been paying more attention to the time."

"Are you going to get in trouble?"

"I'm the boss, so there's really no one to get in trouble with."

"Oh, well then what's the rush?"

"It's still my job, so I really need to get there. I've never been late before."

"Never? I'll take that as a compliment then."

"You should," she said, smiling at him.

As they walked out to the street, he volunteered to drive her to Target Field.

"It's the least I can do for keeping you," he said.

She wanted to insist he didn't owe her anything, but instead she just accepted the ride. It gave them more time to talk anyway. Conversation just came so easily for them, and Kate wished it didn't have to end.

"If you want, you could come to the game," she said as they arrived at the ballpark.

"I wish I could, but I have hockey practice in a few hours," he said.

"Oh, okay," she said, surprised at the disappointment she felt.

"I'm sorry," he said. "If I'd known I would like you this much, I would have made sure my weekend was free. Next time I will."

"Really?" she asked.

"Really," he said, nodding.

He leaned over and put a hand on her neck, sliding it up behind her ear. Kate knew what was coming and she leaned over to meet him halfway. It started off as tentative and awkward as any first kiss, but once their mouths lined up, all of that changed. Neal's lips were soft and inviting, and Kate's responded eagerly. It had been months since her last kiss so she wasn't sure if it was the drought or if Neal was really that good. It was probably a bit of both that made it difficult for her to pull away. When she finally did, he was still touching her face gently. The way he looked at her seemed to say he wanted more. She did too, but she knew she couldn't. She smiled and pulled away slowly.

"I have to go to work."

"Right. So I guess I'll see you ..."

"I'll be back here just after the All-Star Break."

"And when is that?"

"The last week in July."

"That's two months away."

"Yeah."

"I don't know if I can wait that long."

"Maybe you could come see me."

"Yeah, maybe," he said.

His tone was not very convincing, and Kate's joy ebbed a bit. This wouldn't be the first time her career created obstacles for her dating life. She should be used to it by now, but it never ceased to disappoint her. Even when she lacked investment in a guy and wasn't interested in a relationship, it was still a tough pill to swallow.

"We can talk about it another time," she said. "I really have to go."

"Okay, yeah. I'll call you," he said.

His tone was a little more reassuring this time and it helped restore her hopes a little. She gave his cheek a quick kiss and got out of the car.

The third inning was just starting when Kate found her seat. She looked at the scoreboard and saw the Pioneers were up 2-0.

At least something's going right, she thought.

Her gaze drifted to the players and then to the dugout. She wasn't looking for Reid – or at least she told herself she wasn't – but she found him anyway. He was perched on the top step, watching Ben Ramirez, their starting catcher who was currently in the batter's box.

Reid looked really good in his Pioneers uniform. Sure, he filled out jeans and suits just fine, but it couldn't compare to how he looked in baseball pants, a jersey, and a cap. They seemed to be made for his body. She studied Reid for far longer than she should have, and she probably should have been studying Ben. His average had taken a bit of a dip this season, and she wondered if he was hurt or just needed some extra work with the hitting coach. Reid was probably wondering the same thing, but Kate couldn't fully read his expression. He was focused on the batter, and he didn't even flinch when Ben struck out two pitches later and punted his batting helmet into the dugout. Kate watched as Reid wrote a few things down in a little handheld notebook and then walked over to Ben, who was still fuming as he worked to put on his catching gear. He looked up as Reid spoke. He nodded a few times and actually smiled as Reid patted his shoulder and then went to high five Collin Elwood, who had just hit a two-run home run to give the Pioneers a 4-0 lead. The Pioneers' dugout was celebrating, but Kate was still fixated on Reid and his conversation with the catcher.

Ramirez was often described as being temperamental, which she had long ago decided was just man-speak for moody. When he was upset, he festered for a long time. She wondered what Reid had said to get Ben's mood to shift so quickly.

Her curiosity about the conversation lingered for the rest of the 7-1 victory. There was another home run and plenty of good pitching, but she was distracted by Reid and Ben's interaction. Distracted enough that after the game, she headed down to the clubhouse to find Reid. It was the first time since March that she was actually seeking him out.

Reid was surprised when one of the other coaches tapped him on the shoulder and said Kate was looking for him. He was in the middle of a talk with Ian Davis about his follow-through, but he quickly finished up with the infielder and went out into the hallway where Kate was waiting for him.

"You might be good at this coaching thing," she said as he approached.

"Oh yeah? What makes you say that?"

For a moment, he thought maybe she'd somehow gotten wind of the incident with Derek Beaman. He didn't know how though. There's no way Derek would have told her. Maybe someone on the hotel staff mentioned it. Maybe another one of the players overheard them and the word had made its way to her. As his brain was cycling through all the possibilities, she put his thoughts to rest.

"I saw you talking to Ramirez after that ugly strikeout. He was on the verge of a full-on tantrum. Trust me, I've seen a few of them, so I know the signs," she said. "But then you talked to him. He was smiling, and in his next at bat, he took a walk. What did you say to him?"

"Nothing much, really. I just told him to relax a little."

"That's it? Are you sure?"

"I may have said something else, but it's not appropriate for you."

"Why not?"

"Because you're a woman."

"What does that have to do with anything?"

"I try to be respectful about what I say in front of women. Trust me, you don't want to hear what I said. As I said, it's not appropriate."

"Oh. Well, whatever it was, it obviously worked. So, good job, Reid."

Reid smiled. She'd actually complimented him, with no hint of condescension and no room left to end to backhand him with an insult. It was pure praise, the first she'd offered him since he started this job. He wanted to gloat and ask if she'd finally come around on him. He wanted to grin with arrogance. He wanted to hug her. He even kind of wanted to kiss her.

But he did none of that. He knew there was only one way to preserve civility.

"Thank you."

"You're welcome. See you in Chicago."

Chapter Eight

"Nice save last night," Reid said to Derek as they sat down at Lou Malnati's a few days later.

They had debated the other Chicago pizza places – primarily Geno's and Uno's – but Derek said he heard Malnati's was the best. Reid wasn't about to argue with that selection. The pizza and the atmosphere, in his opinion, were superior to the other options.

"Thanks," Derek said, grinning. "That was pretty wild. I never thought I'd get a major league save."

"It was kind of an unusual situation," Reid said.

During their Monday night game with the White Sox, the Pioneers' starting pitcher struggled out of the gate. He gave up five runs in the first inning, and Manager Don Carroll had to bring in a reliever by the third inning. The bullpen was already taxed from the series in Minnesota, so even though Portland was working on a slow rally, they were running out of serviceable arms.

During the rally, the coach asked Derek if he could get three outs. He nodded and jogged out to the bullpen in the middle of the eighth inning. Reid had been nervous for the kid. Derek had just started the game on Saturday – the same day he found out about Keely's engagement – and it hadn't been a good outing. He was done after just four innings. On top of that, he hadn't come out of the bullpen in years, and he'd never been in a save situation. Still, Derek showed no signs of doubt as he took the mound in the bottom of the ninth to protect a 9-7 lead.

He started out kind of shaky, walking the first batter on five pitches. Reid watched Derek kick the dirt and circle the mound as the runner trotted to first. Derek looked around at the infielders. Ian Davis nodded at him as if to say, "you got this." Derek sucked in a breath and settled back on the rubber, looking at Carson Slater, his catcher, who punched his mitt a few times and signaled for the pitch he wanted. Derek exhaled as he got set to deliver what Carson asked for. It was a called strike on the outside corner. It was perhaps a generous call, but Derek and the Pioneers would take the break. Four pitches later, the White Sox first baseman struck out, and Derek relaxed a little. It was just one out, but one out was better than none, especially with Chicago's toughest offensive weapon stepping up to the plate. With one swing, he could tie the game.

Derek the mound again, taking a deep breath as he picked up the rosin bag and tossed it in his hand a few times. He dropped the bag, brushed off his hand, and stepped onto the rubber again. Carson gave him a signal and Derek acknowledged it with a slight nod. He set up, went into his wind-up, and delivered. The batter connected on the first pitch and the ball zoomed past Derek. But he barely had time to turn around before Justin Tanner and Ian Davis turned one of their signature double plays.

Game over.

The Pioneers won. And Derek had just recorded his first ever major league save.

"Yeah, it was crazy," Derek said as he looked across the table at Reid. "I've been a starter almost my entire baseball career. I never imagined I'd have a chance at a save. I never even thought about wanting one."

"Well, now you have one permanently on your record," Reid said.

"It's definitely one of the nicer things on my record," Derek said, raising an eyebrow.

Reid eyed him curiously.

"The drug charges. The assault," Derek said.

"Oh, yeah ... but so?" Reid said.

"So ... I'm not sure I'll ever live those down. Or forget them," Derek said.

"Maybe you're not supposed to forget them," Reid said.

Derek looked at him.

"How can you learn if you forget?" Reid asked.

"You don't think I've learned yet?" Derek asked.

"I didn't say that," Reid said. "But in my experience, substance abuse doesn't go away in one try. It's a constant battle. You've already faced some challenges in your battle. Recently, even. But you have to remember what it can cost you if you fail."

Derek nodded. "That's true."

He was somber for a moment, staring at the table.

"For what it's worth, I don't think you're going to fail," Reid said.

Derek looked up at him. "What makes you so sure?"

Reid shrugged. "I just have a good feeling about you."

Derek smiled. "Thanks, Coach B."

"You know, you can call me Reid, if you want."

"Yeah, but I like Coach B better."

Reid laughed. "It makes me feel old when you call me that."

"You're not though. I heard you were hitting in the cages the other day. Still have some pop in your bat, huh?"

"Surprisingly, yeah."

"Why do you say 'surprisingly'?"

"After the way I played last season in New York, I'm pretty sure no one thinks I can still hit."

"But you can. It was one bad season. It shouldn't define you."

"In this sport, that's all it takes sometimes."

"True. So are you really done playing?"

"I don't know. I mean, I want to play again, but it's hard to say for sure if that'll happen."

"Well, if you want to play, I hope you get another chance."

"Thanks. I hope so too."

Derek took a sip of his water and then changed the subject.

"So you really didn't tell Miss Marks about the other night?"

"Nope. I told you I wouldn't."

"I know, but then I heard Carson say you two are friends, so I thought ..."

Reid sighed and shook his head. He knew Carson had a tendency to talk. He wondered what all Carson had said about him and Kate.

"First of all, I keep my word. If I said I wouldn't tell her, I'm not going to tell her," Reid said. "Second of all, Kate and I are old friends, but we're not friends friends."

"Oh. Carson made it sound like you were close. Said he even found an old prom photo."

Reid smiled. "Yeah, we went to senior prom together. But that doesn't mean we're close."

"But you obviously were at one time."

"I guess you could say that," Reid said.

"Did you date her?"

Reid thought for a minute about Derek's question. He couldn't honestly say he had ever dated Kate. They'd studied together, gone to prom together, and slept together. But he had never really asked her on a real date and picked her up to take her out. He felt a flicker of guilt at that realization.

"Not really," he answered finally.

"Did you sleep with her?"

"That's none of your business."

"I'll take that as a 'no' then."

"Why would you assume that's a 'no'?"

"Because if you did, you'd be bragging about it. I mean, look at her."

Reid smirked. "Yeah, she is pretty."

"She's more than pretty. She's hot. I mean, for an older lady."

"She's my age, so she's not that old."

"That's true. She just seems older than you."

"I'll take that as a compliment, I think. But she probably seems older because of her job. It's a lot more serious than mine, so I guess that's made her older."

"Was she hot in high school too?"

Reid smirked. "She was really pretty. And she didn't seem to know it."

"That's the best kind of pretty," Derek said.

"It really is, and Katie had it. She was really smart too," Reid said. "I guess she's still all those things, so I shouldn't be speaking in past tense."

"Katie?"

"That's what she went by back then. Sometimes I forget and call her that now. She doesn't like that very much."

"She doesn't really look like a 'Katie' anyway."

"She does to me. But I'd like to keep my job, so I'll stick to calling her 'Kate.'"

"Good call," Derek said, laughing. "I'd like you to keep your job too."

Their pizza arrived and the conversation turned away from Kate. Instead, the men went back to talking about the previous night's game. Reid smiled as he listened to Derek recount each pitch he threw during that memorable ninth inning. The young pitcher's voice sounded so much different than it had just a few nights earlier. There was more optimism, pride, and hope. It was as if the other night's disappointment and near-relapse had never happened. Reid hoped that trend would continue for Derek.

As silence followed her date with Neal, Kate tried very hard not to be *that girl*. She really did. There was no reason she should be checking her phone every few minutes. But she couldn't resist that little device. Every time it rang or chimed to indicate a text, she checked the display hoping it was Neal. But it wasn't. It had only been two days since their lunch date, so it was probably too soon to read into his actions – or inactions in this case – but she couldn't help it. She was on her way to convincing herself he was no longer interested in her – and not because he didn't like her, but because he couldn't see her enough. That would not be anything new. Even though she understood and knew it wasn't personal, it was still disappointing and discouraging.

True to her nature, Kate turned her attention to work. With the season in full swing, she had plenty on her plate. The midseason trading deadline was fast approaching, and she needed to evaluate the team and the division to see where she should and could make changes to help the Pioneers down the stretch. They were currently sitting in the middle of the pack in the American League West, six games behind the Texas Rangers and ten games behind the division-leading Los Angeles Angels of Anaheim. But they were ahead of Seattle, Oakland, and Houston, so that was encouraging. There was still time to make up ground. But only if the Pioneers could keep playing strong.

Kate was trying to figure out if they needed some front office help as she sat on the balcony of her Chicago hotel room with her laptop and a large coffee, looking over the roster and latest stats. The team had been playing so well this season it was hard to say they needed any changes. But Kate knew there was always more to the story than just the record. She needed to look for weak spots and areas that could use a boost. Their offense was consistently putting up solid run totals, and too often their losses occurred because the pitching staff had a meltdown. She decided to start there, looking at each pitcher's lines to see which ones gave her the most concern.

Their number two starter, Chris Wimberly, seemed to be struggling – only one great game on his record so far this season. The rest were forgettable, and there were a few she wished she could forget. They were disastrous. Wimberly had won the number two spot the previous season when he notched 17 wins and finished with an ERA under four. She didn't know what had caused his decline, but he was very frustrating to watch. She wasn't quite ready to bump him from the rotation, but she considered the idea that maybe he needed to be moved down a spot or two. Her eyes traveled a little further down the sheet and one name caught her attention. Derek Beaman. He had been outstanding lately with the exception of one disaster start on Saturday. She'd been especially pleased with the way he handled the stress of closing the previous night. Given his history, she hadn't been sure he could step up in that unorthodox opportunity, but he nailed it. He looked calm and poised the entire time. Maybe Beaman could handle a bit more heat. She decided she might be comfortable swapping Wimberly and Beaman in the rotation. She would to consult with the pitching coach and the manager before making the change, but in her mind, it was already done.

Kate made a few notes about possible pick-ups and trades and then looked at her phone again. At least she'd killed an hour between phone checks. That was progress, but she was rewarded with a few work-related e-mails and nothing more. With just a few hours left before she needed to be at U.S. Cellular Field, she decided to give her brain a break and put her body to work. She changed into her workout clothes and headed down to the hotel fitness facilities. She'd been a little relaxed about her workouts lately. Then again, that usually happened with road trips. The rigors of travel were exhausting and they disrupted any routine she might try to establish. And she still hadn't learned how to prioritize her time so she could get everything in – even when her schedule got hectic.

The new Maroon 5 album filled her ears and the city stretched out in front of her as she jogged on the treadmill. She stared straight ahead, focusing on her breathing. Running had always been a good way for her to zone out and find some peace of mind. Somehow, the cardio helped her relax and go to a different place in her head. She was on her way to finding it when she sensed someone on the treadmill beside hers. After a few minutes, she glanced over to see who her workout neighbor was. She did a double-take when she discovered it was Reid. Any beginnings of peace and relaxation were immediately undone.

"Hey Kate," he said, grinning at her.

Even with her headphones on and her music blasting, she

received his greeting. She nodded and removed one ear bud, but it was more out of politeness than a real desire to talk to him. Sure, they had managed a civil conversation a few days earlier, but she was pretty sure that was just a fluke. And it hadn't changed much for her. She was still affected every time she saw him. This moment was no exception. She immediately felt the tension rise.

"Hi," she replied, hoping she sounded calmer than she felt.

"Haven't seen you in a few days. How'd your date go?"

"Pretty good."

"That doesn't sound very promising. Was he ugly? A jerk?"

"No. He was very handsome and very nice."

"So then why was the date only 'pretty good?'"

"It was just one date. First dates are rarely better than that."

Kate didn't bother to tell him they'd actually had two dates. It didn't seem relevant. Or any of his business. None of this was any of his business, actually.

"I guess that's better than 'fine.' But seriously, what was wrong with him?"

"Nothing. Nothing is wrong with him."

"Well, then what's the problem?"

"Who said there was a problem?"

"Well, your lack of excitement about him tells another story. It's okay if you didn't like him. Just say that and move on."

"I did like him. I do like him. I just haven't heard from him."

"Well, then there's the problem. He's an idiot."

"Nah. I guess he just can't deal with my job and the travel."

"Well, then he's still an idiot. You're worth the hassle."

Kate grew flustered at his words. Mostly because it didn't line up with his past decisions. But she didn't comment on that. She wasn't about to say anything that would make them revisit their past.

"Whatever. It's fine," Kate said with a shrug. "I don't need a relationship right now anyway. I have a baseball team to run."

"A pretty good baseball team at that," Reid replied. "The guys look good this year."

She was glad he seemed content to change the subject. She wasn't comfortable discussing her dating life with him. Baseball was much safer. She even turned up the speed on her treadmill, matching his pace as they began discussing the team and various memorable games. His insight was good, and he remembered a few game moments she'd forgotten. She also enjoyed hearing his impromptu mid-season reviews of each player. She agreed with most of his assessments, and he had solid facts to back up each one of his opinions. It helped pass the time, too. Before she knew it, they'd been talking and running together for almost half an hour.

"It really is a good team right now," she agreed. "I've been trying to decide what we need to do midseason, and the answers aren't as obvious as they were in previous years. That's a good thing."

"Starting pitching might be the biggest weakness," he said.

"Yeah, that's what I've discovered, and I don't think there's going to be much available at the deadline. None we can afford anyway. We'll have to get creative with internal candidates."

"Like who?"

"I've been thinking about moving Derek Beaman up a few spots in the rotation."

"Really? That's not a bad idea. I think he can handle it."

"After the way he closed the game last night, I think he can too. I didn't know how he'd deal with pressure, but he was fantastic. The kid impressed me."

"Make sure you tell him that."

"I'm sure he's heard it from plenty of people."

"Well, he can't hear it enough. Derek could use some reassurance."

Kate studied Reid for a moment.

"What do you mean by that?" she asked him.

"I've gotten to know him well," he said. "He's a talented pitcher and a good kid, but he's definitely got some issues he's dealing with. I think a few kind words from the big boss would go a long way."

Kate nodded. "OK, I'll say something next time I see him."

"I think it's great you want to move him up in the rotation," Reid said. "He was once projected to be an ace. Maybe he can still get there."

"I'd love to see that happen, but I don't think it's possible," she said.

"Why not?"

"Because I think his past will always be a barrier."

"It doesn't have to be."

"Derek is lucky he's still alive let alone playing baseball, but I think he blew any chance he had of becoming a top pitcher in the league. He's a recovering addict, Reid. That's bound to mess with his focus and long-term health."

"Or maybe it'll be the motivation he needs to prove everyone wrong."

There was something in his voice that made her slow the treadmill down to a walk and turn to look at him. It wasn't quite anger, but it was close.

"There's no need to get upset, Reid."

"Well, I am upset. Derek's a good kid. He's overcome a lot, and I think we've only seen a little bit of the strength and talent he has in him," Reid said. "You better be ready to fight other clubs when he becomes a free agent because I think he's going to draw a top dollar contract. And if you don't gain some faith in him, he'll leave. I'll make sure of it."

For the first time, Reid was the one to walk away from their conversation. Before she could come up with a response to his rant, he had stopped the treadmill and was out of the workout room. Kate was stunned as the door closed behind him. She hadn't heard that kind of indignation in Reid's voice in a long time. Clearly she'd struck a chord with him. She was struck by his fierce devotion to one of the players. It was perplexing and endearing at the same time. As she finished her workout, she tried to make sense of the conversation and Reid's actions. But after two more miles, she still didn't have any answers. She gave up and went to shower and get ready to head to the ballpark.

It was Reid's turn to avoid Kate.

He steered clear of her for the rest of the road trip, which took the Pioneers to Kansas City for a sweep after they claimed two of three in Chicago. The team's morale was high, but Reid's mood was not. His brain kept replaying Kate's words from their fitness center conversation, and his irritation deepened with every passing repetition. He still couldn't believe what she'd said.

He'd gone into the hotel fitness center for a good workout, and he'd been glad to see Kate in there. He hadn't seen her since their brief conversation in Minneapolis. Not surprisingly, she was guarded about her date. He still didn't know what to think of that. But that wasn't the part of the conversation that filled his mind. It was her comments about Derek and her lack of faith in him. The remarks bothered him enough that he quit after just a few miles and stormed out of the workout room. But not before letting Kate have an earful about how she would someday regret giving up on Derek. Even though he left in a hurry, he could tell Kate was surprised by his reaction to her comments. She'd been speechless as he stormed out. She didn't know how close he'd gotten to the kid. On top of what Derek was doing on the field, Reid had seen him battle some personal issues and beat them. He believed in Derek.

But it was more than that.

Reid's reaction wasn't just about defending Derek. It was also about defending his own ego. If Kate couldn't believe in Derek's ability to bounce back, how could she believe in Reid? His history was as spotty as the younger player's, and his relationship with Kate was a lot more entangled. So if she believed Derek's mistakes would keep him from achieving success, she must believe the same about Reid. And that killed him. He wanted her to believe in him. Her approval mattered much more than he wanted it to. He thought he'd earned a little of her respect through his work so far this season, but now he wasn't so sure.

By the time they arrived back in Portland for a much-needed home stand, Reid was done stewing in his thoughts and doubts. He knew the only way to gain Kate's respect was to keep doing his job. He also planned to focus a lot of attention and encouragement on Derek. Together, they would prove Kate wrong – about both of them.

With interleague play approaching, Reid had a good excuse to spend extra coaching time with Derek. All of the pitchers were hitting the cages extra hard over the next few weeks as they prepared to face teams from the National League. Most of them were pretty excited about the rare opportunity to swing a bat in a game, and Reid couldn't blame them. Hitting was part of the game they fell in love with as children. It was one reason Reid had never considered pitching. He had a decent arm, but strikeouts didn't excite him. On either side of the ball. Hits were a lot more fun. He wanted to hit. He needed to hit. For him, there was nothing more exhilarating than the sound of solid contact between a wood bat and a white ball with 108 red stitches. He enjoyed the defense part of the game, and he'd had his fair share of highlight reel catches, but if anyone asked, he would much rather hit a home run than take one away.

Reid's Kate-less streak ran out when he and the rest of the coaching staff met with the front office staff and the ownership group. The Pioneers did this at the mid-point of each season to discuss the state of the team as they prepared for the second half run. His morning workout ran a little longer than he expected, so he was the last one to arrive at the restaurant for the lunch meeting. The only empty seat remaining was next to the GM he'd been avoiding for nearly two weeks. He was still irritated by their last conversation, but he didn't have any other choice. He took a deep breath and put on a smile as he settled in the open chair. He noticed that Kate shifted in her seat a little when he sat down. Clearly, she was bothered by his proximity. This was nothing new, but it still caught his attention every time. Usually he was amused, but today he was just annoyed. He decided to spread that feeling to her.

"How's it going, Katie?" he asked as he picked up his menu.

"I've told you several times not to call me that."

"Sorry, I keep forgetting. Old habits are tough to quit. Sometimes they can get in the way. Of course, I don't have to tell you that."

Out of the corner of his eye, he saw her mouth open and close as though she was going to say something but thought better of it.

They didn't speak to each other again for the rest of the lunch meeting. At least not directly. Reid gave his input on a few players as they came up in discussion while Kate took notes and sometimes offered a rebuttal, but it was more like she was talking at him than to him. Her voice sounded different when she addressed him too, but Reid acknowledged that might just be his biased imagination. As far as he could tell, the other people at the table didn't notice any tension between the hitting coach and the GM, and that was encouraging. He and Kate might never solve their issues, but it was important that they were able to discuss the business of the team with some semblance of professionalism. Being friends again was obviously a long shot, but they still had to work together.

When they finished lunch, James Scott pulled Kate aside for a private conversation. Reid stopped briefly to chat with the pitching coach, but he made sure to cut it short so he could escape without another interaction with Kate. He heard her calling his name as he unlocked his car. He briefly thought about ignoring her and just continuing on like he didn't hear her. But he decided that probably wasn't in the best interest of his employment.

"Reid," she repeated as she hurried over to him.

"What can I do for you?" he asked, opening the door and turning to face her.

"Do you have a minute to talk?"

"About what?"

"About why you're so mad at me."

"I'm not mad at you."

"Then why are you avoiding me?"

He smirked and shook his head. "Odd question coming from someone who avoided me for the first several months of the season."

"I didn't ..."

"Oh yes you did, Kate. You can't possibly think I'm stupid enough that I didn't see it."

"I don't think you're stupid."

"Just a loser then, right?"

"I never said that either. Why are you putting words in my mouth?"

"Because you aren't saying much of anything to me, so I guess it's easier to make up my own version of what you're thinking."

She sighed. "So let's hear the rest of this version."

"No thanks. I have work to do."

"Seriously, Reid. You've never been this short with me. What's going on? I know you're upset about something I said in Chicago, but I don't understand why."

"I'm just surprised you'd take such a chance on someone if you think he's just going to fail anyway."

Understanding registered in her expression.

"I never said Derek Beaman was going to fail. I actually think he's going to do just fine. I'm sorry if I don't share your opinion that he's going to be an ace."

"And your opinion is based on what?"

"His history. He's an addict, Reid. I'm pleased with how he's bounced back, but let's face it, he's always going to have issues. And those issues are going to hold him back."

"Do you always judge people based solely on their past?"

"Well, I can't see the future, so the past is the only thing I have. So far, I haven't been wrong. I do know a little something about this business. I thought you agreed with me on that."

"You do know the business. I'm not taking that away from you at all. It's just a shame you don't think people can change and overcome their past. Maybe it's that you're no good at judging people."

Kate took a step back and her expression hardened.

"You might be right there," she said. "Look at you, for example."

"What about me?"

"Well, I trusted you twice and you hurt me twice. The first time was your fault, but the second time was all on me. If I'd based my judgments on your past, I would never have let you back in. So, you've definitely done your share of proving me wrong about people."

Reid shook his head. "How did this get to be about you and me? I thought you didn't want to discuss our past."

"I didn't. I mean, I don't," she said, clearly frustrated. "This is about Derek Beaman. I'm not judging him personally based on his past. I'm judging him professionally. Which is exactly what I've done with you. I hired you because I think you'll do a good job as a coach, not because I trust you in any other way."

"So I suppose that's your professional prediction for me too, right? That I'm a coach now and my playing days are done."

"I didn't say that."

"You don't have to. You've already said guys like Derek who have major issues won't ever get past them to succeed."

"You don't have issues like he does."

"If that's what you believe, you definitely don't know me."

She eyed him curiously. "What are you saying?"

"If you won't discuss our past so I can figure out where I went wrong, I'm not going to discuss my past so you can see where you're wrong. Two can play this game, Kate."

"It's not a game."

"Well, it sure feels like one."

Kate was about to say something else, but Reid didn't care to stick around to hear it. He climbed into his car and pulled away without another word. He fumed all the way to the ballpark where he jogged laps around the perimeter of the field to try and burn off some of his frustration. Preferably before the players arrived to start their pre-game routines. As he plodded around the warning track, he tried to clear his head, but he just kept replaying his conversation with Kate.

No one pushed his buttons like she did. Almost every time they talked, tension rose between them. After their brief civil exchanges in Minneapolis, he thought maybe they were working past it. But no. Apparently those conversations had been anomalies in the grand scheme of their relationship. Clearly, they hadn't made as much progress as he thought and hoped. The strain between them was palpable. He was starting to doubt they could ever be friends.

But the source of his frustration went deeper, and he knew it. He was bothered by her lack of faith in him. Even if it was only implied, it still bothered him. He wanted her to see him as more than just a good coach. He wanted to prove to her that he was more than that. He was determined to show her he was still a good player too. And a good person. He had a feeling the former would be easier than the latter.

For now, Reid intended focus on improving Kate's opinion of Derek.

Fortunately, the pitcher was doing a fine job of that on his own. In his next two starts, he threw seven shutout innings of a 2-0 win and struck out eight batters in a game the Pioneers won 8-3. Derek was making people notice him.

Reid's pride in Derek grew. He was the only one who knew the full extent of the off-field stuff swirling around in Derek's head.

Derek's ex-wife continued to flaunt her new relationship all over Facebook. Recently, she shared a video of a proposal along with multiple photos of her ring and fiancé. Derek was close to breaking, but there was very little he could do about it. He couldn't unfriend her or hide her updates if he wanted to keep tabs on his daughter. And he did. He seemed to be coming to terms with the fact that his relationship with Keely was beyond repair. But there was still time for him to bond with Brynn and be a good father to her. If only Keely would let him. So far, Derek wasn't convinced she would. There was no formal custody arrangement in place. He had always hoped he and Keely could work out a deal without getting the court's intervention. But that wasn't happening. As his requests to see Brynn kept getting denied, Derek realized he would need to contact a lawyer soon. He hadn't done it yet, due in part to his travel and game schedule, but he was getting closer. In the meantime, his only glimpse of his daughter came through Facebook photos, which unfortunately were mixed in with posts about Keely's new love.

Reid could tell the separation from Brynn and watching Keely move on was taking a toll on Derek, but that only made his pitching performances even more remarkable. Somehow he was able to put his personal problems aside when he went to the mound. Or maybe he used them as motivation. Reid wasn't completely sure, but he was impressed.

Kate was too. She wasn't yet ready to admit Reid might have been right about Derek, but he was outperforming all the expectations she had for him. Even if this was a fluke or a mere hot streak, Derek was making a huge mark on the Pioneers' season. It gave her more conviction in her decision to move him up in the rotation. When she approached Don Carroll about the switch, he was more than a little surprised.

"Are you sure you want to do that?" the manager asked her.

"Absolutely. Beaman's one of our best pitchers right now. He's earned this."

"I agree he's been pitching well. But this ... it might be too much for him with his history."

"It seems his history is just that. I admit, I never thought he'd be more than a back of the rotation starter, but I'd love to be wrong about that. In the last few weeks, he's shown he isn't afraid of pressure or a new challenge. I think he's ready for this."

"I sure hope so."

After the game that night, Kate went down to the clubhouse to watch the manager's post-game press conference. As she was going into the media room, she heard her name being called. She turned and saw Derek walking toward her.

"Miss Marks, I'm glad I caught you," he said once he finally reached her. "I wanted to thank you for moving me up in the rotation. It's probably a small move to any other pitcher, but it's a huge deal for me."

The gratitude and sincerity in his voice nearly melted Kate on the spot. Always the professional, she kept her emotions from her face.

"You've had a great season so far. You've earned this."

"Coach B said you're a good judge of players, so I know this move is a huge vote of confidence. I can't tell you what that means to me."

"You've been working hard, and it shows. You are a major part of the Pioneers' success."

Derek grinned at her compliment. "I promise I won't let you down."

"Just keep doing what you've been doing and you'll be fine."

"Yes, ma'am."

Kate couldn't help but smile as the young pitcher disappeared into the locker room. She loved knowing she'd made a young player's day. It almost made up for the days when she had to do the opposite – send a player down to the minors or dismiss them from the team completely. Those conversations never got easier, but exchanges like the one she'd just had with Derek reminded her there were some good moments in her job as well.

Chapter Nine

Kate eased into the media room to catch the end of Don Carroll's post-game press conference. It had been a good, clean game, so the manager was in a favorable mood. He spent a lot of time complimenting his players, and the reporters didn't pose any questions that could result in negative answers. As a coach whose moods went with the team's ups and downs, Don's good spirits were encouraging and welcome.

It was a perfect reflection of the season thus far. There had been a few rough games, but the Pioneers were in the middle of a nice stretch, and Kate hoped the momentum would carry through the All-Star Break. She had a few players headed to the mid-season exhibition, but she was trying not to worry about players' ability to keep their focus on the games that really counted. While she appreciated the tradition of the All-Star Game, she did not share the opinion that it counted for much. The game would decide home field advantage in the World Series, but that was only significant if you reached that point in the postseason, and the Pioneers had some work to do before that was a reality. She trusted the managers and the athletes to establish and maintain their focus on the big goal. It wasn't her job to motivate them. She just needed to provide them with the tools they needed. So far, it seemed she'd done a decent job of that.

As she listened to the media room chatter, Kate checked her watch more than once. Usually, she didn't care how long the press conferences were, but tonight she did. As soon as she was done at the ballpark, she was headed to the airport for a flight to Minnesota. Neal had finally gotten in touch with her. After a week of radio silence, he called her and admitted the distance and her schedule had presented a daunting obstacle.

"But you knew about my job before we even went out," Kate had said to him.

"I know, but I got so caught up in getting to know you that I didn't really think about the logistics. I was just enjoying your company," Neal replied.

"And now?"

"Now I want another chance."

"Why? Nothing about the situation has changed."

"True. But I really like you."

"How can you be sure that's enough?"

"I can't be sure, but I want to try. Look, I know it's not ideal, but it's not like I've had much luck with anyone local either. I'm ready to try something new. Maybe I need to step out of my comfort zone."

"What are you saying?"

"I'm saying I'm willing to try and make this work. I know it's going to be hard, but you're an amazing woman. I think you're worth the extra effort."

His words were perhaps the best compliment she'd ever received. It was even better than being called beautiful or kind or smart. Knowing someone thought you were worthy of the hard work involved in maintaining a relationship across distance and busy schedules was an incredible feeling. It warmed her enough that she forgave his brief silence. She also decided she needed to meet him halfway, so she would miss the final series before the All-Star Break in order to spend more time with him. She and the rest of the front office staff had already held countless meetings about mid-season trades. They knew what they needed to do, but there wasn't much they could do about it for a few more weeks. While she still had plenty of work responsibilities, she could complete them via phone and internet. A few days away from wouldn't hurt the team.

It would also provide a break from Reid. Then again, he hadn't been much of an issue since their most recent argument over Derek Beaman. On the rare occasion their paths crossed, they merely exchanged the occasional greeting or discussed team-related issues. That was it. She found the silence a bit unsettling. And it shouldn't have been. She should have been thrilled to be on this level with him. It was what she'd wanted when she hired him – distance and civility. But this just felt wrong. And it bothered her that she was so preoccupied with how Reid was or wasn't regarding her.

She tried not to dwell on her strained relationship with Reid as she boarded a red-eye to Minneapolis. It was time to put work

᷄ hours, relax, and prepare for a weekend with Neal. had some good things planned, but the lack of details ᷄er uneasy. She'd asked him several times over the week, but ᷄ just kept saying he wanted to surprise her. Surprises made her anxious, but she was trying her best to let go of that for now and just enjoy the next few days.

When she saw Neal – and his smile – at the baggage claim, her mood immediately shifted. He hugged her and kissed her cheek in greeting, and her nerves melted away completely. They chatted idly about her flight, the Pioneers, and the weather while they waited for her bags, and then he led her out to his car, where she gave him the name of her hotel. She felt completely at ease as he drove through the city. There was something so utterly and noticeably laid back about him. It was easy to be with him, and she could feel her stress dissolving as they drove to the hotel.

"I figured you'd want a few hours to rest, so I'll be back to get you around two," Neal said. "Dress in comfortable clothes and shoes."

"How comfortable?" she asked. "These heels can be comfortable sometimes."

"I'm sure they can – although I can't imagine how," he said. "But aim for jeans and walking shoes."

"Sounds good," she said. "I can't wait to see what you have planned."

He just grinned and gave her another cheek kiss in response.

After a nap, a shower, and a light lunch via room service, Kate was not only relaxed, but feeling refreshed and ready for her date. She headed down to the lobby in jeans, running shoes, and a plain kelly green t-shirt, which set off her fair skin and green eyes. She'd gone light on makeup, since his instructions implied casual, but she'd left her hair down. As soon as she saw Neal, she knew she'd made the right choices. He wore long shorts, a t-shirt bearing a Minnesota Wild logo, tennis shoes, and a huge grin.

They exchanged compliments and then they were in his car, headed out of downtown. While he drove, Neal asked Kate about the Pioneers' season. Normally, she wouldn't enjoy talking work on a date, but she sensed that he was inquiring as a way to get to know her better, not because he actually cared about the team's record and playoff chances.

"We're only eight games back, which isn't too bad going into the All-Star Break," Kate explained. "We're in a really tough division, and we're going to have to play out of our minds to overtake first. I'd like to say without a doubt that we can do it, but I'm not sure. There are a lot of things that will have to go perfectly for that to happen."

"But you seem pretty happy with your roster. At least that's what I gathered when we talked the other night," he said.

"I am," she said, nodding. "I think we need to make a few adjustments, but ... I'm not going to worry about those for the next few days."

Neal smiled. "Really? You're going to ignore work while you're here?"

"Not ignore. Just delay. Unless it's an emergency, it can wait," she said.

"Given what you've told me about your work habits, I feel pretty special right now."

"As you should."

They shared a laugh, and then he pulled his car into a parking lot. The signs told her she was at Lake Como. She saw trees, water, and a concrete trail winding through all of it. It was peaceful, but it was far from desolate. There were people everywhere – fishing in the lake, reading on the shore, biking, running, and walking.

"I thought we could go for a walk and just get to know each other," Neal said. "I bet you rarely get to just enjoy being outside."

"You're right," she said. "The only time I'm usually outside is in a ballpark. And I enjoy that, but I think this will be a little more relaxing."

"Aha, you're onto my plan."

She gave him a curious look.

"In the time I've known you, it sounds like you are always busy and on the go. I decided what you needed this weekend was relaxation. So that's what I've planned."

"You've planned relaxation? That sounds a little ... odd."

"True, but as adults, we kind of have to plan relaxation or it never happens."

"Good point. I think you already know me better than you think."

"But not as well as I want to."

He winked at her, and Kate felt a slight tingle of anticipation trickle through her.

She waited while he grabbed a bag from the backseat, then she took his hand and they set out for a stroll. He was taller, so his stride was a little longer than hers, but she was in decent shape, so she was able to keep up. Over the next several hours, he talked about his hockey league and his job as they traveled the trail. The small zoo on the grounds gave them new things to talk about, although that really wasn't a struggle. Their conversation flowed as easily today as it had on their first date. There really wasn't a whole lot of silence. None that was uncomfortable anyway.

After they left the zoo, they found a patch a grass so they could sit down. From his backpack, Neal pulled out a blanket, a box of crackers, a bag of grapes, a bottle of wine, and two plastic cups. She smiled as he unpacked the food while she sat back on the blanket, just taking in the park. She could hear children laughing in the zoo, a few splashes in the lake, and the occasional greeting exchanged by people meeting on the trail.

"It's nice out here," she said, breaking the brief silence.

"It is," he agreed. "I run out here a lot in the summer."

"I think I would too, if my schedule allowed," she said. "It's populated enough to feel safe, but serene enough that you can zone out."

He nodded, handing her a glass of clear white wine. "That's my favorite part of running – zoning out. It's the perfect stress relief after a long day."

"Same," she said. "But I'm usually on a treadmill instead of a trail."

He made a face. "I'm not a fan of the treadmill. I call it 'the dreadmill,' and I avoid it at all costs. When it's too cold to run, I get my exercise on the ice."

She shrugged. "I really don't know any different, so it's okay with me."

"I suppose that's true of a lot of areas of your life," he said.

"What do you mean?"

"Whenever we talk about your job, how you rarely get to see family and how hard it is to date, you never seem too upset by any of it. I suppose that's because you're just used to it, so you've become complacent with all of it."

"I don't know if I'd go so far as to say 'complacent.' I'm used to it, yes, but there's more. I love my job, so I don't mind the hours it takes. I miss my family, but I do my best to keep up with them and spend extra time with them in the off-season."

"And dating?"

"I still haven't figured that out, but I don't think I'm the only one."

He laughed a little. "That's true. Dating is tough."

"I think we're doing fine today though," she said, smiling at him.

"We are, but there's just one thing missing," he said.

"What's that?" she asked.

In response, he leaned in and brushed his lips lightly against hers. Her breath caught for a moment and then his lips were there again, nudging against hers. She brought her hand up to his face and tilted her head, slanting her mouth under his, encouraging him to take the kiss deeper. He was very good – at taking cues and at kissing. Kate legitimately thought she was going to run out of air, and yet she didn't want him to stop. When he finally released her, she took a deep breath as though trying to replenish what he'd stolen. For a few moments, she didn't know what to say. It was the first awkward silence of the day.

"Yes, that was definitely missing," she said finally. "I'm glad you fixed that."

He grinned at her. "Me too."

After they finished their mini picnic, they sat for a bit longer, just enjoying the fresh air. As the sun started to dip, they packed up and got in the car again. Their next stop was Bryant Lake Bowl, where she teased him about ordering something called the "Bad Breath Burger" while she enjoyed a delicious grilled cheese made with white cheddar.

After dinner, he popped a mint and winked at her as they claimed a lane for two games of bowling. They were both competitive, but Neal was undeniably better at this game. Kate beamed with pride when she actually broke 100 in the final game.

"Victory is mine!" she cried out.

"What? I won," Neal said.

"Yes, but I got my highest score ever, so that's a win for me."

"Fair enough. Want to grab one more drink before we call it a night?"

"Ready to be rid of me already?"

"Not at all, but I know you traveled all night, and I still have a few more days with you. You'll need the rest."

Kate nodded, and followed him to the bar. He didn't seem to mind when she checked the TV for the Pioneers score. She also checked her phone for the first time all day and was glad to see only a few messages, none of which were urgent. At the end of the evening, she was treated to another one of his breathtaking kisses as they said goodnight at the hotel elevators.

Neal showed Kate a lot of the Twin Cities over the next few days. They walked around downtown Minneapolis, shared Montego Bay Jerked Chicken and sangria at Chino Latino, tasted wines at St. Croix Vineyards, and checked out the view from the endless bridge at the Guthrie Theatre. There was a nice balance of relaxation and exploration. She enjoyed seeing new parts of the city, but not nearly as much as she enjoyed simply getting to know Neal. She grew very familiar with the fit of his hand in hers and the feel of his kiss. He didn't pressure her for more, and Kate was equal parts impressed and disappointed. The way he kissed made her curious about his skills between the sheets, and it had been a while since she'd had sex with anyone. On the other hand, she had never been one to initiate sex, and she wasn't about to start with Neal. She liked where they were, so she decided not to rush it. The sex would happen. Eventually.

She only thought about the Pioneers a few times each day during her trip, and she found it was easier to leave her phone in her purse than she previously thought. She felt more relaxed than she had in a long time. She was delighted as they made plans for him to come visit her in Portland in a few weeks. She was eager to entertain him on her home turf.

Kate had been hesitant about him in the beginning, but as she rehashed the weekend with Jill the phone at the close of her trip, she realized she really liked Neal. He was exactly what she needed in her life – the perfect distraction from work and everything that came with it.

Reid was a little surprised when he didn't see Kate in the stands on Friday. Her usual seat was empty, and at first he thought maybe she was just running late or dealing with business, but as he kept checking throughout the game, she never showed up. He was puzzled when he still didn't see her on Saturday. He even looked for her in the clubhouse, but there was no sign of her anywhere on the grounds. By Sunday, when her seat was still empty, he was concerned. The Kate he knew rarely missed a game, let alone an entire series – especially now, in the midpoint of the season with the Pioneers still very much in the thick of a division race. He finally expressed his concern to Don Carroll, although he tried to make it sound casual.

"I noticed Kate hasn't been around this weekend," he said to the manager as the Pioneers took the field in the fifth inning.

"I noticed that too," the manager said.

"Is this typical for her?" Reid asked.

"Not really," Don said after a brief pause. "I don't think she's missed a series in my entire time working for her."

"Weird. Have you heard anything about why she's gone? Is she sick? Did something happen?"

"I don't have any idea. The boss' whereabouts are none of my business."

"You aren't concerned?"

Don shrugged. "Not really."

"What if something bad has happened?"

"I'm sure she's fine. In fact, I know she is. I got an e-mail from her about some prospects yesterday."

"So she's still working, but that doesn't explain why she's gone. What if there's been some kind of emergency?"

"Then she'll handle it. In case you haven't noticed, Kate can take care of herself and a lot of other people."

Reid knew Don had a point. Kate was very self-sufficient, almost to a fault. Whatever was going on, he knew she could handle it, but Reid couldn't stop wondering. He tried to imagine what could possibly make Kate miss three games in a row. His mind immediately went to her family and his worry escalated. Family was the only thing Kate cared about more than baseball. Someone had to be sick, or maybe someone had died. His heart began to ache for her and whatever situation had pulled her away from the team and her job. Especially if it involved her family. He cared about her parents and siblings as if they were his own.

He thought about calling her or sending a text, but he wasn't sure that was a good idea. Their interactions had been civil lately and he didn't want to ruin that. And with his luck, he'd say the wrong thing. He decided it was best if he didn't contact her. But he still looked for her every day when he went to the ballpark.

Even though it was the All-Star Break, Reid still reported to the stadium each day. Only three of the Pioneers had been selected to play in the midsummer classic. While some of the other players took advantage of the break to spend time with family, there were several who wanted extra cage time and workouts. Reid had no problem with this. He admired their work ethic, and he was sure some were motivated by their place in the standings. The sports media seemed to have crowned the Angels as division champs already, but the Pioneers were not out of the running yet. They sat eight games out of first place and five games out of second place, and there was plenty of time to make up ground, especially with more than a dozen head-to-head games left with their division foes. As far as the Pioneers were concerned, the American League West was still very much a three-horse race. The team had gone into the break on a hot streak, and he was certain the players hoped regular workouts would keep it going once the season resumed.

Between sessions with the players, Reid found time for his own workouts. A half-season of coaching was under his belt, but he hadn't lost his interest in playing. If anything, it was even stronger. His sense of longing grew with each pitch, each hit, and each inning he watched from behind a fence. Being in the dugout was fine for now, but he fully intended to be back on the field in the next season. He enjoyed coaching, but he knew he wouldn't be content until he was between the chalk lines again.

Some of his former teammates had been texting him in recent weeks, asking how he was doing. A few even lamented that he was not with them. The Mets were currently leading the National League East and showed no signs of giving up their lead either. Every time he saw the standings, it made him feel worse about his decline. It seemed as though the team had improved without him. Logically, he knew one player didn't always make a difference, but it was hard not to let his mind go there. The mere idea that he had been holding the team back was a blow, but he decided to use it as motivation. He was a good player, and he would be a better ballplayer when he got back on the field. He was determined to make sure the next team he landed with would be glad they gave him a chance.

On the last day of the break, he was on his way in for an early workout when he spotted Kate's car in the garage. *Finally*, he thought. Instead of heading for the weight room, he turned in the other direction and took the elevator up to the corporate offices.

Kate's assistant's desk was vacant, so Reid stepped right up to the door of her office. He could hear music playing softly inside and as he pressed his ear closer, he could hear her singing along. He waited until the song was over, knowing she wouldn't want to know anyone had heard her. Besides, he liked those few moments of just listening to her. She sounded upbeat and happy. It reassured him that whatever had pulled her away from work hadn't been too terrible. But now it made him even more curious. When the last refrains of the song faded away, he waited a few moments into the new song before knocking.

"Come in," Kate beckoned.

He opened the door and stepped inside. She seemed surprised to see him, and he couldn't tell if it was a bad surprise or a good one.

"Good morning. You're here early," Reid said.

"I could say the same for you."

"Our players have kept me busy. You've got some hard workers on the squad."

Kate's approval showed in her smile. "I knew that, but it's always good to hear."

"I've barely been able to get my own workouts in."

"Oh?"

"But I'm not going to complain. I like the work."

"Good. So, did you just come up here to reassure me about my players' work ethic?"

"No," he said. "I noticed you missed the last series. That doesn't seem like you, so I wanted to make sure everything was okay."

"Oh, yes, everything's fine."

"So there was no emergency that took you away?"

"Nope."

"So why were you gone?"

"That's none of your business."

Reid blinked. "Sorry, I was just curious. And worried. I thought something had happened in your family. I almost called you even."

"No, it had nothing to do with my family. They're fine."

"So where did you go? Was it something for work? Were you checking out a prospect or a new player for trade? You usually send scouts out for that, right?"

"Yes, I do. And, no, it wasn't for work."

"You still haven't told me where you went."

"Because I don't owe you an explanation."

"So you're not going to tell me where you went, and I'm just supposed to accept that?"

"Yes, you are. Do you question all of your bosses like this?"

"Only the ones who do something completely out of character – like abandon work and take off for several days without telling anyone where she's going."

Kate sighed and rolled her eyes. "I went to Minneapolis for the weekend. Alright?"

He frowned for a moment, trying to figure out why she would go to the Twin Cities. Then he remembered their last time there, and that smokin' hot dress she'd been wearing.

"The guy?" he asked.

Kate nodded.

"He must be pretty special," Reid said. "Nothing takes you away from baseball."

She shrugged. "I make time for things that are important to me."

"And he is? Already? You've only just started dating."

"It's really none of your business. How many times do I have to say that?"

Reid shook his head in disbelief. "This isn't like you."

"I wish you'd quit pretending you know me so well."

"And I wish you'd quit pretending we have no history at all."

"Oh, I'm not pretending that at all," Kate said. "But it's history. Ancient history, as far as I'm concerned. And I'd like to leave it there."

"You keep saying that, but the fact that you can't put it aside so we can be friends tells me it's not as ancient as you wish it was," Reid said.

He saw her stiffen and frown. But she didn't object to his comment. Instead, she did just as he should have expected – she shut down.

"I have work to do and so do you," she said. "Close the door behind you."

Reid stood there for a few moments just studying her. He didn't want to go back to work. He didn't want to leave her office like this. He wanted to talk to her more. He wanted to force her

168

into a conversation about their past and whatever was keeping her at a distance from him. He wanted to know what he'd done so he could issue a proper apology instead of just a vague blanket one that didn't seem to be working.

"I wish you'd tell me why you're so angry with me so I could make it right," he said.

She kept her head down, focusing on her computer. Her face remained set in a frown, and he could see her chest rising and falling rapidly. Clearly, she was trying to contain her frustration or anger or whatever emotion it was that he seemed to evoke in her. And those weren't the feelings he wanted to evoke in her. Not even close.

He sighed and turned to go. When he reached the door, he paused and looked back at her again, but as far as he could tell, she had yet to look up from her desk.

"Kate, I know you probably don't believe it, but you're pretty important to me. For a lot of reasons. If you weren't, I wouldn't keep trying to be your friend again," he said. "I'll get back to work now, like you asked, but this isn't over. I may not know you well anymore, but I guarantee you still know me, and you know how I am when I set my mind to something."

She didn't look up at him once as he spoke, but he could tell his words rang through her. He saw it in the expression on her face. Kate was stubborn, but so was he. Before the season ended, he was going to get close to her again.

As soon as the door clicked shut, Kate leaned back in her chair and closed her eyes, breathing deeply. Reid had gotten under her skin again. He seemed to do that without much effort. Then again, he'd always had that power. It was foolish of her to think it'd ever go away, but that didn't stop her from hoping. And it didn't stop her from being blindsided every time it happened either.

Like today.

She'd been in a good mood when she arrived at her office, with her favorite coffee in hand and the latest Ben Rector album playing through her iPod speaker. She sat down at her desk, smiling as she reminisced about her time with Neal. As she clicked through e-mails and the transaction wire, she'd been humming and singing to herself. The time away had been good for her, she'd enjoyed her time with Neal, and now she was eager to get back to work. Peace and productivity were on her agenda for the day.

And then Reid walked in and destroyed her calm demeanor. At first, his visit was fairly innocuous. When he expressed concern about her absence, she'd been touched. Even though she wanted to keep him at a distance, she had to admit it was nice to know he cared. But when he kept asking questions about her whereabouts, his visit took an unwelcome turn. Reid sounded irritated when he asked about "the guy." Kate grew irritated as well, annoyed with his questioning.

She hadn't intended to tell Reid – or anyone – about Neal. Not yet. There was nothing to share right now. They were still just getting to know each other. But she didn't clarify that when Reid asked if this new guy was important to her. She didn't know why that mattered to Reid, but admittedly she had enjoyed testing his reaction. It hadn't been a good one. If she didn't know better, she'd almost say he was jealous. His eyes narrowed, and she saw his fists clench. A reddish tone had been creeping up his neck, and she was certain it would have reached his face if the conversation had continued. But she'd cut it short, put out by his interrogation and even more by his constant presumption to know her and her behavior – even if he had nailed it.

He was absolutely right in his assessment of her spontaneous trip. It wasn't like her. And it bugged her that he knew her that well. With the way he'd pushed her aside so many years ago, he didn't deserve to have that insight. He had dismissed her from his life – over the phone, no less – and never looked back. He didn't get to do this. He didn't get to go away and then come back like he knew all her secrets and all her quirks. Except he did. Even with the years that had gone by since she last saw him, Reid was still the person in the world who knew the most about her. Their time together had been disjointed and brief, but in that time, she'd shared a lot with him – things she hadn't shared with anyone else before or since. She supposed that was another reason she still resented him. Not only had he rejected her; he'd also taken with him parts of her she could never get back.

She sighed and shook her head. She had spent far too much time thinking about Reid – in the past and the present. She needed to break that pattern, but she was certain it wouldn't happen anytime soon. Not with him on her payroll. And, as he'd mentioned on the way out, he was going to be persistent in his efforts to be her friend again.

Friends.

Hrmph.

How could they go back to a place they'd never really been?

Chapter Ten

Reid took out his frustration in the batting cages. He had planned on running and lifting first, but after the conversation with Kate, he needed a different outlet. With every pitch from the machine, he aimed to drive the argument out of his mind. He wished he could drive Kate out too.

He still didn't have any clue as to why she was so angry with him. He'd gone over and over it in his mind, but he was still completely confused. More perplexing than her anger was the fact that he couldn't let it go. Why couldn't he just accept her animosity, do his job, and move on? There was just something about her that made her hard to forget. He'd been trying to do that for years and had never quite succeeded.

No one had ever gotten under Reid's skin like Kate, and she'd done it seemingly without trying. When he accepted her offer of math help all those years ago, he had no idea he'd get more out of it than just a better grade.

As a teenager, Reid had resolved never to fall in love with anyone. He didn't want anything to do with love because it only got in the way of goals and dreams. He learned that early, and it'd been reiterated often in his life.

It had happened to his parents. They'd both had to put their career plans on hold when he came along. He remembered how hard they had worked and struggled during his childhood. Reid had decided long ago he wasn't going to be like them. He was going to get out of his hometown and make something of himself.

When he started playing baseball, everyone marveled at how good he was. In his earliest years, pitchers stopped pitching to him after the first two at bats. When he was in eighth grade, he was invited to play on the junior varsity squad. He was a varsity starter before the end of his freshman summer. The game came easily to him, and he decided that was it. This was his calling. Scouts started coming around, and Reid decided right then and there that baseball would be his life. He didn't want or need anything else.

Then he met Katie Marks.

He'd been surprised when she offered to help him with his pre-calc, but he accepted the offer because he knew she was smart and a good student. She was also safe. She was kind of plain looking, and she definitely wasn't one of the so-called popular girls. There would be no complications of attraction nor would he have to worry about her gossiping about their study sessions. She would help him with his math and that would be it.

As they spent more time together, his view of Katie changed drastically. Or rather, he realized that while he'd passed her in the halls dozens of times, he'd never truly seen her. During their evenings together, he witnessed her fierce independence, her quiet sense of humor, and her genuine nature. She never put on a show or tried to be something she wasn't. She was blunt, honest, and real. He also started to notice how pretty she was. And how unaware she was of her beauty. She was the kind of girl who didn't wear a lot of makeup. And she didn't need to. Her skin had been kissed by the Arizona sun, but only slightly. Her lips were a light shade of pink and usually had the slight sheen of gloss, but she rarely wore lipstick. Her dark hair had a slight wave and fell to just below her collarbones. But her most striking feature was those eyes. The first time he'd looked up from his math homework and straight into those green orbs, his breath caught in his throat. She didn't seem to notice as she went on explaining the problem he was working on, but it took him several moments to get his composure back. Sheepishly, he had to ask her to repeat her instructions. She was always patient with him during their study sessions, and she never made him feel stupid. Quite the opposite. When he studied with her, Reid actually felt smart, which was why he chose to continue studying with her even after his math skills and grades had improved. At least that was what he told himself, but it was a lie. Or, at the very least, it was only part of the reason he went over to the Marks house on almost a nightly basis.

He really liked spending time with her. He liked the way she looked at him and talked to him. It was so different than the attention he received from the other girls. Their fawning was nice for a while, but it quickly got annoying. Katie never fawned over him, and she definitely never annoyed him. She was fun, and it was easy to be with her. And she smelled really good. Oh Lord, she smelled amazing. He became even more aware of that when he danced with her at prom. He still remembered her reaction to his invitation. She'd looked stunned only for a moment, but then recovered and casually accepted. And he'd never forget how she looked when he picked her up for the evening, how she'd felt in his arms all night long, or the soft sweet scent that had enveloped him when they danced.

He had intended the night to be platonic and friendly, but somewhere in the course of the evening, something shifted inside him, and he decided not to fight it. Her hand felt too good in his, and the urge to kiss her built all evening until he finally found the right moment at the after-party. His friend's voice had broken the kiss and a little of the haze Reid had been in all night. As he drove Katie home, he could tell she was confused by his sudden distance. He couldn't explain it, and he figured he'd only hurt her more if he tried. So instead, he avoided the discussion that night and for the rest of the school year.

He immediately went off to summer league baseball and college. Katie was out of sight, but she was never out of his mind for very long. When they reconnected that one summer, Reid did not expect to pick up where they'd left off on prom night, but that's exactly what happened. He went to her house to watch a movie with her, but being that close to her brought back all those desires. Once again, he decided not to fight what he was feeling around her. He still didn't know if that decision conscious or an unconscious, but he wanted to kiss her, so he did. He didn't expect it to go further than that, but he couldn't help himself, and she didn't push him away. He didn't want to be pushed away either. Undressing her and touching her had felt incredible. And so very right. When he slid into her for the first time, he felt like he belonged there. Inside her. With her.

In that moment, Katie simultaneously represented a sense of security and a vulnerability he'd fought to avoid. He battled those two emotions even as he continued to spend more time with her. He knew they would both be going back to their separate schools soon, but he didn't want to waste a single day that he could be with her. When he agreed to try a long-distance relationship, he was sincere, but after he went back to college, his fears won out, especially after Tony's suicide. He couldn't get so lost in a girl he lost everything else, so he let her go and returned to the only other place he felt he belonged, one where he had no fear — the baseball diamond.

Here he was again, trying to use baseball to push Kate out of his mind. The only difference was that now she was part of his baseball life. She was his boss, so he couldn't exactly ignore her. As he smacked another pitch from the machine against the back of the net, he realized ignoring Kate was the last thing he wanted. The years apart had done nothing to diminish his pull to her, but apparently they had the opposite effect for her. Whatever had happened to her in that time had caused her to put up some imposing walls and she didn't seem eager to let them down.

Admittedly, he was surprised when he had learned she was still single. Less admittedly, he was pleased about it. He figured Kate would be married by now or at least be on her way there. She was a great catch, and he didn't know why some guy hadn't scooped her up yet. Based on what he'd heard from people around the organization, she hadn't had any recent serious relationships. When Reid asked why, no one really seemed to have an answer.

"I've seen plenty of men ask her out," said Jed Howser, the clubhouse manager. "And I've heard about some of the men who asked her out."

He was an older gentleman with gray-white hair. He was short and slightly overweight, but he clearly loved his job. The clubhouse was one of the cleanest Reid had seen, and the equipment for each game was always ready ahead of time. The younger players enjoyed hearing Jed's tales about all the players he had worked with over the years, and Jed always told them, "Someday, I'll be telling stories about you." He said it with such sincerity that Reid knew he believed it, so the players did too. They believed they'd be memorable and special.

"Miss Marks rarely goes out with anyone, and when she does, it's usually a dinner or two and that's it," Jed explained to Reid. "I guess she works too much to get serious about anything except baseball. I suppose that's why she's so good at her job. No distractions."

Reid nodded in understanding. He understood too well. But he knew that's where the similarities between he and Kate ended. They were both single and focused on their careers, but Kate was clearly better at her job than he had been at his. He'd been booed and fired when he failed to meet expectations. Kate, on the other hand, was admired and respected by everyone in the field. She was smart, savvy, and ambitious.

She was also as beautiful as ever. Maybe even more beautiful. Her hair was just a little longer and richer in color. She wore more makeup, but it was still subtle and classic. Skirt suits seemed to be her favorite attire, and while they were completely professional, they also showcased the curve of her hips and her shapely legs.

Reid knew he wasn't the only guy on the payroll who noticed either. He saw the heads of players and coaches turn when Kate entered a room, crossed between two practice fields, or simply walked through the tunnels after a game. He'd also noticed a few men from opposing teams appreciating her, but she never seemed to notice any of the attention. Clearly, she was still unaware of her beauty. And she seemed to be dead set on denying anyone the privilege of seeing what was under her skirt suits and, more importantly, what was behind her professional front. She was content with the single life and pouring all of her energy and focus into the Pioneers. At least that's what Reid had decided until her spontaneous trip to Minnesota. He wondered what kind of guy could change her mind.

He arrived at the ballpark late one morning to work out before meeting with Will Batt, a young player who had been called up from AAA a few days earlier. One of the starting outfielders was injured and the new guy was having some trouble catching up with major league pitching, which was ironic given his name. Reid knew that feeling and approached the kid to see if he wanted some cage time. Without a moment of hesitation, Will agreed.

Reid was in total work mode when he heard Kate's unmistakable laugh. He smiled at the sound and followed it, eager to see what had amused her so much. But as he turned the corner toward the indoor batting cages, his smile fell. Kate was leaning against the wall and a man was leaning into her. Their faces were just inches apart, and Kate didn't seem to mind the intrusion. One of her hands was intertwined with his and they were talking softly. Kate laughed again and Reid felt something twist in his stomach. The twist tightened moments later when the man kissed Kate. Reid could do nothing but watch as the kiss deepened and Kate raised her free hand to caress the back of the man's neck. The level of intimacy and familiarity between them told Reid this was not a first date or a casual thing, and that bothered him. A lot.

He thought about backing away quietly and going to the field to run, but something stopped him from doing that. Instead, he continued down the hall, making plenty of noise as he headed for the batting cages. The pair looked up at the sound of his presence, apparently startled to learn they weren't alone in the ballpark.

"Reid," Kate said. "What are you doing here?"

Her voice sounded strange, but Reid couldn't be sure if it was embarrassment or something else.

"Good morning," Reid replied, hoping his voice sounded cool and nonchalant. "I'm working. Usually you're here for the same purpose, but I guess you have a different agenda today."

He thought he saw Kate blush a little.

"I hope we're not in your way," the man spoke.

Reid glanced at him, studying him now up close. The man holding Kate was just a few inches shorter than Reid and had broad shoulders. He looked mildly athletic, but in a more casual way than most of the men Kate saw every day.

Maybe that's intentional on her part.

The thought disappointed him a little although he wasn't sure why, and he didn't want to try and figure out why either.

He shook it off and continued his study of the man standing in front of him.

"Reid, this is Neal. He's visiting from Minnesota," Kate said. "I was just showing him around the ballpark."

"Nice to meet you, Neal," Reid said, offering his hand. "So you're the one who convinced Kate to take a few days off last month. I didn't think anyone could do that."

Neal laughed and Reid wished it were an annoying laugh. He wished for the guy to snort or sound like Janice from *Friends*. Reid wanted something to dislike about Neal – other than the fact that Kate seemed so enamored with him. Sadly, it was just a normal chuckle.

"I guess so," Neal said. "We had some fun that weekend, but she kept up with work and the team. Trust me on that."

"I'm not surprised," Reid said. "Kate's built this team and she's done a fine job of it. We were fine for a few days."

"Would you guys stop talking about me like I'm not here?" Kate said. "We'll leave you to your work now, Reid."

She took Neal's hand and started leading him away.

"See you around, Reid," Neal called over his shoulder.

"Sure thing," Reid said.

Damn it, the guy actually seems nice.

He watched them walk a few steps, but then quickly went into the batting cage. He'd seen enough of those two for the morning.

Out of sight didn't mean out of mind though. Reid was distracted for the rest of the day. His workout didn't feel as good as usual, and he felt bad for the young hitter he was supposed to be helping. He was so caught up in his thoughts he didn't see half of the swings the kid took.

His preoccupation even stretched into that evening's game and, if he was being honest, through the rest of the series. With Texas in town, Reid should have been paying attention to how his hitters were responding to the tough Rangers pitching. Instead, his gaze and thoughts kept drifting to Kate and Neal as they sat in Kate's usual seats. To Kate's credit, she kept appearances very professional and almost platonic, but Reid knew better. He saw how relaxed Kate appeared with Neal and how comfortable they were together. Worse yet, he couldn't stop imagining Kate and Neal touching and kissing the way they had in the hallway. As if that wasn't bad enough, he also began picturing them in more intimate settings and activities. It made him feel sick and uneasy. It made him feel a lot of things he rarely felt. Things he didn't want to feel.

He and Kate were long since over, and as cold as she was to him, it didn't seem like there was any chance of reversing that. Until now, Reid wasn't even sure he wanted that. But after seeing her kissing Neal, Reid was eaten up with envy. That realization surprised him. And scared the hell out of him. Envy made a man vulnerable. Reid didn't do vulnerable.

He wrestled with his realization and mixed emotions for the next few weeks. Neal was gone, so Reid hoped his envy would leave too. He tried to get lost in his work, and work was busy, but not busy enough. Even though the Pioneers were in second place in the division and rosters were expanding to prepare for the playoff hunt, Reid still had too much time to think. And he didn't like the direction his thoughts had gone.

Baseball wasn't doing enough to keeping his mind off Kate, so Reid decided he needed to find another method. There was only one other way he knew to quiet the thoughts in head.

After the Pioneers finished a sweep of the Seattle Mariners, Reid changed into street clothes and walked to a bar a few blocks from the ballpark. He sat down at the bar and ordered a whiskey and Coke with an emphasis on the whiskey.

"And keep 'em coming," he said to the bartender.

Reid put a large bill on the bar to underscore his request. The bartender, who didn't look much older than most of the guys on the Pioneers roster, was happy to oblige the request. As Reid downed the brown liquid, he didn't look at anyone – except to the bartender when he was ready for another. One man recognized him and tried to make conversation about the Pioneers, but Reid quickly shooed him away. A few women tried to flirt with him, but Reid barely glanced in their direction so they took the hint and moved on.

He was four drinks and as many shots in when Derek Beaman sat down next to him.

"Hey, Coach B. Some guys said they saw you come in here."

"Yep. Gotta celebrate, you know?"

"Yeah, we had a good win."

"You pitched lights out tonight. You should be celebrating too."

"I had a late dinner with the guys. You taught me that was a better way to celebrate."

"Did I?"

"Yep, which is why I'm confused to find you here with your breath reeking of alcohol."

Reid shrugged and took a long pull of his drink. He signaled for another, and Derek sighed.

"Not too long ago, you talked me out of making a really bad decision. I'd like to return the favor. Let me drive you home, Coach."

"I don't want to go home."

"Then I'll take you anywhere you want to go, as long as it's away from here and not another bar."

Reid looked at his drink for a few moments, then quickly finished it and laid some money down on the bar. He waved to the bartender as he stood and turned to Derek.

"Let's go then."

Derek seemed a little shocked at Reid's quick agreement, but he didn't say anything. He just walked out to his car and got in the driver's seat. Reid leaned back and gave Derek an address.

"Sounds fancy. Is that your place?"

"No."

"Then what is it?"

"Don't worry about it. Just drive."

"I told you I'm not taking you to another bar."

"It's not a bar. Now, start the damn car and take me there."

The younger man hesitated for several moments, just studying Reid. With a sigh, Reid reached for the door handle.

"If you're not going to take me there, I'm going back in the bar to drink."

"No," Derek said quickly. "No, I'll take you."

The tone in Derek's voice told Reid he was having doubts. But he started the engine anyway and put the car in gear, driving them away from the bar and across town to the mystery destination Reid had chosen.

Kate had just fallen asleep when her doorbell started ringing. A loud pounding followed the chimes and then the pattern repeated. She pulled a short robe over her nightgown as she made her way downstairs to investigate all the noise, which was continuous. She flipped on the outside light and when she looked through the peephole in her door, she groaned.

"Katie, I need to talk to you," Reid shouted.

He sounded drunk, and she really didn't want to deal with him. But she didn't feel like she had a choice. If she didn't let him in, he would wake her neighbors ... if he hadn't already.

She pulled the robe tighter and barely had time to step out of the way as Reid grinned at her and stumbled forward into her foyer.

"How did you get here?" Kate asked as he pushed past her. "Please tell me you didn't drive in this state."

Only then did Kate see Derek standing on her front porch. She tightened her robe a bit more.

"I'm so sorry, Miss Marks. If I'd known this was your place, I wouldn't have brought him here," the young pitcher rambled. "He was at the bar, and I just wanted to get him out of there, so I told him I'd take him anywhere he wanted to go."

"It's OK, Derek. You did the right thing," Kate reassured him.

"You should get home. Are you alright to drive?"

"Yes, ma'am, I haven't had a drop to drink this season thanks to Coach B," he said. "That's why I was surprised to find him so blitzed."

"He'll be fine. I'll take care of him from here," she said. "Good game tonight."

"Thanks," he said.

But he didn't move from the step. He craned his neck to look beyond Kate, apparently reluctant to leave Reid there.

"He'll be OK. Reid and I are old friends. I know how to handle him," Kate said. "Have a good night."

Derek nodded, turned slowly, and headed back to his car. Kate heard the car start and pull away from the house as she locked the door. She took a deep breath as she prepared to face Reid, who was sprawled out comfortably on her living room couch. She crossed her arms as she stood across the room from him.

"Make yourself at home," she said sarcastically.

"Being with you is kind of like being home," Reid said.

Kate rolled her eyes. "You are definitely drunk. Why are you here, Reid?"

"To see you. We have unfinished business."

"We do? I'm pretty sure you took care of finishing things years ago."

"You don't understand, Katie."

"I gave up on understanding you a long time ago. I don't need to, and I don't want to."

"But I want you to. Please, hear me out."

"Of course, because it's always been about what Reid wants."

"Katie, whatever I did to hurt you, I am so sorry, and I honestly didn't mean to."

"You've said that a few thousand times this year. You can stop anytime."

"Not until you believe me and forgive me."

"I do forgive you."

"No you don't. And you don't believe me either. But maybe if I knew for sure what I was apologizing for, it would clear things up."

"As I've said before, if you don't know then you probably aren't really sorry."

"Damn it, Katie," Reid said, standing up.

Or at least he tried to stand up. The whiskey had clearly messed with his center of gravity. Kate watched as he wobbled. This was not a familiar sight for her. Reid had always been so strong, athletic, and in control. It was strange to see him unbalanced. Kate didn't like it. The steady, confident version of Reid rattled her, but this version just made her sad.

Even though he was still wavering a little, Reid made his way toward Kate. With overly deliberate steps, he slowly crossed the distance, as if he was expecting Kate to bolt or back up. But she decided to stand her ground. She could handle him – especially in this state. He was less intimidating like this.

"Katie."

He was close enough now that she could smell the booze on him. And the way he drug her name out gave her an extra dose of his breath. She made a face, but didn't budge.

"Katie, please. Tell me why you are so mad at me."

"Reid, I think you need to sleep this off."

"My ride is gone. You're stuck with me."

"I'm calling you a cab."

She pulled out her phone and quickly made arrangements for a pick-up. She was dismayed that a car wouldn't be there for almost half an hour. That was half an hour more than she wanted to spend with Reid. Then again, with this much whiskey in him, she figured he was pretty harmless.

"How long are you going to avoid this conversation?" he asked.

"What conversation?"

"About our past."

"Forever if I can."

"What are you so afraid of?"

"I'm not afraid of anything. I just don't want to talk about our past."

Reid smirked a little. "Then maybe we can relive some of it."

She wasn't sure what he meant by that, and she was caught off-guard when he reached out and touched her cheek. His coordination suddenly didn't seem the least bit compromised as his thumb gently stroked her skin just to the left of her mouth.

Now it was Kate who felt off-balance. She knew she needed to pull away, but her brain was not relaying that message to the rest of her body. Or maybe it was, but her body was not listening. The messages got even more muddled when he leaned in to kiss her. It was Kate's turn to feel intoxicated. Reid's kisses had always floored her, and this one was no exception. She could feel her knees weakening and her pulse quickening. Her body was betraying her and she felt powerless to stop it. Reid's lips and tongue currently held all the power, and Kate couldn't help but melt against him. As nice as Neal's kisses were, they were nowhere near the caliber of Reid's.

At the thought of Neal, she knew she needed to stop this. She put her hands up to his chest to push away, but her body's betrayal continued. Instead of creating distance, her hands slid along the strong muscles of his upper body and met at the nape of his neck, pulling him closer. The thin layers of her satin robe and cotton nightgown provided very little in the way of a shield. She was keenly aware of every inch of him that was pressed against her. He was all heat and muscle. She heard a moan and was surprised to realize it had come from her.

"Now that's the Katie I remember," Reid murmured against her lips.

His voice broke through the haze, and Kate finally managed to back out of his touch. Her lips still tingled and her body was alight with arousal, but her strong resolve was returning.

"No, no this isn't me," she said.

"Sure it is," Reid said, seeming more sober. "And I kind of like it. I think you do too."

"No, no, no," she said, shaking her head.

She had found the will to resist him, but the logic side of her brain was still a little impaired.

Reid laughed, clearly amused by this, and took another step toward her, putting a hand on her waist.

"Come on, Katie," he said. "Let's have some fun. We used to be good together. I bet we'll be even better now."

"No," she said, pushing his hand away. "I'm with Neal, and besides …,"

"What?"

"This would be a disaster," she said, gesturing between them as she accentuated the word "this."

"Why do you think that?" he asked.

"Because I've been through this before with you."

"Through what?"

"You and me. The insane chemistry."

"Right. I don't understand why that's so bad," Reid said, as he reached for her again.

"Of course you don't. You got what you wanted. That's all that matters to you. You just played me and left. You've done that twice, and I'm not going to let you do it a third time."

The lust and desire that had been coursing through her body were now replaced with anger and fury. The change was evident in her tone, face, and body language.

Reid dropped his hand and took a step back.

"What did you say?"

"It's true, Reid. I used to think you were different than other guys – smarter and kinder. But you're really not. You are just like them – selfish and mean," Kate said. "I was stupid enough to give you my virginity before I learned my lesson. That was my second mistake with you. There won't be a third."

"Katie … that's not how it was."

"Maybe not for you, but that's how it was for me. You have no idea what you put me through," Kate fumed. "Did you know I got pregnant?"

Reid's eyes widened and his face went white. He looked like he'd been hit. Well, in a way she supposed he had, but his expression made it seem like he'd been physically hit. He appeared to sober up even more.

"You what?" he asked. "Why didn't you tell me?"

"You had broken my heart. And then I miscarried, so what was the point?"

"You still could have told me. I would have …,"

"You would have what?"

"I would have been there for you."

"I handled it just fine on my own. And don't worry, I didn't tell anyone so your reputation is safe."

"I'm not worried about that."

"I don't want you to worry about me either. You didn't care about me back then, so don't start now."

"Yes I did, Katie. I wish you had told me."

"Why? I'm really not sure why I'm even telling you now," she said. "It's not like you've ever cared about me, and the last thing I need is for you to realize the kind of power you have, I mean had, over me. I have no desire to stroke your ego … or anything else of yours for that matter."

"Katie …"

"Stop calling me that!" she shouted.

"Kate …" he tried again.

"I don't want to hear it, Reid. I just want you to leave. Your cab should be here any minute."

She walked over to the front door and looked out the window. Her driveway and the street in front of her house were both empty. She wasn't sure exactly how long it had been since she called the cab. A lot had transpired since she made that phone call, making it feel hours later even though it was probably only a few minutes. She just knew she needed to get away from him. Her emotions were swirling, and her mind was a jumbled mess.

Naturally, Reid followed her into the foyer. She heard his footsteps behind her as she peered out into her quiet neighborhood. Every house was dark, indicating her neighbors were all still in bed – just as she should be. She wished she felt as calm as the scene before her. She wished she'd never opened the door for Reid. She wished she'd never told him the secret she'd kept between herself and Jill all these years. She took a deep breath and turned around to face him, crossing her arms in front of her.

"You've had a chance to explain your side. Let me tell you mine," Reid said.

"I'm not interested in hearing it," she said. "I don't need some lame excuse about why you did what you did. What's done is done, and nothing you say can undo it."

"I just want you to understand. There's a lot about me you don't know."

"And I don't want to. I know enough."

She heard a car pull up and honk.

"Your cab is here," she said, opening the door. "Good night, Reid."

He stared at her for several moments, unmoving.

"If you don't leave, I will call the police," she said. "So you can go home or you can spend the night in jail."

Kate didn't know if she actually would call the police on Reid, and thankfully, she didn't have to make good on her threat. He left without another word. He didn't even look at her as he walked out the door and folded into the waiting cab. She closed the door, but watched through the window as the cab backed out of her driveway and started down the street. She kept waiting for it to stop and for Reid to storm back up to her house, but it didn't and he didn't. They both disappeared into the darkness.

Kate locked up and headed back up to her bedroom. She climbed under the covers and tried to relax again, but it quickly became apparent sleep wasn't happening that night. As she tossed and turned, she cursed Reid.

Damn him for asking me to tutor him back in high school.

Damn him for asking me to prom.

Damn him for kissing me at the after prom party.

Damn him for breaking my heart.

Damn him for inviting himself over to watch a movie over Christmas break.

Damn him for being so good in bed.

Damn him for breaking my heart again.

Damn him for coming over here drunk.

Damn him for kissing me senseless.

But even during her inner diatribe about Reid, Kate knew the blame wasn't all his. It was easy to just blame him, but Kate knew she was plenty guilty.

Damn me for letting him in.

And she wasn't just referring to her house.

Chapter Eleven

Too late, Reid realized he hadn't reset the alarm on his phone. It went off at an ungodly hour the next morning. He groaned and rolled over, but that proved to be a bad decision as he landed on the floor with a thud.

"Ow, damn it," he grumbled.

As he sat up, he grimaced. His head felt as though there were two tiny people in there taking turns hitting each side of his skull with a hammer. He closed his eyes and leaned back against the couch, waiting for the pain to subside a little so he could get up. He didn't need to be at the ballpark until noon but it appeared he would need every moment between now and then to recover from his hangover.

His bladder kept him from staying on the floor all morning. He didn't know how long he laid there like that, but the sun was definitely a little brighter by the time he finally got up. The pain seared through his head as he pulled himself off the floor and made his way to the bathroom.

As he washed his hands and splashed water on his face, Reid made the mistake of looking at his reflection in the mirror over the sink. He looked even worse than he felt. His eyes were puffy and a little bloodshot. He needed a shave, and his skin looked dull.

The alarm went off again and as he silenced it, he looked at his phone and saw he had two missed calls and several texts. They were all from the one person he dreaded facing today – Kate.

He couldn't pinpoint the moment he'd decided to go to Kate's house. It was tempting to blame the whiskey, but he couldn't be sure the thought hadn't entered his mind when he was still sober. At some point during the evening, he'd decided he wanted answers from her about their past. And, boy, did he get them.

For some reason, he had naively believed she would tell him she was mad because he had made some stupid comment. Or because he hadn't called her back once. He should have known better. Kate wasn't the kind of girl to get bent out of shape over something petty. While other girls in their high school were fighting over someone wearing the same sweater or looking too long at a guy, Katie had always been drama-free. Even when the girls tried to toss insults her way, she just let them roll off her back and continued on like nothing had happened.

No, Kate had very good reasons to keep him at an arm's distance.

His drunkenness may have clouded his judgment the previous night, but it had done nothing to dull his reception of Kate's words.

The news of her pregnancy and miscarriage hit him hard, and even now he wondered what would have happened if she hadn't miscarried. Would she have kept it? Would he be with her now? What would their child look like? Be like? He wasn't sure how he felt about any of that.

Her assessment that he was a selfish jerk hurt and made him feel terrible. He had never intended to mistreat her, and he had no idea she had felt used. Looking back now, he could see how it might have seemed that way to her, and he wished he could go back in time and do things differently.

But it was more than just her words that got to him. The real sting was in her delivery. Piercing didn't even almost describe the look in her eyes. She may as well have been looking at her sworn enemy who had just killed her family and burned down her house. And tone of her voice packed more punch than a Clayton Kershaw fastball. He had heard his share of anger from fans in recent years. Conversations with his family lately had been laced with disappointment. Kate's voice held a mixture of both of those things and had an edge that cut right through him.

Their conversation had sobered him up considerably. As he rode home in the cab, he kept replaying her words in his mind. All the whiskey in the world hadn't been able to numb the pain from that. Even now, as he thought about it, he felt an ache in his chest that had nothing to do with his hangover.

And yet, there was one part of the evening that made other parts of his body ache in a good way.

That kiss.

Going to her house to talk may have been a semi-conscious decision, but kissing her had been much like every other big moment between them – an impulse. And it wasn't a mistake. It proved to him that their chemistry had not been a fluke or merely a thing of their youth. It was still very real and very alive. He thought it might even be stronger than ever, but he couldn't be sure if that was because the time that had passed or the other lingering emotions between them. Either way, it felt incredible. He hadn't had a kiss like that since … well, since her. And he had kissed his share of women in recent years, but no other kiss he'd experienced had felt like that. His entire body came alive in those moments, hardening against her as she melted against him. They fit just right, just as they always had. If she hadn't pushed him away, he would have pulled open her robe and taken her right there on her living room floor. He had no doubt it would be even hotter than their past encounters.

More than once during their conversation, he'd wondered what she was wearing underneath that robe. His imagination gave him visions of satin and lace. He also pictured lots of skin. Kate still had a bit of a sun-kissed glow about her and Reid remembered the curves of her body well. And he had a feeling they had only gotten better with time. Her work attire was always conservative, but it didn't hide the fact that she had taken very good care of her body. And he had a brief memory of the night he'd seen her heading out on that date in Minneapolis. The dress she'd worn that night showed off her killer figure, hugging every inch of her body and putting her cleavage on full display. The mental image, however brief, made him groan.

He groaned again when he realized he would have to face Kate in a few hours. It was a much different groan. That kiss and the information she had dumped on him about their past would only add to the tension that previously existed. And now there was likely to be a degree of awkwardness as well. No matter how amazing that kiss had felt, it probably hadn't been his best career move. The fact remained that she was his boss. Not only that, but he could not forget that she had given him a new leash on his career. And this is how he thanked her, apparently – by getting drunk, showing up at her place, and kissing her.

He didn't know why she was trying to contact him this morning, but he was certain he didn't want to hear whatever she had to say. Reid put the phone back down as he began the work of nursing his hangover.

Kate's number showed up on his display again while he was

devouring a greasy breakfast at a local diner. This time, he decided to answer.

"It's about time you picked up," Kate snapped. "I've been trying to get ahold of you for hours. After last night, I ..."

"Look, I'm not ready to talk about last night yet," he said.

"Well, you don't have a choice. Someone took photos of you and posted them online. They're everywhere. We need to do damage control."

"It can't be that bad. All I did was sit at a bar and down drinks."

"That's not the only photo they got. Life would be easier if it was."

"Then what did they get?"

"You. Leaving my house."

"What? How?"

"Someone must have followed you from the bar to my place," she said. "Someone else decided to do a little research, and now the media knows we have a history. Our prom photo is making a real splash."

"OK, so we knew each other in high school ... that's not bad, right?" he asked.

"It wouldn't be bad if these photos didn't show me standing in the doorway in my robe," she said. "Thankfully, Derek isn't in any of them. That kid doesn't need to be in the middle of this ... not any more than you already made him part of it anyway."

Reid sighed. His headache was starting to come back.

"So what do you want from me?"

"You need to be at the ballpark in an hour. I'll work on a formal statement for both of us. You'll read it, and you'll apologize for embarrassing the organization."

"Is that it?" he asked.

"For now, it is," she said. "After that, I have a meeting with ownership to clear everything up."

"Oh shit," he said. "Am I going to be fired?"

"I don't know yet," she said. "You've created a real mess for me, Reid. This is exactly what I asked you not to do when I offered you the job."

"Right, right ... I'm sorry, Kate," he said.

"Save it," she said. "I've heard that word from you so often it doesn't even mean anything to me anymore."

Reid was about to say something else – what, he didn't know – but she hung up. He still had half a plate of food, but he pushed it away. Between the hangover and the distressed phone call from Kate, his stomach was likely to protest anything he put in it. He put some money on the table and left, heading straight for Pioneers Stadium. During the drive, he tried to figure out how he could fix this.

When he got to the ballpark, he went directly to Kate's office. She was waiting for him, along with James Scott and two men he couldn't name but recognized as front office staff. Kate's scowl was the strongest, but the others didn't look happy to see him either. He'd been in plenty of meetings like this in New York, but he'd never before experienced this level of shame and embarrassment. He'd really messed up this time.

Kate crossed the room and handed him a sheet of paper.

"Read this over a few times so it sounds natural when we go down to the press room," she said.

He hadn't thought her tone could get icier than it had been in recent months. But he'd thought wrong.

Reid looked down at the words on the page and began skimming them.

"Read it aloud," Kate ordered.

"I'm here today to apologize for embarrassing the Pioneers. Last night, I made the decision to drink at a local bar. I have no explanation or excuse for that decision, and I accept that I've made a mistake that could be costly. I will also accept whatever punishment the Pioneers front office sees fit, even if it means the termination of my employment. Once again, I am sorry to the organization, the players, and the fans, for my lapse in judgment."

He looked up at her. "So, this only addresses the drinking. I thought you said there was another photo. Of me at your house."

"There was," Kate said. "I'll be handling that statement."

"What are you going to say?" Reid asked, glancing at the men in the room.

He wondered what she had told them about their past.

"Don't worry about it," Kate said. "The press will be here in 15 minutes. Read your statement a few more times and meet me down in the clubhouse. We'll walk into the press room together."

Kate, James, and the other men left the room, and Reid sat down, staring at the sheet of paper in his hands. Between the hangover, the bombshell Kate had dropped the previous night, and this media nightmare, he was having a hard time focusing on the words.

A short while later, he was sitting at the table in the press room. Reporters filled three rows of chairs while James and the two front office men stood at the back of the room. He glanced at Kate on his left, but she was staring straight ahead.

"Thank you all for coming today," she said. "Mr. Benjamin and I each have a statement to read, and that will conclude the press conference. There will be no questions."

She nodded at him, and he began speaking. Even though he hadn't written the statement, it effectively summed up his feelings. When he was done, he folded the sheet and sat back, listening as Kate began reading her statement.

"As some of you have recently learned, Mr. Benjamin and I graduated high school together. We were friends until college, but we lost touch after that. But our shared history is not why I hired him. Mr. Benjamin is extremely knowledgeable about batting and the psychology involved with stepping up to the plate. When I interviewed him for the position, I knew he would be an asset, and he has proven me right. Our offense has improved greatly with his guidance," she said. "When he made the decision to drink last night, he knew he'd made a mistake. Because of our long-established bond, he decided to come to me directly to admit his error in judgment before I could hear it elsewhere. This resulted in photos of him at my home. While I was not thrilled at his condition upon his arrival, I appreciate the fact that Mr. Benjamin has owned his mistake. He has also agreed to seek counseling for his drinking problem. We support him in his recovery, and he will remain the Pioneers hitting coach at this time."

She took a breath and then looked at the reporters.

"I hope that clears everything up," she said. "Thank you for coming today. We'll see you later tonight at the game."

Without another word or even a glance at him, Kate left the press room, followed by the owner and the other front office executives. Reid followed their lead, although he headed to the clubhouse instead of upstairs to the management offices.

He didn't see Kate for the rest of the day. At least not up close. She was in the stands during the game, but she seemed to be steering clear of the clubhouse, batting cages, and everywhere else

Reid might be. He decided not to push it by seeking her out. Besides, he still didn't know what to say to her after everything that had transpired, so it was probably best to let her have her space.

He did have another person to apologize to though. After the game, he waited outside the clubhouse until he saw Derek Beaman emerge.

"Hey Derek," he said. "Do you have a minute?"

Derek nodded and followed Reid through the tunnels underneath the ballpark.

"What's up, Coach?" Derek asked when they finally stopped a safe distance away from where all the players and staff were.

"I just wanted to apologize for last night," Reid said.

Derek shook his head. "We've all been there. It's no big deal."

"Yes it is," Reid said. "It was stupid of me to drink that much and then make you drive me. You shouldn't have had to deal with any of that. I'm supposed to be the mature one here."

Derek laughed a little. "We're ballplayers, maturity is hard when you play a game for a living."

Reid couldn't help but laugh. There was a degree of truth to what Derek had said.

"It's really OK, Coach B," Derek said. "I mean, I don't understand why you were drinking or whatever, but clearly it had something to do with Miss Marks, so I get it. Women make us do crazy things sometimes."

Again, Reid had to agree with the younger player. That reasoning was why Reid had done his best not to let any woman get to him over the years – several had tried and failed. The only one who had broken through them had done it without trying or even realizing what she'd done. She still didn't have any idea. In fact, she thought he'd used her. Reid knew he needed to set things straight at some point, but he still needed time to figure out how to do that.

"And don't worry," Derek said, pulling Reid out of his thoughts. "I'm not going to tell anyone about what I heard or saw last night. You kept my secret. I'll keep yours."

"I appreciate that, Derek," Reid said. "But it's not going to stay much of a secret thanks to the press."

Derek looked confused until Reid told him about the photos and the press conference.

"Wow. I bet Miss Marks is really mad," Derek said.

"She is, but I'm used to that by now," Reid said with a sigh.

"So do you want to go grab dinner?" Derek asked.

"Sure, let me get changed and we'll go," Reid said.

Reid was grateful when Derek didn't push him for more details about his drunken night. As they ate, they simply discussed the season, the team, and their thoughts on the next series.

Out of the blue, Derek also mentioned that his ex-wife had been in touch with him. There was no hope of reconciliation, and Derek seemed resigned to that, but Keely wanted to make sure he was still in his daughter's life. She still didn't trust Derek completely, which he understood, so any visits with Brynn would be supervised. Fortunately, she did trust Derek's family. During their conversations, Derek and Keely had made arrangements for his parents to keep Brynn for a week, during which they would visit Portland to see Derek. That visit was just two weeks away, and Derek could not hide his excitement.

"She's gotten so big," he gushed, showing Reid a picture of the little girl on his phone. "I guess she's talking now and everything."

"I'm glad you'll get to see her," Reid said.

"Yeah, I'm just afraid she won't really know me," Derek said. "Keely said she can be kind of shy, and I haven't been around her."

"So she might not know you at first, but I'm sure she'll get used to you," Reid said. "If you work to make her a priority and visit her more regularly, you'll be fine."

Derek nodded. "That's what I intend to do. I plan to spend as much of the off-season with her as I can. I even told Keely I'd like to keep her while she and her new husband go on a honeymoon."

"Wow ... that can't have been easy to say," Reid said.

"It wasn't," Derek admitted. "I still love Keely, and I think I always will. But I messed up. I let her believe I didn't care enough about her, so she found someone who will treat her the way she deserves. I'll regret that forever, but there's nothing I can do to change it now. The only relationship I can still save is the one I have with Brynn, so that's my focus."

Reid nodded as he listened. And the look in the younger guy's eyes as he talked about regretting the way he treated his wife, the woman he loved, hit Reid hard. Maybe it was too late for him to fix things with Kate too, but he at least had to try. He needed to apologize and explain to her what had happened to him all those years ago.

It seemed the hardest part would be finding an opportunity to talk to her. Work was insanely busy, and he'd started seeing a therapist about his drinking and other problems.

Plus, he couldn't find Kate. The only time he saw her was in her seats during the game. He went to her office a few times, but each time she was in a meeting or on the phone. At least that's what her secretary said. He didn't know how true it was. He thought about going to her house, but that hadn't gone so well last time, so he decided against it. That would be a last ditch strategy, and as the weeks went on, it looked like he might have to use it.

The season was quickly winding down. The regular season, that is. The postseason was on the minds and tongues of everyone in baseball, including the Pioneers staff and fans. For the first time in franchise history, the team was poised to play beyond game 162.

The Angels had crumbled, losing 13 straight games and surrendering their division lead to the Rangers. Now the Pioneers were in second place, just three games behind the Rangers. The two teams would face off for a four-game set to end the season, so the Pioneers still had a chance to win their division.

There was also a wild card at stake. The Pioneers had grabbed the top spot at the end of August and hadn't let go. As long as they won 15 of their next 24 games, they would retain that lead and stamp their first trip to the postseason.

As a result of the team's success and also by her own design, Kate was a very busy woman. There were some increased demands on her time at work, but she'd also returned to the Reid avoidance strategies she'd employed when he first arrived in Portland. She realized now – too late – that she should never have stopped avoiding him. Now he was under her skin again. If she was being honest, she would have to say he'd always been there. But now he was even deeper. His drunken visit had rattled her more than she wanted to admit to anyone – and not just because of the press attention.

The media had dropped the subject, but she was fielding questions from other sources – namely her family and a few friends.

Jill called Kate one night to ask why she'd broken things off with Neal. Kate tried using the excuses about work and distance – the same ones she gave to Neal – but Jill pressed on.

"Neal seemed to think there was someone else," Jill said. "And then that story about you and Reid came out …"

"There's no one else," Kate said. "I promise you. I don't have time for anyone else. And there's nothing going on with Reid."

"You know, I know your history, so I was surprised when I heard you hired him," Jill said.

"He knows baseball, and he's a good hitting coach. That's why I hired him," Kate said. "That's it."

"Are you sure?" Jill asked. "I mean, I wouldn't blame you if there were still some lingering feelings."

"Oh, there are lingering feelings – mostly anger," Kate said. "Seeing him has brought back memories of the way he just used me and left me."

"But he was your first love, Kate," Jill said. "You can't tell me you don't still have a little of that for him. And you told me about how hot you two were together. Aren't you a little curious about if that's still there?"

"No," Kate said.

And she wasn't curious. After the way he'd kissed her, she didn't need to be. The heat between them was definitely still there. She hadn't slept much after he left that night. Part of it was from the emotions and memories he'd stirred up, but there was more. Reid's kiss had awakened parts of her that had been dormant for years – parts even Neal's expert kisses hadn't been able to rouse. And she hadn't even been aware of it until his lips and tongue had coaxed them back to the surface. Her body had been buzzing with desire and the mere thought of that kiss still turned her on more than a kiss from any other guy. In fact, Reid's kiss had affected her more than most of the sex she'd had since him. So, yes, there was certainly still plenty of heat between Kate and Reid, but she wasn't about to let herself get burned again.

Even though she did not intended to explore things with Reid, she knew she had to break up with Neal. Staying with him wouldn't be fair to him or her. She'd dropped the news on him in a phone call, which she realized made her just as bad as Reid. Neal had pleaded with her to give it more time and even suggested more frequent visits, but Kate knew that wouldn't change anything and she told him as much. He finally stopped calling and texting, although she still wasn't sure he'd accepted the break-up. She had a hard time accepting it too, and she hated that she had let Reid ruin this for her.

Thankfully, she only needed to avoid Reid for a few more weeks. She had already been looking into hiring a new hitting coach. It wasn't that she planned to fire Reid. She certainly had grounds for it after the incident at her house, but she had opted not to exercise it to spare her own humiliation and any extra media speculation. She didn't expect him to stay on as hitting coach, however. Reid's agent had contacted her already to discuss his contract. Reportedly there were at least four teams interested in Reid's services – as a player. Kate knew there was no way Reid would stay on as a hitting coach when he had a chance to play. As soon as the season was over, he would be out of her ballpark and her city. She just had to steer clear of him until then.

Her reprieve ran out when she arrived at the ballpark early for Fan Appreciation Day. He was just getting out of his Mercedes when she pulled into the parking garage. She took her time parking, hoping he would head on inside. Of course, that was not in Reid's plans. As she got out of her white Audi, she saw him waiting near the elevator.

"Good morning," he said. It sounded more like a question than a statement.

"Good morning," she answered, keeping her tone even.

She pushed the button on the elevator, and her hand inadvertently brushed his arm.

"Kate, we need to talk," he said.

"There's nothing to talk about," she said.

"I want to apologize again," he said.

"I don't want to hear it," she said.

The elevator arrived, and she stepped on. Reid wasn't about to let her escape. He scrambled into the elevator just before the doors shut, and Kate sighed in annoyance.

"You need to hear it," Reid said. "I'm sorry about the way I handled things years ago. I had no idea it hurt you so much."

Kate felt her whole body tense up. She hated that he had affected her then, and she especially hated that he affected her now. She wanted to say that, but she said nothing. She didn't want to have this conversation, so she was fine letting it be a one-sided affair. Let him say what he needed to say and then he could just go away.

"A lot of things happened to me back then. I went through

some tough times and I didn't handle them very well."

"Oh, and my life was a piece of cake," she spat. So much for just letting him talk.

"Fair enough. But will you give me a chance to tell you?"

"I really don't see the point. It won't change anything."

The elevator stopped on the floor where her office was. She stepped off without looking in his direction. He followed her down the hall and into her office, shutting the door behind him.

"You're right. It won't change anything. I can't change what I did, but maybe you'll understand why I did what I did."

"I don't want to understand," she said.

She finally turned to face him as she spoke. She was determined to stare him down.

"I don't want to understand what makes someone treat another person like that," she continued. "I don't want to understand why you thought it was okay to just toss me aside like I was no one. I'm not no one, Reid. I was not one of your little groupies. I deserved better than that."

"I know you did, but you scared me," Reid said.

"Scared you?" Kate asked. "What could I have possibly done to scare you?"

"You existed," Reid said simply.

Kate frowned in confusion. "Are you drunk again?"

"Not at all," Reid said.

"Well, you aren't making any sense right now," she said.

"I'm trying, trust me," he said. "Here's the deal, Katie. I decided a long time ago that I was never going to fall in love. It just messes up people's plans and steals their dreams. I saw too many people get hurt."

Kate could not disagree with that reasoning. She had experienced plenty of that.

"But then you happened," Reid continued. "When you offered to tutor me in math, I had no idea I would start to like you so much. But you were so smart and nice and funny and beautiful. Damn it, the worst part is that you didn't know you were any of those things. That just made me fall harder. When I kissed you that night after prom, I knew I was in danger of losing myself in you. That's why I left without saying anything. I thought it would be easier."

Kate just blinked, too stunned to speak. Plus, he was clearly not finished. Even though she'd been fighting this for weeks, she suddenly wanted to hear what else he had to say.

"I really thought I would be able to forget all of that when I went to college. Out of sight, out of mind, you know? And it worked a little. But when we got together that summer, everything came back to me. I realized I was absolutely in love with you and that scared the shit out of me. You were everything I wanted and everything I feared all in the same package."

He paused and Kate swallowed hard, trying to figure out how to respond. She had not expected any of this out of him. Just as she opened her mouth to say something, Reid stopped her.

"My roommate in college committed suicide over a girl. I'm the one who found him. Everyone else thinks his death was an accident, but I know it wasn't. He ended his own life," he said. "Kate, he was one of the best pitchers I'd ever seen. There was no chance he wasn't going pro. And he threw it all away over a girl. I decided I never wanted to let a girl have that much control over me. I knew the only way to make sure of that was not to fall in love. So I had to let you go."

"Reid, I don't know what to say," Kate said.

"You don't have to say anything. It was my turn to talk," Reid said. "I'm really sorry I hurt you back then. You deserved better, and I regret that I couldn't give it to you."

He waited for a few moments, but Kate still didn't know what to say to him.

"So ... that's everything. And I'll leave you alone," he said. "I need to get downstairs anyway."

Kate nodded and watched him turn to go. She felt like she should say something, but she still couldn't find the words. After the door closed behind him, she leaned against her desk and let out a long breath. She sat like that for a long time after he was gone, still letting all of his words sink in.

In the elevator, Reid leaned against the back wall and closed his eyes. He let out a shaky breath and was suddenly grateful for the slow elevator. He needed time to reflect on what he'd just done and get himself together again.

He had never poured his heart out to someone like that before. It had been a little scary when he started, but by the time he was done, he felt good. He'd heard that saying about getting something off your chest, but he always thought it was just a saying. Now he knew why the saying had been born. He felt decidedly lighter after saying all of that to Kate.

Kate had looked a little shell-shocked at his spiel. He didn't blame her. He had unloaded a lot on her. If he was still reeling over it, there was no doubt she was as well. When all of his words were out, he'd waited for a response from her, but she'd been silent. He decided maybe she needed a little time. Or maybe she would never have a response. But now she knew how he felt and hopefully understood why he'd acted the way he did in their younger years. There were no guarantees, but he'd done his part and said everything he needed to say. What she did with the information was up to her.

He exhaled as that realization washed over him. He felt a little more composed by the time the elevator doors opened on the main concourse, but his relief was short-lived. Standing there, apparently waiting for the elevator, were Kate's parents. And they weren't alone.

"Mom? Dad?" Reid managed to choke out. "What are you doing here?"

His parents glanced at each other but didn't answer him. Kate's mom spoke up.

"I got in touch with them after we talked in Arizona and invited them to come with us this weekend," Sharon said.

"We kept reading and hearing about how well you're doing, and we wanted to see it for ourselves," Sam said.

It was the first time he'd heard his father's voice in months and the first time he'd heard it in person in more than a year. And it'd been much longer since he'd heard any semblance of pride, but there seemed to be a little in there.

"It's not like I'm playing," Reid said. "There's really nothing to see."

"We wanted to see you, Reid," Kathy said. "We've missed you."

He looked at his mother for a few moments as though trying to gauge her sincerity.

"We're on our way up to see Kate," Ron said. "We'll give you three some time to catch up."

He took his wife's hand and they stepped into the elevator. Reid watched the doors close on Kate's parents before he turned to face his own.

"Do you want a quick tour of the ballpark?" he asked them.

Sam and Kathy nodded, and Reid pushed the button for the elevator. As they waited, none of the Benjamins spoke. It wasn't an uncomfortable silence though. Quite the opposite. As Reid showed his parents the clubhouse, press room, batting cages, and dugout, he almost felt as though the last few years had disappeared. All of his mistakes that had brought his parents shame seemed to have been washed away.

They ran into a few of the players who had shown up early for the day's festivities. Each one stopped to chat with Reid and shook hands with his parents when they were introduced. Carson Slater lingered the longest with Reid, talking about his swing and timing. Reid agreed to meet him in the cages early the next morning.

"The players really like you," Kathy said.

They were seated in the dugout now, just looking out at the field. Some members of the grounds crew were out getting the field prepped for the game even though first pitch was still four hours away.

"Yeah, I think so," Reid said. "They're a good group of guys. They listen well and take my advice. Carson's deal really isn't his swing or timing. He's just in a little bit of a slump, so I think it's gotten to his head. I'm going to try and get him to relax."

"They trust you," Sam said. "That's huge."

"I guess," Reid said shrugging. "It's going to be hard to leave them."

"You're not going to stay here next season?" Kathy asked.

Reid shook his head. "Coaching has been fun, but I'm not done playing yet. My agent said there are a few teams interested in me. I won't talk to any of them until the season's over, but … I definitely plan to play again next season."

"I see," Kathy said. "Have you talked to your boss about that?"

Reid thought about Kate. They really hadn't talked about anything work-related lately. They'd both been too preoccupied with their personal past.

"No, but I'm sure she won't be surprised," Reid said. "Kate knows I want to play."

And he wasn't completely sure Kate wouldn't be glad to see him go, but he wasn't going to tell his parents that.

"Well, you should probably discuss it with her directly," Sam said. "After the favor she did you by hiring you, you owe her that."

"I know," Reid said. "And I will discuss it with her. Right now though, we're both just focused on our playoff run. No one's even talking about next season yet."

Maybe it wasn't the whole truth, but it wasn't a lie.

"We always liked Kate," Kathy said. "I thought maybe you two would date at some point. Is she still single?"

"Yes, but … that's not going to happen, Mom," Reid said. "I'm not interested in a relationship and I don't think she is either."

"You've always said you're not interested in a relationship, but I don't get that at all," Kathy said. "Don't you want someone to share your life with?"

Reid shrugged. "I don't really have time, Mom. I need to focus on baseball."

"And what will you have when baseball's over?" Sam asked. "You know it won't last forever."

"I'll still have friends and maybe I'll even come see you two more often," Reid said, hoping it would lighten the mood and change the subject.

It didn't work.

"It's not the same. And if you ask me, it's not enough," Sam said. "Sooner or later, your friends will all be married too. And we'd love to see you more, but we aren't going to be around forever either. And then you'll be all alone."

"I've been fine alone," Reid said.

"Well, I want you to be better than fine," Kathy said. "Have you ever even been in love, Reid?"

He stared out at the field unblinking. It was odd she would ask that on the day he first uttered that word to anyone.

"It doesn't matter," he said after a few moments. "I've chosen my career, my dreams."

"It doesn't have to be one or the other," Sam said. "You can have your dreams and love."

"Oh? How did that work out for you two?" Reid asked. "Because of me, you didn't get to go off to college."

"That doesn't mean we gave up our dreams," Kathy said.

"Right," Reid said, his voice heavy with sarcasm.

"We didn't," Kathy said. "It's true we had to delay our career dreams a little, but it was worth it to have you. Family was always part of our dream. You just came earlier than we expected is all. But we still got everything we wanted."

Reid turned and studied both of his parents.

"She's right, Reid," Sam said. "We didn't give up anything to have you. At least that's not how we look at it."

"Well, I'm sure you haven't felt that way the last few years," Reid said.

"You've made mistakes, but we still love you," Kathy said. "We were only disappointed because we expected better out of you."

"I did too," Reid said. "I don't know what happened to my bat."

"We're not talking about baseball here. You'll always be an All-Star in our eyes," Sam said. "Your off-field antics were what bothered us."

"Oh," Reid said. "Yeah, I didn't deal with the pressure and stress well."

"Clearly," Kathy said. "Are you sure you want to go back to that? The pressure of playing?"

"Definitely," Reid said. "A year away from it has been really hard. I'm ready to go back."

"Have you found a new way to cope with stress?" his father asked. "Other than alcohol and women?"

Reid opened his mouth to say he had, but then he remembered the night he went to Kate's. That night had been about jealousy, but that was just another unpleasant emotion, right? Maybe he really hadn't learned a new stress management strategy.

"I'm seeing a therapist now," Reid answered finally.

"That's a good start, but maybe you should be sure you're ready to handle the stress before you get back on the field," his dad advised.

"I'll be fine," Reid said firmly.

He was glad when his parents dropped the subject. They didn't have much choice. Their visiting time was over. Reid had obligations with Fan Appreciation Day, and he was due at an autograph table. He walked his parents back to the main concourse so they could go meet Ron and Sharon. A quick phone call told them the elder Marks couple was still with their daughter on the executive level. Reid gave his mom a hug and shook hands with his dad before they got on the elevator.

There was already a line at Reid's table, which surprised and humbled him. All season, some of the players had told him he should be out there signing autographs with them before the game, but he thought they were just teasing. Surely no one wanted his signature. This line said otherwise. He waved to the gathered crowd and sat down. For the next few hours, he wrote his name more times than he could count and his cheeks hurt from smiling for so many photos.

When a security guard told him his time was up, Reid looked at those still in line. There were still about 20 people, and they looked sincerely disappointed that they hadn't made it to the table. Reid didn't like disappointing people – despite what his track record might imply – so he quickly went down the line and signed for the last few people.

He heard a familiar voice call his name as he handed the last baseball to a fan. His parents and the Markses were walking toward him.

"I'd love to chat more, but I have to get to work," Reid said to them.

"We know. Kate just told us the same thing," Sam said. "But we're all going to dinner after the game."

"Who is?" Reid asked.

"All of us plus Kate," Ron said, gesturing to himself and his wife, Sam and Kathy, and then Reid.

"Is she on board with that?" Reid asked.

"Of course," Sharon said. "Why wouldn't she be?"

All four of the elders looked at Reid curiously. He could see the questions whirling in their minds. He didn't want to give them enough time to voice them.

"No reason," Reid said shaking his head. "I'll see you guys in a few hours."

Reid hurried off before they could press him for answers. And he prayed they would forget about his comment before the end of the game.

"Did something happen between you and Reid?"

Kate looked up from her phone in surprise. She'd been checking the scoreboard and standings while they waited for Reid, but her mother's question caught her off-guard. She hadn't expected that. Their visit in her office earlier had gone smoothly and there hadn't been much talk about Reid then. Why were they bringing him up now? What had happened between the time they left the executive offices and the end of the game? The other three adults were also looking at her, awaiting her response.

"Why?" Kate asked, hoping she sounded casual. "Did he say something?"

"Not really," Sharon said. "He just seemed surprised that you agreed to have dinner with all of us."

"What exactly did he say?" Kate asked.

Sharon recapped the conversation they'd had with Reid after his autograph session.

"I don't know why he would say that," Kate said, looking back at her phone quickly.

Honestly, she'd been hesitant to go to dinner with both families, but when her parents suggested it, she didn't have a good reason to decline. She couldn't tell them why she didn't want to face Reid. Her conversation with him – or rather his monologue – had shaken her deeply. His words were still fresh in her mind. She just kept hearing, *"I was in love with you, Katie."* Her whole body had warmed at those words and she was surprised he didn't notice the change in her. Then again, he'd bolted as soon as the words were out. Typical Reid. Get a little closer and then run away. Things had always been that way between them.

Hours later, she still didn't know what to say when she faced him again. She'd have to figure it out, and now she'd have to make extra effort to appear normal with their parents as an audience and a suspicious one at that.

Thanks a lot Reid.

She hoped they could manage friendly conversation long enough to convince their parents nothing was going on. It was only an hour or so. Surely they could pull that off, right?

Her mental pep talk did nothing to prepare her for the moment Reid walked up to them.

"Anyone else hungry?" he asked. "After a win like that, I'm starving."

They all started talking about the game as the group headed out to the parking garage. Reid sounded proud as he talked about the solid hits and plays from the Pioneers, who had needed a walk-off home run from Ian Davis to secure the victory.

They split into two vehicles – the men in Reid's SUV and the women in the rental car. Kate prayed the mothers wouldn't ask her more about Reid. Thankfully, the women were more focused on getting to the restaurant than inquiring about any awkwardness between their children.

At the restaurant, the baseball talk continued for a while. After they placed their orders, Kate asked her parents about her siblings, hoping to keep the conversation in a safe zone. She was hyperaware of Reid's presence. He was at the other end of the table and she had barely looked in his direction all night, but she could still feel him there.

She was relieved when dinner was over and the parents declared their eagerness to get back to the hotel to sleep. The only downside was that their hotel was in the opposite direction of the ballpark where her car was still parked.

"I can give you a ride back," Reid said, addressing her for the first time all night.

They hadn't talked directly to each other, but there really hadn't been a need for it either. With their parents there, it was easy to talk to the whole group. But now they would be alone in a confined space. She didn't know how she felt about that, but it really was her best option for getting back to her car. Calling a cab would be silly and it would probably require more waiting than she wanted to do. So she accepted Reid's offer and tried to keep her reluctance hidden from their parents, who were watching the interaction.

After a few hugs, the group split up again. Kate climbed into the passenger seat of Reid's car. His scent was everywhere in the vehicle and apparently he still wore the same cologne as he had in high school. She was immediately inundated with memories of prom and their first kiss, which segued into a mental replay of their most recent kiss in her living room. Reid was silent as all of this ran through Kate's head. She wondered what he was thinking about but then decided maybe it was better she didn't know. In fact, part of her wished she could go back to not knowing how Reid had felt about her all those years ago. Somehow, believing he hadn't cared was easier than knowing he'd been in love with her and left anyway. While she understood his fears, especially after losing a friend, it still didn't justify the way he'd ended things with her.

"It was fun seeing our parents, huh?"

His voice pulled her out of her thoughts.

"Yeah, I didn't realize your folks were coming too or I would have given you a heads up," Kate said.

"That's alright. It was a nice surprise," Reid said.

"I know you hadn't seen them in a while."

"No, but it won't be that long again. I feel like we put the past behind us today."

"That's good."

"I wish you and I could do that too."

Kate didn't know how to respond so she just looked out the window. Reid didn't push her either, and neither of them said another word until he stopped his vehicle next to her car.

"Here we are," Reid said.

"Thanks for the ride," Kate said to him.

"No problem," Reid said. "And Kate …"

She was halfway out of the car when he said her name. Against her better judgment, she turned back to face him.

"I know it might take time, but I do hope we can put our past behind us at some point. You still mean a lot to me," he said. "I'll wait as long as it takes and be ready when you decide you're not mad at me anymore."

"Reid, I'm not mad at you," she said. "Trust me, I wish I was."

Chapter 12

Kate meant what she said to Reid. She wished she could be mad at him. That would be so much easier to deal with than what she was really feeling.

Mostly, she was just hurt. That's really all she felt when it came to him. Years after his actions, she was still just hurt. Even though he had apologized numerous times, she still couldn't let go. She was starting to think she might never, and that bothered her more than her anger. Why couldn't she invest her emotions in someone who actually deserved it? Someone more like Neal.

She tried to be mad at Reid, but it was no use, and she knew it. She had tried to be mad at him for years, but she never quite mastered it. There were times she thought she was mad at him, but when she looked closer, she realized she only wanted to think she was mad at him. It was better than facing reality.

Reid wasn't to blame. She was.

Reid had broken her heart, but she'd never bothered to repair it. Instead, she just put up walls in the name of protecting herself. But it hadn't made her stronger at all and she had only hurt herself more in the process. She had allowed Reid to control her emotions and every dating decision she'd made in the meantime. Or non-decision, as it was in some cases. In addition to rejecting a few suitors, there had been many she simply avoided. She'd always thought that made her look stronger and more in control. Now she realized it was quite the opposite. She'd never been in control. She had given that over years earlier and never really took it back.

She didn't need closure from Reid. She didn't need an apology from Reid. She needed those things from herself. And that was way harder than getting them from Reid.

Believing Reid had been the bad one all these years had been comfortable for her. She still believed he had done her wrong and she would probably always believe that. But she also needed to admit and accept that she'd been wrong too. And she didn't like that. She'd never been good at accepting when she made a mistake.

In this case, it meant she'd been wrong more than once and she'd made the same mistake over and over for a very long time. There had been no strength in her decisions and actions. Only weakness. Admitting she'd been wrong and weak for so many years was rough. It made her doubt her judgment in many areas, and she wondered what all she had missed out on because of her bad decisions. Dwelling on that was just as pointless as blaming Reid. And also quite exhausting. But she did it anyway.

While Kate battled her inner emotions and thoughts, the Pioneers were battling for a postseason berth. This meant she spent a lot of time at the ballpark – looking at contracts and numbers during the day and watching games in the evening. There were even a few extra inning affairs that kept her in her seat until after 11.

She didn't mind those long days at all. The team was exciting to watch and the fact that they were playing meaningful games in September was even more exciting. In the final week of the season, the Pioneers enjoyed their first-ever champagne celebration in the clubhouse as they clinched a wild card spot. October baseball was coming to Pioneer Stadium.

Kate was grateful for the distraction. The busy days left her too exhausted to deal with her Reid-related worries. Most days anyway. She occasionally ran into him in the ballpark, which seemed smaller than ever lately. Their interactions remained civil, but Kate could tell Reid wanted to continue the conversation about their past and how it had leaked into their present. The way he looked at her and lingered a little longer after their brief business discussions seemed to let her know the door open for that conversation. She just wasn't ready for that yet, and she was glad when he didn't push it. He wasn't shying away from her either. He was letting her decide when she was ready.

Maybe he wasn't such a bad guy. Sure, he'd been selfish and made some bad decisions, but that didn't mean he was inherently bad.

The players certainly didn't seem to think he was. In just a few months, Reid had made a powerful impression on the team. Kate shouldn't have been surprised. After all, Reid had gotten to her pretty easily too – even if it was in a completely different realm. Reid just had an aura about him that made him easy to like. People gravitated to him without realizing it or understanding why.

As talk began swirling about the possibility of Reid leaving after the season, several Pioneers players approached Kate and begged her to do whatever she could to keep him. No one was more insistent about it than Derek Beaman. He even offered to transfer some of his pay – which was at the major league minimum – to Reid if it meant he would stay.

"That's quite the sacrifice," Kate said to Derek. "It's not possible for me to do that, but I'm glad you like Reid that much."

"Is he leaving because of his past with you?" Derek asked. "I saw some of the stories that came out after that night at your house, and he's told me that you two have a bit of a rocky past."

Kate's face flushed a little. She didn't know what Derek knew, but she sensed it was more than she wanted him to know.

"I hope you haven't mentioned that to anyone else in the clubhouse," she said.

"No ma'am," he said. "I told Reid anything he told me that night was between us. Just like he's kept secrets for me."

Kate nodded, and now she wondered what all Reid had said. And what secrets of Derek's Reid had kept. She decided none of it was relevant at the moment.

"Good," she said. "And for the record, my past with Reid has no bearing on his employment – one way or the other."

"I didn't figure … but I had to ask," Derek said. "I think you could convince him to stay though. He obviously listens to you. Please. We need him. I need him."

"Reid and I will have that discussion when the time is right," Kate replied. "But at the moment, I don't think Reid is thinking much about next season. And neither am I, honestly. We're both just focused on the postseason. That's what you need to be focused on too, Derek. Especially since you're starting the first game."

Derek grinned. "Yeah, I know. Trust me. I'll be ready."

Kate smiled and nodded. "You worry about the Tigers. Let me worry about Reid."

The young pitcher seemed to feel better when he left her office. Kate hoped her answer hadn't given him a false sense of optimism. She hadn't decided whether she wanted Reid to stay or not. On one hand, he had given their offense the boost it needed and clearly his impact reached beyond just field performance. Players trusted him and counted on him. On the other hand, she wasn't sure she could take another year of her emotions being in such upheaval. Then again, she had let her feelings for him rule too many decisions in her past, and it hadn't done her any favors. She needed to approach this issue from a purely professional angle. With that in mind, she knew she needed to at least offer him another year as hitting coach. With that in mind, she knew what she needed to do.

Kate couldn't think about next season yet though. The Pioneers' current season was still very much alive.

Derek kept his promise to Kate. He was lights out in in Comerica Park. He shut down the Tigers' offense almost completely, allowing just four hits through seven innings. He wanted to finish the game, but the manger didn't want to take chances with Derek's arm, so he let the bullpen take over. They quickly gave up three runs, but the Pioneers' offense had already put five runs on the board. Derek and his team won the wild card game, enjoyed another clubhouse party, and advanced to the division series to take on the Yankees.

New York scored eight runs in the first inning of the series and went on to win game one by a score of 11-3. Kate wasn't sure how the players would respond to such a beating, but they showed their character and rallied for an extra-inning 5-4 win in the second game. Then it was back to Portland, where the home team again won the first game. There were plenty of Yankees fans in the crowd, the roar at the end of the 7-4 win proved the Pioneers fans had come out to support their boys in their first postseason game in Portland.

Pioneers fans were back in force the following night too. Derek was on the mound again in the most important game in Portland baseball history. And his career. Kate didn't see any sign of nerves from her young pitcher. Only focus and determination. He retired the first twelve batters he faced, including six on strikeouts. No one went near him in the dugout, and he sat at one end of the bench just staring at the field.

Kate always wondered what went through a pitcher's head in those moments.

Were they even seeing their own batters or were they already mentally prepping for the next half-inning?

The Yankees pitcher was matching Derek pitch for pitch. There had been no base runners for either team through four innings. The zeroes on the scoreboard continued until the seventh inning, when Ian Davis hit a leadoff double through the middle. The Portland crowd went crazy. The excitement died a little as the next two batters struck out. The noise returned when Carson Slater snuck a two-out single by the first baseman and down the right field line, allowing Davis to round third and cross home plate.

Derek went back to the mound for the eighth with a 1-0 lead. He looked just as calm and collected as he had the entire game and that demeanor carried through in his pitching. He notched his ninth strikeout and the infield took care of two easy hits to keep the bases empty for their pitcher. They weren't able to give him any more of a cushion in the bottom half of the inning though, so the score remained the same as Derek headed back out for the ninth. He immediately got a strikeout and a ground ball out.

The tension in the ballpark was palpable. Fans didn't seem to know whether to be loud or quiet.

Derek looked at his catcher, Carson, for a long moment before delivering the first pitch – a strike on the inside corner. He went outside with the next pitch, but it was a little too outside. He missed the strike zone with the next pitch too. And the next one. Kate saw the first signs of nerves on her pitcher's face as the batter trotted to first base on a walk. Derek's bid for perfection was over, and more importantly than that, the Pioneers' lead was in danger, especially when the next batter hit a blooper to left, putting runners on first and second.

Carson trotted out to the mound to return the ball to Derek. Kate couldn't read the catcher's lips, but she saw him say something to Derek and pat his shoulder before heading back to his spot behind the dish. The next Yankees hitter got a piece of the first pitch, but fouled it back into the stands. That continued for three more pitches until one hit went fair but right into the glove of shortstop Justin Tanner.

It seemed to take a moment – but only a moment – for the players and fans to realize what had just happened. Suddenly, the stadium erupted with noise. Chaos of the best kind ensued as confetti flew and there were camera flashes everywhere. The Yankees players had disappeared quickly and only a sea of brick red jerseys remained. Jerseys that were quickly turning an even deeper shade of red as the players doused each other with water.

Derek Beaman's jersey was the most saturated, and – if it was possible – his smile was the biggest of all the players. And rightfully so. This was quite possibly the best night of his life. He had pitched a complete game shutout to help his team win their first American League Division Championship.

Kate smiled, happy for the young pitcher, as she remained at her seat, taking it all in. This was Pioneers history and she didn't want to forget a moment of it. For the first time, the stream of people leaving the stadium was just a trickle. No one wanted to miss out on this. Music blasted over the loud speakers. There were high fives and hugs on the field and in the stands.

She caught sight of Reid in the middle of the fray. He almost blended completely in with the players. He mirrored their joy more than any other member of the coaching staff. It only proved to Kate that he was still a player at heart. As she watched him, she was surprised at what she felt – pride and and happiness. Any bitterness, anger, or hostility she'd once had for him was gone. None of it remained. She wondered when the negativity had left her.

Was it just chased by the joy of this moment?
Or had it just slowly melted away over the past few weeks?

Then she realized she didn't care. She was just glad. The freedom from those feelings made this moment a lot easier to enjoy.

"They're going to make a movie of your life someday, kid," Reid said to Derek as they embraced.

"I'll make sure they cast someone good for you," Derek said, laughing. "Brad Pitt, maybe."

"He'll be too old by then," Reid said. "Maybe Chris Hemsworth."

"I think he's a little too big," Derek said.

"What are you saying?" Reid asked, pulling back and flexing.

Derek just laughed.

"In all seriousness, you pitched a hell of a game," Reid said. "I knew you had that in you somewhere. I'm just way impressed you pulled it out tonight."

"I don't know where it came from," Derek said, shaking his head in disbelief.

"Maybe from her," Reid said, pointing to the family section of seats.

There, standing at the railing, was a little girl with brown curls, eyes exactly like Derek's, and a tiny Pioneers jersey that said 'Beaman' on the back. Reid watched as Derek looked up at his daughter, flanked by his parents, and his eyes filled with tears. The older man said something and the little girl waved. Derek took a few steps toward the edge of the field, still surrounded by his teammates but oblivious to anything except that little girl.

He patted Derek on the back and did his best to clear a path so the pitcher could get to his family. It wasn't easy though. The other players, coaches, media, and fans, were eager to get a word with the big game winner. Reid knew Derek wasn't getting up to the stands.

"You go to the press room and give your interview," he said to Derek. "I'll bring her to you."

Derek nodded and gave his coach a grateful look. Reid was able to get away from the crowd more easily. He took the best route he knew to the family, whom he'd already met. Brynn wasn't so sure about this strange man but after some coaxing from her grandparents and a promise that she was going to her daddy, she finally went into Reid's arms.

"It's going to be kind of loud down here," he warned her as he made his way back to the clubhouse with her. "Just cover your ears if you need to."

The little girl followed his instructions as the cheers echoed off the tunnel walls. Reid walked as quickly as he could to get her out of the ruckus, finally finding the media room. Derek sat at the front table with his manager, his catcher, and a few other players, fielding questions from local and national reporters.

"Daddy!" Brynn exclaimed as soon as she spotted him.

Derek looked up, grinned, and nodded at Reid, who squeezed through the crowded room to hand over the little girl.

"To answer your question," Derek said, going back to his interview. "This little angel and the guy who brought her to me are a big part of my success this season. I was determined to be someone she could be proud of, and Reid told me I could be. All of my coaches were great this season, and I appreciate all they did for me, but Coach B was the only one who really got to me. Once he believed in me, I started to too. I would not have made it through this season without his guidance."

Reid was humbled by the praise. Almost embarrassed. He ducked to the back of the room while Derek and the others finished the press conference. He didn't even notice Kate was beside him until she spoke to him.

"I knew you'd be good for him," she said softly. "You deserve every compliment he just gave you."

He looked over at her in surprise.

"Thanks," he said. "He's a good kid. I didn't do anything special. I was just there for him."

"Exactly. You were there for him when he needed it most," Kate said. "I don't know the specifics, and I don't need to. But I know you took care of him. You did a good job, Reid. Just believe that and accept it."

Reid nodded and for a few moments neither of them said anything.

"Should we meet tomorrow about my contract?" he asked.

"No," Kate said. "Not yet. The Pioneers still have baseball to play. Until they're done, you're still a Pioneer."

Reid nodded again and left to get cleaned up. He didn't know why he'd suggested meeting so soon about his contract. He wasn't ready to talk about next season. He wasn't ready to say 'goodbye' to her or this team. He also wasn't ready to say 'goodbye' to his playing days. In other words, he still hadn't made a definitive decision about what he wanted from baseball in the future.

Fortunately, the Pioneers gave him a little longer to think about that as they rode their momentum into Texas for a showdown with their division foes. The first two games were absolute slugfests, which ended in a split. Back in Portland, there were two great nights of pitching and low-scoring games, but the Pioneers only won one of the three home games. They trailed three games to two as they headed back to Texas to finish out the seven-game series. But their trip was a lot shorter than any of them would have liked. Rangers pitching completely shut down the Pioneers offense. The middle of the order had a few hits, but they couldn't string enough together to score any runs. Texas handed them a 2-0 loss in game six and promptly ended the Pioneers' season.

There were lots of tears in the clubhouse that night, and it was hard for Reid to take in as he walked among the players. He wished he knew what to say to cheer them up and remind them to take pride in what they'd done this season. But he didn't have the words. The sting of defeat was still fresh, and he knew nothing he could say would take away what they were feeling, so he remained silent.

Silence prevailed during the flight back to Portland early the next morning. They were all eager to get home and at the same time, they were in disbelief that the season was over. There had been so many emotions in the recent days and weeks. Everyone was still reeling from the highs and lows, and it seemed no one really wanted to talk about them.

Reid hung around the ballpark for the next few days, talking to the players as they cleaned out their lockers and left to embrace the off-season. His heart was heavy as they all said they hoped to see him again in March. Reid didn't make any firm statement about his plans, but he did promise them he would stay in touch. And he meant it.

The season had been over for a week when Reid finally sat down across from Kate in her office. They were the only two in the ballpark, but she was still in a business suit, making him glad he'd chosen black pants and a grey button-down. He always dressed nicely for travel, and his flight to New York was leaving in three hours.

"So here we are," he said as he looked at her across the desk.

"Yes, here we are," Kate said. "I want to start by clearing the air about our personal history."

"Fair enough," Reid said. "Let me have it."

He leaned back, waiting for a lecture, a tirade, or a guilt trip. It had been almost a month since their last discussion about their past. He figured she'd have something good worked up by now.

"I don't hate you, Reid," she said.

He didn't expect that.

"I'm not even mad at you."

Another shocker.

"Yes, you broke my heart years ago, but if I'd have been smart, I would have just let you go and moved on," she said. "Instead, I clung to the pain and let it rule my life for way too long. I'm done with that now. Our past is the past, and I've decided I'm not going to hold it against you anymore."

"So what are you saying exactly?" he asked.

"I'm saying I want to try and be friends again."

He grinned. "I'm on board with that."

She let out a long breath and her tone changed a little.

"Now, let's talk business," she said. "This season was a pretty wild ride."

Reid nodded in agreement. "Thanks for letting me be part of it."

"You had a hand in it," Kate said. "You exceeded my expectations as a first-year hitting coach."

"Thank you."

"You gave a lot to those guys," she continued. "Even though I'm pretty sure your heart is still set on playing, you never made them feel like they were your second choice. You never made this organization feel like we were second choice."

Reid nodded again, watching her carefully, wondering what she was going to say next. She seemed to be trying to figure that out as well. There was a long pause. He started to wonder if she was going to speak again or if that was just it. Surely, she wasn't done yet.

"We'd like a chance to be your true first choice," she said. "I've talked to your agent and a few other people around here, and we'd like to offer you a contract for next year."

"I really appreciate that. I really don't want to sound ungrateful as I say this," Reid said. "I've enjoyed coaching, but I really want to play again."

"I know," Kate said. "And that's exactly what we're offering."

Reid straightened and sat forward in his seat. He hadn't even considered this option. He didn't know it would be an option. His mind tried to figure out how it was possible.

"What? You don't have room for me on the roster," he said.

"Collin Ellwood is entering free agency. His agent wants to try and get him big money, and I don't think he'll be in our price range," she said.

He appreciated her honesty, but also wondered if that was a slight to him. *If they couldn't afford Ellwood, what were they offering him?*

"Now, I'm not guaranteeing you playing time. You'll have to earn that in spring training like anyone else," she continued. "We're offering you a chance to earn that."

"Of course, but … why would you sign me instead of pulling someone from the minors?" he asked.

"Like I said, you gave a lot to the guys this season," she said. "I think your mentorship for the younger players is needed in our organization – whether you're on the bench or on the field with them."

Reid was quiet for several moments.

"I don't know what to say," he said finally.

"You don't have to give an answer now. I've sent a copy of our offer to your agent, and you can take this one. Look it over and give me a call," Kate said.

Reid glanced at the contract. He only skimmed it, but he saw the dollar amount. It was fair. He was still in shock at the offer.

"I don't know how to thank you, Kate," he said. "For giving me a chance when I thought I was done with baseball. Or rather that it was done with me."

"You've already done enough to thank me," Kate said. "You helped this team get to postseason."

"I had good players to work with," he said.

"And believe it or not, dredging up our past was good for me too. It helped me move on," she said.

Reid nodded, unsure of how he felt about that. He believed her though. There was a peace about her today that hadn't been present the last time they talked about their past.

"Enjoy your off-season, Reid. You've earned it."

Kate had been more than ready for her meeting with Reid.

In the days since they returned from Texas, she'd waited for her turn to talk to him. When he told her he wanted to stay until all the players were gone, she was impressed. It seemed Reid was just as attached to them as they were to him.

All morning, she'd waited in her office, going over her notes again and again, preparing for the moment when he sat down across from her.

She wasn't nervous about any lingering personal feelings or negativity. She'd been relieved to see those were completely gone when he walked in and she felt no effects whatsoever. When he appeared in her doorway and folded that athletic frame into the office chair, just as he had done on the day of their interview back in January, she felt some slight déjà vu, but it passed quickly. There was no stomach turning, no heart fluttering, and no sense of dread. In fact, she had been glad to see him.

She wasn't scared about the contract she was offering him, and it was a good one. She had worked hard on it. Hours of research, phone calls, and negotiations with Mr. Scott had gone into drafting what she considered a very fair offer. It was slightly more than what they would have offered Ellwood, but probably less than what other teams might offer Reid. And Kate was prepared for that. But at least she had tried, and in doing that she was keeping a promise she made to Derek Beaman. He had stopped by her office before leaving for the season and she told him about the offer. He was the only one outside of the team owner who knew there was a possibility Reid could come back as a player instead of a coach.

If he chose to come back.

Kate hadn't been able to gauge his decision from his reaction to the contract. He'd seemed genuinely stunned, but beyond that, she had no idea if he was interested. She would have to wait on that.

Waiting on Reid.

Again.

This time didn't feel the same as all the other times she'd waited for him. This time, the playing field was equal. They both had much to lose and much to gain from his decision. Everything had been said and spelled out clearly. There was no uncertainty. About anything.

As the door closed behind him, Kate sat back with satisfaction and spun her chair around to look out at the baseball field. The chalk lines had faded. The grass was a little longer than it was during the season. The scoreboards were blank. It would be months before the stands were full again. It had been a long season, and Kate was looking forward to the break, but a part of her was also already longing for the new season to begin.

A new season meant a clean slate. A chance to start over for a different ending.

Then again, she didn't need to wait until spring for that. And she wasn't going to. She closed up her office and drove straight to the airport.

A new season was waiting for her in Minneapolis.

Glossary

Here are some of the baseball terms and phrases used in this book.

Ace – The best starting pitcher on the team and nearly always the first pitcher in the starting rotation.

Batting average – The average performance of a batter, expressed as a ration of a batter's safe hits per official times at bat. It is usually reported to three decimal places and read without the decimal: A player with a *batting average* of .300 is "*batting* three-hundred." A point (or percentage point) is understood to be .001.

Blooper - A weakly hit fly ball that drops in for a single between an infielder and an outfielder.

Bullpen – The relief pitchers for a baseball team and also the area where relief pitchers warm-up before entering a game.

Double play - The act of making two outs during the same continuous playing action. In baseball slang, making a double play is sometimes referred to as "turning two" or a "twin killing."

ERA – Stands for earned run average. The mean of earned runs given up by a pitcher per nine innings pitched (i.e. the traditional length of a game). It is determined by dividing the number of earned runs allowed by the number of innings pitched and multiplying by nine. An ERA lower than 3.00 is considered outstanding.

Farm system – Comprised of minor league teams affiliated with a single major league team. The teams are separated by division, from "Rookie" to "Triple A" (AAA). The purpose behind such a franchise system is to allow baseball organizations to train their own talent and to control the destination of that talent, either by trading valuable prospects for skilled MLB players from other teams or by moving players from the farm team up through the ranks into the major leagues.

On base percentage - A measure of how often a batter reaches base. The full formula is OBP = (Hits + Walks + Hit by Pitch) /

(At Bats + Walks + Hit by Pitch + Sacrifice Flies). Batters are not credited with reaching base on an error or fielder's choice, and they are not charged with an opportunity if they make a sacrifice bunt.

OPS – Stands for on-base plus slugging. It's calculated as the sum of a player's on-base percentage and slugging average (total bases divided by at bats).

Range – The more formal term is range factor, and it is calculated by dividing putouts and assists by the number of innings or games played at a given defense position.

RBI – Stands for runs batted in.

VORP – Stands for value over replacement player. This statistic demonstrates how much a hitter contributes offensively or how much a pitcher contributes to his team in comparison to a fictitious "replacement player, who is an average fielder at his position and a below average hitter. To calculate VORP, one must multiply the league's average runs per out by the player's total outs; this provides the number of runs an average player would have produced given that certain number of outs to work with. Now multiply that number (of runs) by .8, or whatever percentage of average the replacement level is designated to be; the result is the number of runs you could expect a "replacement player" to put up with that number of outs. Simply subtract the replacement's runs created from the player's actual runs created, and the result is VORP. For example, if a hitter has a VORP of +25 runs after 81 games, he has contributed 25 more runs of offense to his team than the theoretical replacement player would have over the same span of games.

Wild card – Two teams in each of the leagues (American and National) that have qualified for the postseason despite failing to win their division. Both teams in each league possess the two best winning percentages in their respective leave after the three division winners.

Coming soon

Behind in the Count
A Portland Pioneers Novel

By Micah K. Chaplin

Derek Beaman had it all — a career in baseball, a marriage with his high school sweetheart, and a newborn daughter. When he suffered an injury that sent him into a downward spiral, he lost it all. After a break and some time to recover, he gets a second chance at his Major League Baseball aspirations with the Portland Pioneers. His future as a pitcher is bright, but he's still contending with the demons of his past.

Zella Hansen is pursuing her lifelong dream of a career in baseball management. Her role in the Pioneers' front office introduces her to Derek. Zella soon realizes her feelings are more than just an admiration of his talent, but Derek's history may be enough to end the game early.

About the Author

Micah K. Chaplin lives in Des Moines, Iowa, where she works in the exciting world of insurance and spends many weekends running 5Ks, making fast runners look good. She's also a lifestyle blogger who occasionally gets caught dancing by herself to good music, drinks locally-brewed beer, and has strong feelings for the Texas Rangers. Her other published works include *You'll Never Know*, *A Promise Worth Breaking*, and *Riffs of Regret*.